Sign up for our newsletter to hear
about new and upcoming releases.

www.ylva-publishing.com

OTHER BOOKS BY
KD WILLIAMSON

Pink

Cops and Docs
Blurred Lines
Crossing Lines
Between the Lines

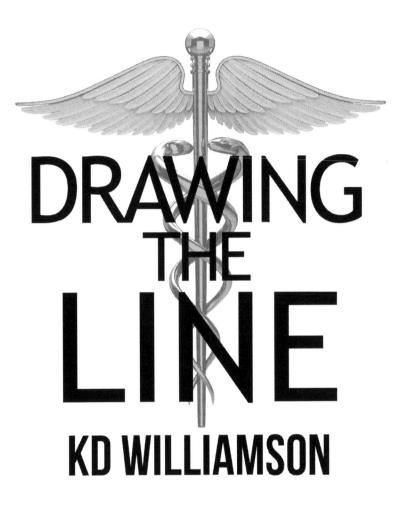

DRAWING THE LINE

KD WILLIAMSON

DEDICATION

To my wife, Michelle. Thirteen years hasn't been long enough. You're my best friend and an all around badass of a woman. Thank you for doing the things that I can't and the things I won't...like manual labor.

ACKNOWLEDGMENTS

Thanks to Amy and Anne who helped pull the words out of me, and to Lee Winter who helped me refine and shape the characters inside.

To Astrid, that Facebook DM changed my life.

CHAPTER 1

Dani's eyes fluttered open. It took her a minute to adjust to the darkness of her bedroom. God, she loved those blackout curtains. Best invention ever. She yawned noisily and stretched, lifting her arms toward the ceiling and pointing her toes toward the far wall. Dani was still tired, but there was no fog weighing her down. The term well rested didn't apply to her, but she had learned to savor the days when she got to be in her own bed and sleep for more than a few hours.

Something brushed against her. She gasped and recoiled. A soft hand, a woman's hand, snaked its way up Dani's torso.

"Well, last night must not have been all that memorable. You forgot I was here?"

Dani chuckled. "Yeah, sorry." It should have been hard to forget that a woman like Sandra was in her bed. She was all pouty lips, bedroom eyes, and blatant innuendo. Had it really been that long? "If it's any consolation, I slept like a rock."

"Mmm. What time is it? I picked up an extra shift. The regular charge nurse had to go to a wedding. Have to be at the hospital by eight thirty." Sandra pressed against her from behind, bringing a sudden combination of hot skin, curves, and hard nipples with her.

Dani shivered and gasped for a whole different reason. She squinted at the clock on her nightstand. 6:03, maybe? She couldn't be sure without her glasses. She patted around the area near the clock until her fingers hit pay dirt and slid her glasses on. It was 7:13 a.m. She'd been way off. "It's a little after seven."

"Damn it." Sandra sighed. "But maybe it's enough time to leave a lasting impression." She slipped an open palm over Dani's breast, dragging it across her nipple. Dani sucked in a breath and arched into the touch.

Sandra's fingertips plucked at aroused flesh as her teeth sank into Dani's shoulder. Her body drank it all in as if she'd been close to dehydration. It really had been *way* too long.

Less than an hour later, Dani was laughing and pushing Sandra out of her bedroom. "You're gonna be late."

"Well, it'll be your fault. All you have to do is answer me." Sandra grinned. There was a glint in her eyes making them bluer than usual.

Dani crossed her arms over her chest. "Fine. Yes, maybe we can do this again, but I don't know when. I'm always—"

"Busy. I know. You're in residency, but don't be surprised if I drag you into one of the on-call rooms sometime soon."

"Ahem."

Sandra turned.

Dani blinked at her roommate and best friend. His hairy, deeply bronzed chest and legs were on full display. The rest of him was tucked into a grey pair of Jockey boxer briefs. The stool he sat on, in front of the built-in breakfast nook, creaked as he leaned forward and lifted the bowl in his lap higher. He brought the spoon to his mouth and chewed the contents quietly.

"Oh, hey, Rick."

Rick tilted his head and smiled slowly. "Mornin', Sandra." He practically sang the words.

Dani glared at his obvious teasing.

In return, Rick's brows rose, making his forehead wrinkle.

Sandra pressed a quick kiss to Dani's lips and was out the door.

Dani didn't say a word as she slid on the stool beside Rick. He turned toward her slightly and continued to eat his breakfast.

"Is that my Raisin Nut Bran?" she asked finally.

Rick scowled but it changed to a grin. "Damn right, it is. I could eat a whole bowl of those raisins by themselves."

She reached for the bowl. "The box was almost empty."

He snatched it away. "Well, it's completely empty now."

Dani was a step away from being hangry. Rick's life could very well be in danger. "You could at least share."

He sighed. "Fine, but go get your own spoon. I know where your mouth has been."

Dani groaned. "You just couldn't let it go, could you?"

"No, I could not. I'm just glad somebody knocked the dust off it."

Her face heated and there was no way to hide it. Sometimes she hated being so pale. Despite his encouragement to get her own utensil, Dani took his spoon and the bowl back and dug in. "Shut up," she mumbled around a mouthful of cereal.

"I bet bats flew out when you spread your legs. Did they squeak?"

Dani bumped him with her shoulder, hard.

Rick laughed. It was deep, warm, and hard to resist. Dani leaned against him and joined in.

A few minutes later, she finished off the bowl of cereal and glanced up to find Rick staring at her. He pressed his lips together and rubbed a hand over his bald head.

"What?"

"Uh, maybe I should let you digest your food a little first."

"Oh my God, what?" Dani set the bowl on the counter. "Just spit it out."

Rick huffed. "Okay, just promise me it won't keep you from doin' your thing."

"My thing?"

"With Sandra, if it's goin' there. You know? A little ass when you need it." Rick held up his thumb and forefinger. They were barely a centimeter apart.

"Whatever. I don't do the flavor-of-the-week club. I don't have the time or the interest."

"You don't do any kind of club…short or long term. I'm just glad you settled for somewhere in the middle." Rick's eyes were soft as he looked at her.

Dani shrugged. "No matter how many times or ways we have this conversation, I'm not capable of giving someone that much focus and attention, not with the hours I work. At least I've learned to take care of myself better."

"If you say so."

"Hey! What's that supposed to mean?" Dani glared.

"You really want me to answer that?"

No, she really didn't. Instead, Dani changed the subject. "Anyway, I don't know where you get the energy to chase women."

"Me neither sometimes, but that's so not the point."

"What is then?" Dani put her elbows on the counter.

"I know you don't have anythin' against it, but you know Sandra's bi, right?"

"Yeah, so? What does that have—" Realization crept up the back of her throat and left a weird taste there. "No… You didn't. Here? In our apartment?"

Rick threw his hands up. "I did. It's been a couple months. We kinda had a regular thing until it fizzled out. Every once in a while here, but mostly at the hospital."

So, Sandra had a thing for on-call rooms. "Oh, ew. Was her mouth all on your…" Dani looked down at his crotch.

So did Rick. He smiled.

Dani cringed. "God, it's like I gave you a blow job by proxy." They'd stumbled into a similar situation before, but Rebecca stood out as a special case for them both. She pushed thoughts of Rebecca away with only a small amount of difficulty and met Rick's gaze, giving him her full attention.

"That's way *too* incest-y." Rick scrunched his nose.

"I know, right?"

"I just wanted you to hear it from me in case she brought it up. Now, I wish—"

"Not another word." Dani pointed at him.

"Yeah, for real."

"Wait. One more thing. Did you guys use protection?" Dani had to ask.

Rick's eyes widened. "I get tested regularly. I don't have anythin', but hell yes! Did you?"

"Definitely."

He stood. "Good. Now, I've gotta go."

"Where are you going? It's early. We hardly ever have the same day off anymore, and it's Saturday too."

Rick turned and met her gaze. He smiled. "Aww, you miss me."

"I do. Besides a few nurses, you're the only one I—"

"Uh-huh, and whose fault is that?"

Hers. It was all hers, but Dani was doing what she thought she had to in order to get through her last year of residency, even though she had an additional three years ahead for her fellowship in pediatric oncology. "Yes, well."

"The other residents really aren't all that bad long as you don't get sucked into drama."

Dani shrugged. "I don't have—"

"You don't have it in you for socializin'. I mighta heard that a few times even moreso in the past couple minutes," Rick finished for her. "May not seem like it, but you're still liked despite the cold shoulder you give almost everybody. They remember how you used to be."

She shrugged, not caring either way.

"With everythin' that happened, sometimes I really think it would have been better for you to transfer to another residency program and start fresh."

Leaving was never an option. She only had a few more months left in her residency, and it was way too late to apply for a fellowship somewhere else. Besides, her demons would probably follow. This conversation was taking her to a somber place, and she didn't want to be there. Humor was the better way to go. "You say that now, but what would you do without me?"

"Sandra, again?" Taking the bait, Rick wiggled his eyebrows, showcasing his ability to be funny and douchey at the same time.

"Oh, God. Stop." Dani covered her face. This was going to be hard to live down. She had no business dipping into the company ink anyway. Driven by her career goals, Dani was still human, and all the flirting Sandra had been shooting her way had finally hit its mark. She didn't think of giving in as weakness. It was more of a biological imperative and a matter of convenience after a long dry spell.

Rick pulled her hands away. "You'll get over it."

"So, where're you going?" Her voice lilted upward at the end as curiosity took hold.

"Meetin' a friend. I should only be a few of hours."

"Who?"

Rick looked away. "No one you'd know."

Interesting. "Maybe I can come too?"

"It's a funeral."

"Oh." She was pretty sure it would be rude to crash a funeral.

"Yeah, I'm the moral support, so I might be a while. But I'm all yours when I get back. Promise. Maybe I'll cook and we can put a dent in the DVR. It was at ninety-five percent capacity last time I checked."

"Wait. You're choosing me over your afternoon pick-up game with the guys?"

Rick shrugged. "They'll do fine without me. I'm sure."

"Well, your team might actually win anyway." Dani couldn't resist teasing him. "I know you at least turn heads running around shirtless, so that has to be a bonus."

"Whatever." He huffed and waved her comment away. "The rest of the guys aren't that good either."

"True. So, will you make that chicken dish, then?"

"Which one?" Rick asked.

"The one with those little green salty things?"

"Capers?"

"If you say so."

"Okay, you'll go get what I need if I leave you a list?"

Dani sagged in her chair and groaned, "You're already gonna be out."

"Well, shit. You want me to clean your room too? I got just about everythin' else covered."

"No, we're good." She smiled.

Rick gave her a hard stare and turned away, walking toward his bedroom.

Damn. Well, she could always read for a few hours to pass the time. Maybe something not medicine related. At this point in her career, her head was full to bursting, but regardless, she had to find room to learn even more. She'd get back on that train tomorrow. Even she had to come up for air every once in a while.

"Hey?"

Dani looked up as Rick poked his head out of the bedroom door.

"How does that thing Sandra does with her tongue translate to girl parts?" Rick smiled so hard his eyes crinkled.

"Shut up!"

He threw his head back and laughed.

Dani looked around for something to toss at him.

CHAPTER 2

THE WIND, BLUSTERY AND LOUD, blew through the collection of skeleton-like trees that filled the graveyard. Empty branches groaned and clacked against each other, nearly drowning out the sound of the preacher's voice. Rebecca could have focused more, but she didn't want to. She'd already said her good-byes three days prior. While expected, Aunt Felicia's death still had to have been a welcome relief for her after so much suffering.

The funeral itself was a technicality at this point. It didn't seem like much, but it was all Rebecca could afford even with the money her great aunt had saved. She could have gone with cremation, but the thought of Aunt Felicia being forever on her mantle or the coffee table didn't sit well. A graveside service was a thousand dollars less than the pomp and circumstance of a church. Her aunt had never been religious: Rebecca didn't remember dressing up for church on Sundays. Christmas, for some reason, was a different story. So, the preacher was a stranger and part of the funeral home's package.

Only a smattering of people gathered around the plain pine casket, hovering over the opening of its freshly dug, permanent home. Rebecca was very familiar with three of them, including the live-in home-health nurse who'd been taking care of Aunt Felicia since her diagnosis the year prior, but the others not so much. They were family friends who'd come out of the woodwork. Thankfully, no relatives had bothered. They hadn't had anything to do with her years ago, and there was no point now.

Rebecca stood away from everyone, near the knee-high mound of dirt, blanketed with a green tarp. She wasn't sure what the point of that covering was. Hiding it didn't shatter the finality of the situation.

She scanned the faces of everyone around her. None of them were crying, and Rebecca remained stoic as well.

Aunt Felicia would've wanted it that way.

One sniffle and she'd probably rise up out of that satin-lined box and yell at them all.

Rebecca almost smiled. Instead, the wind took her away again. She glanced up at the sky. The sun made a valiant attempt to burst through a section of clouds, making them brighter, almost white compared to the grayish tinge of the rest of the sky. It didn't matter if the sun broke through completely. Nothing would change. Mid-September was shaping up to be unseasonably cool. Even though it was in the high forties, it was still too cold for her taste.

Her eyes started to burn as grief seeped in. Aunt Felicia had been a hard woman, never affectionate or overly kind. Rebecca was grateful, even though growing up with her hadn't been easy. At times, it was downright barren. Her aunt was strict and believed in being blunt with the truth as she saw it, which included her view on Rebecca's sexuality. They'd only spoken about it once when she was in high school and got caught grinding on her girlfriend. Though "speaking" implied a conversation was had. There'd been more yelling than anything else. After that, Rebecca knew exactly where she stood, and she did all her grinding away from her aunt's. She refused to stop living her life.

The sun lost its battle and disappeared. Rebecca adjusted the collar of her leather jacket to cover her neck. She should have worn something thicker, but the black mid-length coat went better with her pantsuit and the corresponding situation. She shoved her hands in her pockets and scolded herself for not wearing gloves as well.

Someone eased up beside her. Instinctively, Rebecca stepped to the side. The person's hand pressed against the small of her back, bringing with it a familiar warmth and distinctive cologne. She turned slightly and looked up at Rick. His eyes were dark, his expression gentle. Rebecca relaxed against him. She hadn't really expected him to come. Grateful that he had, she hooked her arm around his and squeezed.

"Sorry, got caught up behind a wreck," he whispered, and kissed the top of her head.

Rebecca nodded and sank into him even more.

Long minutes later, the preacher came up to shake her hand. "Ms. Wells, I wanted to reiterate that I'm sorry for your loss."

"Thank you," Rebecca said in return. Then, one by one, everyone else came to her, offering condolences. Those who were known to her attempted additional contact, a hug, but she stiffened her body and rebuffed them without a word.

When they were alone, Rick stepped closer again. "You okay?"

Rebecca glanced at him and nodded. She moved forward, grabbed a handful of dirt, and sprinkled it on top of the now lowered coffin.

"I need to hear you say it."

She clapped her hands together to get rid of excess soil. "Yeah." Her voice was thick, hoarse from disuse. Rebecca cleared her throat. "Yeah, I'll be fine."

Rick tilted his head and eyed her for a few more seconds. "Okay. Good. Now, I know you haven't eaten. Let me treat you to breakfast."

Rebecca walked toward her car. The older, dark-blue Toyota Camry stood out next to the nicer cars pulling away. "You paid last time I was here, and I make more than you."

Falling in step beside her, Rick snorted. "That won't be forever."

She grunted.

"Home Grown?"

Rebecca actually started to salivate. No true Southerner could turn down homemade biscuits, especially with gravy slathered all over them. "Mm-hm."

"I'll meet you there and save a spot if I get there before you. Counter or table?"

"Table," she answered.

"Got it."

Trying to find somewhere to park, Rebecca circled the block. Just as a spot opened up, the car in front of her zoomed into it. "Fuckin' asshole!" She slowed down and glared at the guy getting out of the car. He paid her no attention whatsoever. That just made her grumble more.

Her phone dinged. When she stopped at a red light, she picked it up.

Just got here. Got a booth. It's in my name.

Rebecca responded to Rick's text. *K.*

She found a space farther up the street. Rebecca got out and typed her license plate number into the Park Mobile app on her cell, paying for at least a couple hours of parking. Then she walked quickly toward the restaurant. When she entered Home Grown, the hostess smiled.

"I'm with Rick Turner?"

The hostess looked down at the table diagram in front of her and then peered back up at her blankly.

"Really tall, bald, a couple shades darker than me, and good lookin'?"

The hostess turned around and looked at the sitting customers. She glanced back at Rebecca and raised a brow.

Rebecca's lips twitched. She'd just described over half of the people present.

A man walked up behind the hostess. "Thanks, Jaime."

The woman nodded. "Kevin might know who you're talking about. I can't read his handwriting."

Rebecca scanned the room again as Kevin took the seating chart from her. The place was packed. The sounds of laughter, various conversations, and the smell of fried food made it welcoming. The lobby held quite a few people as well. Rick must have flirted or bribed somebody to get a table so quickly

"Can I help you?" Kevin asked.

"Rick Turner?"

Kevin beamed.

So, possibly flirted *and* bribed. The man had no shame.

"Jaime, can you stay for another minute?"

She nodded.

Kevin waved at Rebecca to follow.

Once she was seated, Kevin turned his focus toward Rick.

"Can I get you anything else?" His smile was big, bright.

Rick shook his head. "Nope, but thank you for doin' this."

Kevin's smile dimmed. "You're very welcome."

Rebecca watched the whole exchange in silence. She pressed her lips together to keep from laughing.

As Kevin walked away, Rick looked at her and smirked. "So, what took you so long?"

Rebecca snatched up a menu even though she knew what she wanted. "Someone stole the parkin' spot I was about to pull into."

He chuckled. "You didn't shoot anybody, did you? Or tell 'em off? For somebody so tiny, you can be scary as hell. That road rage problem you have is so unlady-like."

She glared. "I'm not tiny, Bigfoot, and I don't carry a gun off duty."

He snorted. "I got that look enough this mornin' from Dani. I don't need it from you too. Thank you."

Dani. Hearing that name caused a corresponding twinge in the bottom of Rebecca's stomach. The feeling used to be closer to a gut punch. It had taken a long time to become something tolerable. "She's mad at you?"

"Naw, not really."

"Mm." Rebecca bit the inside of her cheek to keep from asking more. "How is she?" The words slipped out anyway.

Rick picked up his glass of water and drank from it. Several seconds passed. "I like the new haircut. Fits you. What made you go short?"

Feeling hot, Rebecca unbuttoned her jacket, shrugged it off, and left it dangling on the back of her chair. She knew what he was doing, trying to divert and protect her. She practically had to pry information out of him at times, even though Dani was really none of her business. Rebecca played along with his subterfuge. "I needed a change." She brushed her hand across her bangs and then over the back of her neck. She was still getting used to having nothing there. Her remaining hair was soft and close to her scalp in the back and on the sides. "I was tempted to go even shorter and completely natural."

"Like Lupita Nyong'o when she started out?"

"Yeah."

He studied her. "Nah. You shoulda lightened the color though. Make those hazel eyes pop. Dani's had the same hairstyle forever. I think she would look good with shorter hair and maybe go blonde, but she's still happy with puttin' it in a ponytail when she needs to."

Rebecca smiled. Some things never changed. She had a picture of Dani in her head, and she didn't want the image of dark, messy, shoulder-length hair and soulful brown eyes to be disturbed. "Maybe you're in the wrong profession."

"I pride myself on knowin' these things."

She wasn't going to agree or disagree. "Rick?" Rebecca swallowed. "Hmm?"

The waiter showed up. "Good morning, I'm Andy. Can I start you guys off with something to drink?"

"Coke with extra ice, and I'll have the biscuits. Heavy on the sausage gravy."

"Orange juice, no pulp, and the chicken biscuit with home fries." Rick smiled at the waiter.

Orange juice would have been better for her, but she needed a fix. Besides, Coke went with everything. When they were alone again, Rebecca continued. "So, she's with somebody? It's been four years. I'm not gonna go all to pieces if she is." Rebecca had been far from celibate, herself.

Rick leaned back in his chair and sighed. "Then why do you ask? I was just tryin'—"

"I know and it was sweet at first, but—"

He held up a hand. "Okay, I get it. She's doin' okay. Still spreadin' herself too thin."

"Mmm." He didn't answer her directly, but even that was telling.

Rick had been Switzerland after the break up and still vacationed there when necessary. No way their friendship would have survived otherwise.

"She hasn't changed all that much. You, on the other hand…" Rick didn't finish. He didn't have to.

"That's a good thing." The sudden dryness in her throat made her reach for his water and take a sip. Apparently, Andy had forgotten to bring hers. "I know you didn't tell her about Aunt Felicia, but you'd think she'd have seen it on Facebook or something." She was fishing. Not the smartest thing to do, but she couldn't take it back now.

"Dani's not into all that. She doesn't even have a Facebook account." He took his glass back. "Just keepin' it real. She wouldn't have come anyway. She didn't really know her, and even after all this time, I can't see her wantin' to be around you."

The waiter set their drinks in front of them. Rebecca unwrapped her straw and stuck it into the tall glass of Coke. She probably deserved everything he said. Only the ass end of the bait she was trying to hook him with remained, and the twinge in her stomach returned. "Yeah."

"Uhm, okay." Dani took a small step back from him. He seemed a little off kilter, but didn't all interns? "Well, this isn't the place for you, then."

He shrugged. "My medical school education needs to be well rounded." His tone lacked luster, as if he were reading from an extremely boring brochure.

"You don't like kids?" Dani shifted a little more to the side.

"God no," he whispered.

At least he had the sense to lower his voice.

"And they don't like me either," Dr. Norman hissed.

They could probably smell his fear. Dani bit the inside of her cheek to keep from smiling. Mostly, she didn't want him to think they were going to be friends. Yet it didn't cost her anything to give him free advice. "Then it's best you let your advisor or someone know."

He nodded.

"Did you need somethin', Dr. Russell?"

For today, at least, Betty had impeccable timing. Dani offered Norman a tight smile and turned to Betty. "Yes, the results of Mark's new blood work aren't in his medical record. I thought I put a rush on it."

Betty glanced in Dr. Norman's direction, and so did Dani. "He was supposed to stay in the lab and try to butter them up."

Dr. Norman's face reddened. He sputtered. "I'm sorry. I, uh, misunderstood. I did tell them you—"

Dani interrupted. "Think of it as your chance to escape for a little while."

"I can do that. Thank you." He'd barely finished speaking before turning away.

Betty rolled her eyes. "Well, bless his heart. Maybe he'll do better if they stick him in research."

"That's not nice." Dani chuckled.

"No, but you know it was funny."

"No comment."

"Good response. Gotta keep that reputation intact." Betty cocked a brow.

Dani pressed the tablet to her chest. "What are they saying now?"

"Apparently, the new crop of residents still thinks you believe you're better than everybody else, but someone had the bright idea that it's because you have money."

"I wish. How do they come up with this stuff?" Dani didn't care what the students and other residents thought of her. Not anymore, but the crap they came up with often left her scratching her head.

Betty shrugged. "You're a woman of mystery."

"No, I'm not. I talk to people."

Betty stared.

"Well, some people. Kids, parents, nurses, and Rick should count for something." The fact that she'd barely seen or spoken to Rick all week came to the forefront.

"You'd think. Speakin' of which, Austin's been lookin' for you all mornin'."

"Has one of the other doctors from his treatment team been in to see him?" Dani asked.

"Yes. He's havin' trouble understandin' that you're not gonna be around as much anymore."

"I know. I'd rather for him to be confused than be back in PICU or oncology. Where is he?" Dani sighed. Getting attached seemed to be an issue for children and parents alike. She didn't mind one little bit, especially if it helped them during a crisis.

"Over by the Avengers last time I checked."

A few seconds later, she walked up beside Austin. Dani brushed his arm but didn't say a thing. They both stood and stared at the mural.

"Why doesn't somebody tell 'em that the Hulk isn't 'posed to be that kinda green so they can fix it?" Austin turned his brown eyes on her. They were clear and bright, a stark contrast to being glazed over in pain, which was the expression Dani'd become used to.

Dani studied the mural. She didn't know anything about comics or superheroes, but she'd lost count of the number of kids who told her the Hulk wasn't supposed to be neon green. "I'm not sure."

"And he's smilin'. The Hulk don't smile. Why's his teeth so big?"

Dani wondered that too. He looked like he was poised to do a toothpaste commercial. "These are questions I don't have the answers to."

Austin continued to look at her. He reached up to scratch the top of his bald head. "Why can't you be my doctor no more? I can teach you 'bout the Hulk if you want."

"Because when Dr. Meda operated, all the bad stuff was taken out so you don't need me anymore. But I'm willing to learn whatever you want to teach me about the Hulk."

"The really, really sick kids are the ones who get to see you the most, right?"

"Right. I make sure they get the right medicine to help them get better." Dani nodded and made sure to maintain eye contact.

Suddenly, Austin wrapped his arms around Dani. She smiled and enjoyed the warmth along with a surge of affection as she rubbed a hand down his back.

"I don't like not seein' you." He sniffled and pressed his face against her chest.

"I know you don't, but you get to go home soon. You can see your dog and play outside. Don't you want that?"

He looked up at her and nodded. "I don't wanna be sick like that again."

"I don't want that for you either."

Austin stepped back, but he continued to lean against her. "Thor's not right neither. He 'posed to have a hammer, not a sword."

She chuckled. "I've heard that too." Dani eased her arm over his shoulders. "C'mon, I'll walk you back to your room.

"Okay." Austin allowed himself to be guided. "Dr. Russell?"

"Hmm?" They passed the monster trucks.

"If I can get my mom to bring it, will you watch *The Avengers* with me? Or maybe YouTube it? The Hulk has the best scenes. I want you to see." Austin looked up at her. His eyes were wide and earnest.

"Well, I have a few minutes and a smartphone. So, let's YouTube away."

Ten minutes later, Dani exited Austin's room with a smile firmly in place. These little moments made her sometimes grueling residency bearable. Saving lives and meeting amazing kids completed the other parts of the magic equation. There was nothing else like it.

Dani sent Rick a text, but fifteen minutes later, he still hadn't answered. She checked the residents' lounge and had been brave enough to pop her head into a few on-call rooms with no success. All she wanted was to have lunch with him. They had been like ships passing in the night the past few days. Typical. The part that hadn't been so typical? Rick's abruptness and avoidance. They usually sought each other out even if it was only for a few minutes.

He wasn't in surgery. Dani had checked the board. When she got to the end of the hallway, Dani pressed the button for the elevator. She hadn't looked in the cafeteria. They needed to talk—reconnect or something.

The elevator opened. Dani spotted Sandra. She quickly brought her cell phone up to her ear and laughed uproariously. She waved in Sandra's direction as Sandra got off the elevator and Dani entered. Yes, she was doing her own avoidance thing, but she had reasons. She had no desire to swim in rivers Rick had dipped into. Nothing against Sandra. That night and morning was still fresh on her mind.

The doors opened a couple times before getting to her stop. Dani let others file out ahead of her. She scanned the hallway; sure enough, Rick was leaning against the wall on the other side as he talked on the phone. He started to pace and gesticulate wildly before wiping a hand over his head. His face was pinched, as though he smelled something sour, and that expression was enough to give her pause. However, his wild eyes said the most, making him look just as anxious as Dr. Norman had been.

In return, Dani's heart rate doubled out of concern and empathetic distress. She walked toward him. Rick looked up. His mouth opened and closed several times..

"Uh, yeah we're good. I'll catch up with you later." He shoved his phone into his scrubs pocket. "Hey." Rick greeted her but barely held her gaze.

She'd had enough. The lack of eye contact was new and alarming. "What's going on? Do I need to make a list of all the weirdness or are you just gonna save me the trouble and acknowledge it?"

Rick glanced away again. He exhaled slowly. His shoulders hunched by the time he was done. "Dani, I…" He shook his head. "I need to get my shit together. What's wrong with me?" Rick looked at her. "Hey, I'm sorry. I thought I'd have more time to—"

"Time? More time for what? What is going on with you?" None of this helped her heart rate, which had yet to slow.

"Becca."

That name used to have such an impact in her world. Now, it conjured up a tiny flutter in her chest laced with old pain and anger. "Becca?" Her breath left her. Being a cop was a dangerous profession. Almost every muscle in her body hardened, leaving her frozen. "Is she—"

Rick grabbed her shoulders and squeezed. "No, it's nothin' like that."

Dani relaxed, but her heart continued to ram against her chest. "Then what?"

Rick's hands trailed down her arms and laced their fingers together, which weirded her out even more. "I'm a coward. I shoulda told you right away. It's only been a week, but still." He shook his head. "That funeral that I went to? It was her aunt's. She left her the house. Becca's comin' back to Atlanta." He tightened his hold on her. "That was her on the phone askin' me to help her move this weekend."

Dani looked down at their joined hands then back to Rick's face. His eyes were glassy, hopeful, and his lips were slightly parted as if he had lots more to say.

Stillness. It went on for several seconds until memories uncurled and tumbled through her. Four years. It had been four years. Apparently, that wasn't enough time to wash herself clean of the whole thing. She'd stored so much away and that hadn't been easy. Now, memories danced around her like shadows. Dani waited for the barrage of feelings to come. They were there, locked away. The pain, the anger; the sense of failure, helplessness, and abandonment. She'd gone through them all during the last legs of their relationship, the end, and beyond.

"Dani? Say somethin'. You haven't brought her up in a long time, but this still has to hurt."

Yes, she should feel something, but a blanket of numbness found its way around her, wrapping her tight. Dani held on to it. This wasn't the time or the place, but those weren't the only reasons. She just didn't want to go any deeper. She squeezed his hands before pulling away.

"Dani?"

She shook her head. "I can't. I have to go." Moving on autopilot, Dani stood in front of the elevator. She stabbed at the button, willing the doors to open, and when they did, the relief that shot through her was almost overpowering.

CHAPTER 4

REBECCA PEERED INTO THE CAT carrier. Peyton's green eyes narrowed, and she had the nerve to hiss. Rebecca rolled her eyes and poked a finger through the front bars of the kitty prison. Peyton growled and swatted. "God! You're such a little bitch. I'll let you out in a minute."

Peyton grumbled again. Rebecca picked up the carrier and looked up at Aunt Felicia's house. It belonged to her now, not any of those other so-called relatives that refused to claim Rebecca after her mother died. Her house. It was a lot to wrap her head around.

She moved slowly up the walkway. Rebecca scanned the exterior as if something had changed miraculously over the past week, taking in the earthy yellow paint and white trim. She decided to get everything painted as soon as possible.

Change could be a good thing. Rebecca knew that for a fact. She opened the screen door. It screeched and then slammed behind her.

The cat yowled in surprise.

"You're fine." Rebecca fished the keys out of her jeans pocket and let herself in. The pungent smell of mothballs was still in the air even though she'd taken the time to search out every stash the last time she was here. She trailed a hand over the plastic-covered couch and made her way toward her old room. When she got there, Rebecca set the carrier on the bed.

Peyton swatted at her again as she tried to open the latch. Rebecca hissed, and the cat responded in kind. She smiled and shook her head as she pulled the carrier door open completely. Peyton stepped out and stretched before sitting down and wrapping her tail around her legs.

Rebecca scratched her behind the ears and stood. "There better not be anythin' on the floor or claw marks in the curtains when I get back, lil miss."

Peyton gave her a slow blink then yawned. Her mouth opened wide, exposing sharp teeth and making her look downright demonic despite her sweet black-and-white face.

"Becca? You in here?" Rick's voice boomed.

"Yeah, I'm comin'!"

Seconds later, she nodded to Rick in greeting.

He leaned against the back of the couch. The plastic crunched in protest as he righted himself. "You left the door open. What's wrong with you?" He glared at her, and his lips were pressed together into a grim line.

"There are no neighbors on either side of me. It's fine."

"Whatever. This is fuckin' Grove Park. You should know better, cop or not." His expression didn't change.

Rebecca met his gaze. He stood tall, rigid, with his hands folded over his chest. Tension rolled off him, and it probably had to do with way more than just her being careless. She swallowed down the guilt that clawed its way up, but it knew a shortcut and ended up right in the pit of her stomach. "Things not goin' well, I take it?"

Rick snorted. "That's a goddamn understatement, and I'm not sure I wanna talk about it."

Her feelings took root and grew. Rebecca maintained eye contact and whispered, "I'm sorry, Rick." Even though she had a million questions about Dani's reaction, she walked past him toward the door. Nothing she could say would fix things.

"She's barely said a word to me in two days."

Rebecca stopped just before she got to the door.

Rick sighed. "I tried to avoid her this whole week and I haven't been completely straight up yet, so I don't blame her."

Surprised, she turned to look at him. He seemed pretty sure about what he wanted to do. Rebecca had expected him to jump at the first opportunity. "You mean you didn't tell her right away? Why?"

He shrugged. "I didn't know how to tell her. It's like I had one fuckin' job to do and I messed it up by waitin' till the last minute and tellin' her at the hospital."

All of this had to be killing him. "What happened?" Rebecca squirmed slightly as she waited for the answer.

"She thought you were dead at first."

Rebecca sucked in a breath. Outwardly, she did her best not to respond and ask for more regarding Dani's reactions, no matter what they were. Inwardly, every little bit fed a part of her that was starving.

"Yeah, and when I told her what was up, she looked at me like I'd slapped her in the face."

So much for him being Switzerland again anytime soon. Rick was smack dab in the middle of all of it now.

"I didn't mean to put you in this position."

"Yeah, well, it's where I am. I think all this really hurt her. I could be wrong though." He threw his hands up. "She could be pissed as hell. I'm just not sure, and I should be. I've known her longer."

Rebecca could only stare at him. She deserved his anger. "Just…go home. I'll just take out the things I need and hire movers as soon as I can."

Rick's gaze dropped to his feet, and he didn't say anything for several seconds. "It's not all on you. This is my fuckin' fault too. Let's do this, but I'm not in the mood to talk about it anymore."

She nodded. Rebecca was fine with that. The only drawback was it gave her more time to think. She'd done plenty of that while a couple guys from her former squad loaded the truck back in Savannah, and the four-hour drive to Atlanta had given her even more.

She'd told Rick the truth during breakfast last weekend: Rebecca did miss home. She also wanted to reconnect, but most of all, Rebecca wanted forgiveness. She had a hard time reconciling the person she used to be with the one she'd become.

Quietly, Rick followed her outside. Rebecca unlocked the U-Haul trailer. The door creaked as she lifted it. Rick moved and went straight to work. He hardly looked at her. Already, she'd shaken things up, and even then, her intent remained to move forward.

Was it selfish? More than likely. Was this going to be difficult? Yes. Big time, but here were the facts—she'd tried a few times to move on, but each time things went to shit where she ended up hurting the men who'd taken a chance on her. It had taken Rebecca a while to realize that in order to go forward, she had to face what she'd done in the past. She hoped that meant forgiveness. She would understand if it meant the opposite, but she'd be happy as hell if it meant some even ground where she and Dani could see each other for who they'd become.

Rebecca pulled the door to the U-Haul closed and locked it with a newly purchased padlock. They still had a few more things to put in the house, but she was dying for a Coke. Despite the chill in the air, she was sweating like someone had thrown a bucket of water over her. She wiped at the mess on her forehead, but all it did was make the back of her hand wet. Rebecca glanced up at the sky. It was still hazy, but none of the clouds looked threatening enough to spit on them.

A white SUV with tinted windows slowed to a crawl as it got closer to the house. After a few seconds, it sped up again.

She wasn't even curious. Any friends she'd made growing up in the area had long since moved away. Grove Park was a somewhat desolate place nowadays. There were a lot of empty houses, and the people who remained had been around for a long time already.

The screen door screeched as it opened. Rick walked up beside her.

"Coke?" Rebecca asked.

He nodded and followed her back in. They passed the boxes stacked in the living room and throughout the house. Rebecca had attempted to get rid of excess crap back in Savannah, but she feared that she hadn't thrown away nearly enough. The house was already cluttered with Aunt Felicia's things. Moving in and getting settled was obviously going to take a while.

Rick leaned against the kitchen island as he guzzled the can of Coke in his hand. He burped and pointed at the remainder of the six pack on the counter. Rebecca gave him another one while she chugged the rest of hers.

"Just to let you know, I'm not helpin' you unpack. Who the hell moves without labelin' the boxes?"

They were the first real words he'd said to her in well over an hour, which wasn't weird for them at all. But given the situation they were in, Rebecca had to admit that she'd rather know what he was thinking and feeling. She shrugged.

He looked at her then. His gaze had weight. It nearly made her shoulders slump. Rick sighed and shook his head. He peered up at the ceiling, and when he glanced at her again, his eyes were sad, concerned. "All this might turn into a shitshow."

"I know," Rebecca whispered in acknowledgement. She wanted to reach out for him, but she didn't. She had to find her own reassurance.

"You made some fucked-up choices back then. I know she hurt you. I know she messed up too, but the way you treated her…the way you left…" He wiped a hand over his head.

"I know." Even though it had been a few years, Rebecca remembered most of the things she'd said out of anger, resentment, and loneliness.

"I wanted to hate you." Rick closed his eyes for a second.

Rebecca swallowed and said nothing. She knew that as well. In fact, she hated herself for a while too, but finding a direction, a purpose, had been the key to changing all that.

"The way things are goin' down right now isn't helpin'."

"I know that too."

"Yeah? What else do you know?" Rick crossed his arms over his chest and waited.

Rebecca met his gaze without hesitation. "Not a damn thing."

His stared at her for several seconds. Then, slowly, a small smile appeared. He reached for Rebecca, pulling her close. "Welcome home."

A loud yowl interrupted the moment. Rebecca looked down at Peyton. "What? You're not gettin' enough attention?"

Peyton blinked and let out a meow that sounded closer to a whine.

"Don't talk to her like that." Rick kneeled and reached for the cat, scratching her underneath her jaw. Peyton stared at him and purred loudly. "She's bein' sweet."

"Yeah, but you know how she—"

"Ow, goddammit!"

Rebecca cringed. "Nevermind."

Peyton brushed and weaved her way around Rick's legs like she hadn't bit the shit out of his hand a few seconds earlier. "I'm tellin' you she's bipolar," Rick whispered.

"She just has personality. Why are you whisperin'?"

"I don't fuckin' know." His tone was only a little louder than before.

Rebecca laughed. It was good to be home.

Dani left their apartment before Rick did. In her opinion, it saved them some awkwardness. Instead of driving, she took public transportation. MARTA was slower and more time consuming, but that's what she wanted, needed. Time to kill. Despite the briskness in the air, Dani loitered around the lake at Piedmont Park. The cooler temperatures helped to ensure that the area was less populated for the moment. She shoved her hands deep into her jacket pockets and slowly walked along a well-defined trail lined with huge, nearly leafless oak trees.

It was difficult trying to dissect emotions she'd worked hard to forget. The first few months after Rebecca had left were trying, for lack of a better word. When they'd ended, everything happened so abruptly that the entire situation left her reeling. Dani stopped walking. There were stronger words for what she'd felt then. Devastated, enraged, and abandoned—a malicious trifecta had taken hold of her, and she remembered all of it well. Needing to sit, Dani walked toward a nearby bench. After taking a few deep breaths, she leaned forward and pressed her hands against her face in an effort to push away a contemptuous tide rising within her. It came anyway.

Dani stepped off the elevator and walked slowly down the hall toward her apartment. It was nearly two a.m., and she had no intention of being so late. She should have called but didn't want the added stress of yet another argument to bog her down while at work. Dani paused. She took a deep breath and tried to center herself, intending to do her best to be solicitous in the face of Becca's belligerence. It would be hard for Becca to fight without much input.

Taking the last few steps quickly, Dani shoved the key in the lock. She opened the door, and darkness was the only thing that greeted her. The TV wasn't even on, which was odd. Still, Dani's shoulders sagged in relief. Maybe Becca was sleeping and she could just slide in bed beside her and pretend that everything was okay, even if it was only for a few hours. As quietly as she could, Dani felt her way toward the bedroom. As she got closer, Dani was a little surprised by the faint light coming from around the half-closed bedroom door. She tensed up involuntarily, hoping that Becca wasn't lying in wait.

Dani couldn't stand there forever. She charged in, expecting the worst. She stopped at the foot of their bed, neatly made, and Becca wasn't in it. Something hot and searing snaked its way into Dani's stomach. She pressed her hand against her abdomen and turned toward the closed bathroom door.

"Bec-ca?" Dani whispered. She was suddenly scared to speak too loudly. Her heart thudded against her chest as she put her hand on the knob. Things were bad between them, but… "Please be locked. Please be locked."

"Becca?" Everything was quiet. She turned the knob easily and pushed the door open. The bathroom was in complete disarray. Toiletries were scattered on the floor and the sink. The doors to the cabinet were wide open.

Dani closed her eyes, and it was extremely hard to open them again. But she did. Her gaze was riveted on the empty side of the vanity. Dani tried to suck in a deep breath and found that she couldn't quite make it. The weight on her chest went from uncomfortable to crushing, making things even harder. Panic set in, and her vision tunneled. Her heart beat was loud enough, hard enough, like a percussion playing in her ears.

She had to get out. Like her body had a mind of its own, Dani left the bathroom and went straight to the closet. The folding doors were slightly ajar, and Dani ripped them open violently enough to pull one off track. She stared at the half-empty space. Part of her curled in on itself, leaving an emptiness behind as well.

The kitchen was her next stop. She flipped on the light. Numbly, she opened drawers and cabinets to find glassware, silverware, and even a majority of the food gone. When she finally made it back to the living room, Dani sat down on the couch. She stared at the cheap Wal-Mart television stand. There was a reason the TV wasn't on. It wasn't there anymore. It had been Becca's. Gone too was the DVD player, and only two DVDs remained on the open shelf.

The numbness was at once replaced by a blistering heat and a simultaneous cold that made her shudder. With shaking hands, Dani reached inside her scrubs pocket and got her phone out to call Becca. She had no idea what to say. Maybe she would yell. Maybe she would cry. Maybe she would beg.

"We're sorry. You have reached a number…"

Dani sobbed. Those two sentences cleaved her in two, leaving her vulnerable parts raw, exposed, and throbbing. She brought her knees up to her chest and continued to stare at the TV stand until it became blurry.

Becca was gone.

The sense of loss made her gasp, but it was far from the only emotion that filled her. With a loud cry, Dani threw her cell phone across the room.

Dani stood up and stumbled back onto the walking trail to get away from the hole that the bench had sucked her into. Breathing hard, she put her hands on her hips and leaned forward to try to gather herself. A jogger muttered an "excuse me" as he stepped around her. A few seconds later, a group of laughing women walked past her.

It had taken over a year for Dani to get to the point where thoughts of Rebecca were few and far between and for the ache they caused to be manageable. She'd poured herself deep into that last year of medical school and was convinced that nothing else mattered. No one else mattered, except for Rick. He'd been there through it all.

She shook her head, pulling herself from the past, and landed smack dab in the middle of the bitterness that had broken free. She could taste it in the back of her throat. Rick had been keeping things from her, and she had a feeling there was a lot more to learn. That knowledge brought a hollowness with it which settled deep in her stomach. She knew it was his way of protecting her, but Dani couldn't help but think he was protecting himself too. He had a life separate from hers, and she didn't begrudge him living it. Maybe they didn't know each other as well as they thought, which wouldn't be the first time she'd made that mistake.

Becca was here.

Dani scoffed silently. Becca coming home was the very last thing she'd expected to hear or have to face. The past that she thought was securely tucked away had been yanked free without an ounce of permission, severely disrupting the peace she'd fought for.

Her emotions were jumbled enough to give her pause. The lack of closure in that chapter of her life only contributed to her overall predicament.

She started walking again. None of this was going away. She had to deal with it, but she'd had enough for today. Hopefully, going to the hospital instead would help her keep it that way.

Instead of going directly to pediatrics, Dani took the scenic route, stopping at the emergency department first. As always, it was bursting with the sights, sounds, and smells of the sick, injured, and possibly dying. No amount of antiseptic could cover all that up. Patients moaned, coughed, cried, and there was even someone yelling. Doctors and nurses zig-zagged around her to get where they needed to be.

As a med student, she'd spent an ample amount of time dealing with adults in various areas of the hospital, and, occasionally, it was nice to reminisce. Having her fingers in so many pies was interesting, but once she'd decided on an area of concentration, Pediatrics, Dani hadn't looked back.

"You look so lost. I can find you somethin' to do."

Assuming she was being spoken to, Dani spun around in the direction of the voice. Dr. Steven Yates, the ER attending, grinned and fluttered his fingers at her. He stood tall, gangly, and reed thin, reminding Dani of a scarecrow complete with a crooked, garish smile.

Dani pressed her lips together to keep from smirking, which didn't work very well. "I'm not actually supposed to be here. I just—"

"Miss it. I know. Trust me you're not the first to wander down here and you won't be the last. Where are you right now?"

"I'm in Pediatric oncology for the next couple months, but before that I was in cardiology," Dani answered.

"Well, we might not have anything that exciting for you, and we're not exactly short handed. Still, pick a corner for the time being." He nodded toward the controlled chaos around them. "Some of these kids could learn a lot from you."

Dani inhaled deeply. Instead of responding, she turned and looked around to find a place where she could belong for the next couple of hours. It meant she had to interact with other residents, and keeping professional boundaries was something she'd become very proficient in. It prevented entanglements and perceived demands that had cost her dearly in the past.

She walked toward a patient who seemed to be the most distressed, denoted by her racking sobs. The left side of her bed was crowded with people who obviously cared. One held her hand, and the other two were reaching out, as well touching her arm and knee. The resident on the other side had her eyes trained on an iPad, reading from it verbatim instead of splitting her attention between the results or recommendations and the patient. There were people involved, and a personal touch was needed. They all looked Dani's way as she came closer.

Dani smiled slightly at the patient and her family before addressing the resident. "Can I talk to you for a minute?"

Instead of responding verbally, the resident stepped to the side. Dani did the same. She held her hand out for the iPad. "You should probably come up for air and actually look them in the eyes while you go over things."

The resident pressed her lips into a thin line, and her face flushed. "Uhm, well, I'm pretty sure she's drug seeking. Look at her records."

Dani scanned the records silently. Irritation rushed through her, and she did her best to swallow it down. "First or second year?"

"Huh?"

"Is this your first or second year in residency?"

"Oh, first." The resident—Dr. M. Salinger, according to her glossy white name tag—smiled, but Dani didn't smile back.

"You're probably right, but reading her diagnosis to her isn't going to fix anything. Don't you think she knows she has cancer?"

Dani didn't wait for Dr. Salinger's response. "Just watch and learn." She moved back toward the bed. "Mrs. Flowers?"

"Y-yes?" The woman's skin was sallow and her features pinched.

"We're gonna do what we can to reduce your pain since it's the weekend, but please contact your oncologist on Monday, okay?" Dani made a notation in the chart and handed it back to Dr. Salinger.

"Thank you. Thank you so much."

Dani nodded and flashed a soft smile at the people near Mrs. Flowers' bedside before stepping away

Dr. Salinger followed her. "But Dr. Russell—"

"She'll be on her way to a hospice in the next few months. She could be an addict, but she's also dying," Dani whispered. Sometimes a doctor had to look past what was written in a chart.

Dr. Salinger's face reddened again. She didn't look happy, but she nodded anyway.

By the time Dani headed up to pediatrics, her focus had sharpened.

CHAPTER 5

BACK WHEN REBECCA WAS STILL only contemplating a return to Atlanta, she had researched and vetted the woman who was now her new boss. Based on her findings, Rebecca had already started to develop a healthy respect for Lieutenant Benz. Not because she was a woman in a position of power, but because she was passionate, intelligent, blunt, and good at her job. It was sort of like looking in a mirror, ignoring the fact that the lieutenant was older and white.

Rebecca waited in front of Lieutenant Benz's desk as she continued to bark into the phone. Her voice dripped with irritation, and her gaze was steely even though it wasn't focused on anything in particular. It almost made Rebecca smile. The sight was so cliché, a cookie cut-out from the cop shows that flooded the major networks. Too bad those shows only scratched the surface.

A few minutes later, Lieutenant Benz hung up the phone and, with raised brows, peered at Rebecca. "So, Detective Wells. You won't need it, but I'm thinking you figured out that I'm not the type to hold your hand on your first day."

"I did." Rebecca switched her box of personal items from one arm to the other.

"Good. Just like with your last squad, we work together and pair off when it's called for. Emmet's gonna help you get your feet wet."

Rebecca nodded.

Lieutenant Benz smiled. It transformed the hard angles of her face into something softer and more approachable. Rebecca decided then and there that she liked her the other way better. "Detective in three and a half years. You hunker down and get shit done. We need that around here. May light some fire underneath certain asses."

Making sure to maintain eye contact, Rebecca nodded again.

"Okay, I'm already tired of looking at you." The lieutenant moved her chair back slightly and opened her top drawer. She reached in and then carefully placed the contents on her desk. "Go introduce yourself, get your service weapon, and get to work."

Rebecca stared at her new shield. She already had a lanyard around her neck ready and waiting. "Thanks." She picked up a new piece of her future and headed for the door.

"Don't talk my ear off or anything."

The statement was so deadpan that Rebecca paused and looked over her shoulder.

Lieutenant Benz grinned. More of a baring of teeth, really. "Emmet is gonna love you."

Rebecca nodded and put her shield in the box with the rest of her stuff. Once more, she stepped out into the squad room. Three sets of eyes looked back at her, staring the same way they had when she'd first walked in.

One man, clean shaven and balding, peered at her over the rim of his coffee mug. He raised a thick bushy brow as she met his gaze. Rebecca moved toward him first and held out her hand. "I'm Rebecca Wells"

He put his mug down and rolled from behind his desk. Staying seated, he took the hand she offered. "Mark Strong. Nice to meet you, Becca."

Rebecca cringed and pushed away the urge to sigh. That name didn't sound right coming out of his mouth. "Just Rebecca, please. Not Becks. Not Becca, B, or ReRe. No offense."

His mouth twitched, and his blue eyes twinkled back at her. "None taken."

As they talked, the other two men got up and came forward. Mark jerked his head toward the right. "That one there is Emmet Thomas."

Rebecca turned toward him. He was on the short side, maybe three or four inches taller than her own five-foot four-inch frame. His arm muscles bulged, but so did his stomach. He sported a goatee and had blond flouncy hair like he belonged in a boy band. Emmet smiled all big and bright.

"You can call me Em. It's cool."

She studied him, wondering if he was teasing, but his gaze was warm, open. Emmet took her free hand, covering it in both of his. He glanced at the box Rebecca held in the other. "Can I help you with that?"

"I got it. Thanks," Rebecca answered.

"All right there, Dudley," Mark mumbled.

Emmet pursed his lips and rolled his eyes.

The other guy snorted.

"Dudley?" Rebecca looked from Mark to Emmet and back again.

Mark grinned. "Yeah, as in Do-Right."

Rebecca cut her eyes in Emmet's direction. "By the book, huh?"

"Yes." Emmet drew the 's' out. He glared at Mark, but smiled slightly.

"Nothin' wrong with that," Rebecca said.

"Boom! Thank you!" Emmet threw his hands high above his head.

Rebecca joined the other two men in staring at him.

Emmet sobered almost immediately.

"Uh-huh." Mark shook his head. "And this is—"

"Alvin," the man interrupted, "Alvin Johnson." He was tall, stocky, and his complexion was much darker than her own. The bottom part of his face disappeared behind a thick but short graying beard that matched the hair on his head. "Hey. Good to have you. Thank God I'm not the token anymore."

Mark and Emmet groaned but didn't say a word.

Rebecca shook his hand. "Yeah, I guess you can look at it that way."

Alvin grinned and then roared with laughter. "I'm just foolin'." He waved a hand toward Mark and Emmet. "They're used to it."

"Yeah, it's taken me forever to figure out when he's kidding. I still don't know fifty percent of the time," Emmet chimed in.

"That's the beauty of it, my man." Alvin looked back at Rebecca. "You can call me Big Al."

Emmet nudged him, hard. His eyes bulged. "No, she can't."

"Why not? Y'all do."

"It'll sound creepy when she says it," Emmet answered in a stage whisper.

"Creepy?" Alvin frowned. Then, his eyes widened. "You mean porny?"

"Big Al," Rebecca cut in flatly. They were obviously used to this being a men's club. She had to show them things really didn't have to change all that much. A club was a club.

A loud bark of laughter shot out of Alvin's open mouth. "Oh, I like her, and that didn't sound porny at all."

Mark looked heavenward and shook his head.

Emmet smiled and sighed in what Rebecca could only assume was relief.

"Mmm, well, if being around us doesn't send you running in a week, I'd say you're a keeper." Mark patted her elbow.

Rebecca wanted to pull away, but she didn't. "Could be." Despite their propensity for unwanted touching, she was starting to like them already, but they didn't need to know that. Not yet. She'd left a group of good people in Savannah, and it bolstered her to know she might have one here in Atlanta as well.

Rebecca scanned the dusty room, made dingier by the harsh fluorescent lights above them. Lieutenant Benz was the only one lucky enough to see the sun. Part of the room was taken up by slate-gray filing cabinets, a huge whiteboard dotted with pictures from open cases, fake potted plants, and a rather fancy microwave cart beside a mini fridge.

The rest contained clunky desks pushed together in twos. Emmet's desk was the only one organized with filing baskets and separate containers for pens and pencils next to a large, sleek computer monitor. The one in front of his was bare except for an identical monitor and phone.

"I hope this is okay." He rapped his knuckles on the new desk. "It seemed better space-wise to push 'em together. It's been the three of us for so long, but if you need more room. I'm sure we can—"

"No, this is fine." Rebecca had the feeling that Emmet was going to try to talk her to death, but she had plans to work on him. He'd learn.

She placed the box on her desk and sat in her chair, adjusting it for her height. Rebecca looked inside, and her gaze landed on a memento she'd kept from her time at the academy. Applying had just been something a little more interesting to do with her sociology degree after her boring-ass job in human resources had been dissolved, leaving her unemployed for a while. The academy experience had been hell on her body, especially for a person who exercised sparingly. Every night, she'd gone back to her apartment and thanked her mattress for its kindness. So while her body wept, her mind woke up. In a way, it had been perfect timing since the world she built with Dani was a step away from falling in on itself.

Rebecca reached in and removed the paperweight she'd been staring at, letting its heaviness soothe her. It was clear, perfectly round on one end, and in the center was the world. Whenever she felt out of sorts or unsure, she held it, and, for that time, she had the world. It didn't have her. The store she'd gotten it from was nothing more than a tourist trap, and Rebecca had paid way more for it than it was worth. Still, she had to have it. She needed something to mark the occasion as the night Rebecca decided to take the academy seriously.

Her coffee mug came next. It was huge, bowl-like, and had a disgruntled-looking black-and-white cartoon cat that bore a likeness to Peyton. Nine times out of ten, she filled it with Coke instead of coffee. By the time the box was empty, her desk was still sparsely accessorized, but it was hers. She took a deep breath and let it out slowly. At least this part of her new beginning had started off well.

Rebecca's pocket vibrated. She fished out her cell phone to see a text from Rick.

I'm done around 8 or so. Ur takin me out for drinks. Still gettin cold shoulder. Tequila will help me figure out a way to warm shit up.

Bile rose in her throat along with a familiar flash of guilt. She texted back. *Ok.* When she didn't get a reply a couple minutes later, Rebecca sent another text.

Sorry.

Dani moved forward in the elevator closer to the control panel as people got off and a few entered.

"Hold the elevator!"

Because she was generally a nice person, she pressed the button. When Dani looked up to see who it was, she decided being nice was overrated. She released the button and ignored the stares of the people around her despite them nearly burning her.

Rick eyes widened, and he practically ran.

The doors started to close. He shoved a hand, then a foot, between the dwindling space, stopping it. Rick gave her a tight smile before moving to the other side. As big as the hospital was, Dani wasn't surprised that they'd run into each other, even though he usually lingered on a completely different floor in orthopedics. Still, his presence must have been her penance for not taking the stairs like she usually did in non-emergency situations.

Dani tried to move to the back of the elevator, but Rick grabbed her arm and ushered them both out.

She pulled away, but he stepped in closer, placing a hand on her back and steering them toward the door that led to the tenth floor landing.

"I don't think I can keep doin' this. For real. We gotta talk."

Her shoulders tightened. None of this should have been happening. Weren't things happy and normal just last week? The power Becca had over both of them could only be described as impressive. It had to be to pull their world out of orbit.

Dani moved away from him.

Rick dropped his hand and looked down at her. "I can't force you, but...roof, please?"

Dani was tempted to just turn around and go about her day, taking the easy way out instead of trying to remove a chunk out of the wall forming between them.

"Please?" He glanced down at his feet and then back at her.

Rick was trying. Dani had to give him that. She nodded and followed him up five flights of stairs. Even though it had only been a few days since they'd talked, it felt like much longer.

They were going to have to sift through this whole mess. Might as well start tending to the wound now rather than later. Otherwise, infection would set in and spread, and left unattended, the tissue around the area could go into a state of necrosis. Regardless of her feelings, she didn't want that to happen to them.

When they got there, Rick paused and looked out at downtown Atlanta. Dani did the same. Various buildings jutted up out of the landscape like sentinels. Despite the chill in the air, the sun, high and bright, beamed down on them. Everything seemed so small from this vantage point, people and cars included. In turn, she felt bigger and so did the problem.

"It's not a big thing now, but back in med school, when I used to let it drop that you're my best friend, people would give me a side eye."

Dani let the words seep into her. Instead of overthinking it, she let her gut do the talking. "Why, because I'm white, or because I'm a lesbian?"

Rick shrugged. "I don't know. Hell, both? Dependin' on the company I kept."

She turned her head slightly, glancing at him. Rick continued to look out at the city instead of at her. "Okay. What does that have to do with this…train wreck?"

"I don't know, but you don't think it's weird how we just meshed that first year?" Rick finally looked at her.

"No, I don't. You made it easy to trust you. Talk to you."

"Same."

"That part of us kinda feels messed up right now."

"I know." Rick peered down at his feet.

Anger roared and swirled inside her. Dani crossed her arms across her chest. "I don't think I've ever been so pissed at you." She exhaled noisily. It felt good to say it out loud.

"I *know*."

"You were like my rock when Becca left."

He didn't say anything.

"I never cared that you guys talked, but the way you've been acting. Is there more?"

Rick pressed his lips together and ran a hand over his head. "Yeah… yeah, there is. I visited her in Savannah, and when she came here we hung out too." He released a long breath like saying all that was some kind of relief. Maybe it was.

Dani's breathing went ragged. "How long?"

He cleared his throat. "Uh, since a few months after she left."

"I'm not a kid!" The words exploded out of her. "You didn't have to keep any of that from me." It wasn't like the information was going to make her fall apart. "She's your friend too. I get that." Dani paused. Her fists clenched. "God, I wanted you to take sides when things first went to shit, but I never asked you to. Never!"

Rick eyes were soft and apologetic. He reached out to her but dropped his hand at the last second.

"If I hadn't dragged it out of you, when were you going to tell me she was back? Or was the plan for her to just knock on the door?"

His head reared back like he'd been slapped.

Dani welcomed the violent rush of emotions. "Oh my God!"

"No! I wouldn't have let that happen. I—"

"Did you want me to say thank you?"

"I was just trying to—"

"Protect me? I didn't need that. I needed to trust you."

"I know! Okay? I fucked up, and I'm sorry. I'll take some responsibility for all this, but it's not just me. It's her and it's you!"

Dani stepped away from him, totally taken aback. "What?"

"Yes, keepin' things from you made the situation easier, but I didn't think you were ready to hear that I was spending time with her. You went from wantin' to know everythin' about what she was doing to actin' like she never existed. I didn't know if it's because you weren't over her or what, but the shit you put yourself through every day? You've closed yourself off—"

"You don't get to tell me I'm not ready. I did what I had to fix—"

"But you haven't! You haven't fixed anything! You've done to everybody else what you did to Becca. It's been four years since..."

Rick's words cut through her. She needed to stop the bleeding. "So I made you lie to me?" Dani threw the blame in his corner, putting a bandage on the additional cut he'd opened so she could ignore it.

"That's not what I'm sayin'!" Rick threw his hands up.

"Then what are you—"

"I don't know. This is all fucked up and it hasn't even really started yet. I'm sorry. I don't want you to be pissed at me. I don't want you to hate me. I thought I was doin' the right thing. I really did at first. It all just got away from me. You're family, both of you, and I've been tryin' so hard to keep things goin' that I didn't see..." He shook his head.

Dani swallowed and realized that he was bleeding too. "I don't hate you."

"I don't know how to fix this. Tell me what you need. I'm down for whatever."

"I don't know."

"Should I j-just..." Rick's voice cracked. With a shaking hand, he rubbed his head again. His faced scrunched up as if he were in pain. She'd never seen him look so lost. "Cut her off?"

The part of Dani that hurt wanted to say yes, but she was still rational. Still an adult. His fear jumped out at her, and Dani didn't want to compound it. How wrong would that be? "No," she said softly. "No." Dani strengthened her tone. "It's all out in the open now. We have to find a way to deal with it."

Rick released a long, tremulous breath. "Yeah, I guess we do."

"Okay, we'll talk more at home. I have to go or I'm going to be late for Noon Conference. We're having a guest who's going to finish out the lecture series on genetics." She stepped away from him.

"I'd better get back too."

As Rebecca sat down on the other side of the restaurant's table, she glanced at Rick. He looked at her, watched her, but his eyes were kind of vacant. Concern tied her stomach in knots. "You been here for a while."

He brought a glass to his lips. The liquid inside it was brown. The smell of alcohol wafted toward her from his Crown and Coke, a very strong one. It was his thing. Rick sucked down the rest of the contents and crunched on some ice. He smiled and laughed. "I'm so lit right now."

"Damn it." Rebecca stared at him.

He laughed even harder.

Had all this broken him? "I'm sor—"

"Stop sayin' that. Doesn't help anythin'," Rick practically yelled.

"I don't know what else to say."

"Then drink and shut up."

That was probably not the best of ideas. One of them needed to stay sober. As if on cue, a waitress came over. Rebecca would have thought they'd end up at a real bar, not some restaurant that was a TGI Friday's knock off. It was Atlanta; there were so many other better places to go.

"I'm Amy. Can I get you an appetizer and start you off with a drink?" She smiled and glanced in Rick's direction as well. "Another Crown and Coke for you, sir?"

"Yeah," Rebecca answered for him. "Get me the same." One wouldn't hurt.

"Will that be all?" Amy asked.

Rebecca was as far from hungry as she could get. "That's it." She peered at Rick. Changing the subject would probably be a good thing. He had more going on than the mess he'd been dragged into. It was downright selfish to act like he didn't. "How are your parents?"

He blinked at her, so she repeated the question.

Rick shrugged. "Same. I guess."

"Bullshit. You talk to them every week, and there's always a story to tell, especially since children that age can be disgustin'."

"But they both teach high school."

"Exactly."

Rick's eyes lit up a little bit. "My dad caught his favorite student givin' some guy a blow job in the boy's bathroom."

"Two guys?"

"No."

"Oh, that would've been more interestin'."

His mouth lifted at the corner. "That's what I said."

Rebecca let out a choked laugh. "Figures. You need to tell your mom to give you the recipe for her macaroni and cheese."

"I have it. I was gonna make it for you as a comin' home surprise, but things kinda went to hell."

Because of her. "Oh. Yeah, guess so."

Amy returned with their drinks.

"Seein' anybody?" Rebecca was grasping at straws which made her feel three different shades of pathetic.

For a second, Rick's forehead scrunched. "You already know the answer to that." Any other time, he would have called her out for not paying attention, but after a few drinks Rick seemed a little sluggish. "I gotta tell you though. Shit's gettin' old."

Rebecca was close to asking him what shit, but she sipped on her drink instead, waiting for him to continue.

"I dunno, wouldn't it be better if I just had the one woman who got me and the whole doctor thing?"

She almost spit out her drink. Dani had said something similar. "That would take someone really special."

Rick gulped down half his Crown and Coke and peered at her over the glass. He set it back down. "Yeah, it would." He fished out a piece of ice and popped it into his mouth, crunching on it. After a few seconds, Rick muttered, "Thanks for tryin' not to be a shitty friend."

"You're welcome." That was pretty much the only thing she could say to that.

"Still shittiness all the way around. I talked to Dani and told her everythin'."

A million questions clogged her throat, but Rebecca swallowed them back down.

"She doesn't hate me, but she doesn't like me right now either." He paused and took a long pull from his glass. "I offered to kick you to the curb."

Is that what this was? After seven years of friendship that had started at some random party, they were at good-bye? Rebecca gripped her glass hard enough to shatter it. Fear closed in on her, and it was accompanied by a sudden sense of loss. Still, she didn't say a word.

"She said no, but maybe that's the best thing…"

She couldn't blame him. She couldn't blame Dani. None of that stopped her heart from ramming against her chest.

They stared at each other.

Rebecca had a chance to be the hero in this scenario, but she didn't want to be. Rick was all she had left here. She had the guys from her former squad. They were all…friendly, but Rebecca only let them in so far. "There's gotta be a way we can work this out."

"That's what Dani said."

She closed her eyes. Hope settled over her. It was thin, fragile, but there.

"No lie though. I don't even know where to start."

After downing the rest of her drink, Rebecca added, "Yeah, me either." Regardless, he was worth the effort, and so was their friendship. Desperately, she hoped that he thought the same.

An hour or so later, Rick stood. "I gotta pee." He stumbled and almost fell while trying to scoot the chair out of the way.

Rebecca jumped up to help him. She wrapped an arm around his torso. He leaned on her and almost sent her sprawling. She righted herself and followed the signs to the bathroom, ignoring the looks they got along the way.

Waiting, Rebecca put her back against the wall. After more than five minutes passed, she made up her mind to stick her head in to make sure he was all right. The door almost hit her in the face.

Rick flailed backward in surprise.

Rebecca grabbed his shirt to keep him upright.

He looked down at her and blinked. "Can you get me an Uber?"

She shook her head. "No, I got you."

"Becca, you can't take me home. She's not ready to—"

"I know that. You're comin' home with me." She wrapped an arm around his torso again. Doing this for him wasn't much, but the small things mattered. Hell, everything mattered. Rick deserved so much more from her. She had to try to be there for him. This was the least she could do.

CHAPTER 6

DESPITE EVERYTHING, DANI WALKED DOWN the corridor of the pediatric oncology wing with positivity perched on her shoulders. Pre-rounds were her favorite part of the day. As a senior resident, she usually had a first year and med student along, so Dani savored the mornings she was able to do it alone while they did their own thing. It wasn't hard to put a smile on her face as she entered her first room. "How are we doing this morning, Lola?"

The eleven-year-old girl in question grunted and twisted the cell phone in her hands this way and that. A few seconds later, she sighed, pursed her lips, and lifted big green eyes to meet Dani's gaze. "Huh?"

Dani continued to grin. "How are you?"

"Bald and bored. Same as yesterday." She sassed, but there was nothing malicious in her tone. Lola dropped the cell phone onto her lap.

"I don't know any magic tricks and my jokes suck."

Lola grinned. "They do. They really do."

"Lola! That's rude." Paul, Lola's father, put his magazine down and pushed himself up from the bedside chair.

"No, it's not, Dad." Lola rolled her eyes. "Look, she's smiling."

Dani turned and slightly extended her smile to him. "Morning, Mr. Green."

"Same to you, Dr. Russell. I'm assuming we're still on track to start the last cycle of chemo in two weeks?"

"Yes, there have been no complications from surgery. She's healing well."

"You sure we can't do it early?" Lola asked with a little whine in her voice.

"Nope, sorry."

Lola huffed. Paul reached for his phone. But his daughter slapped his hand away.

"You have your own phone."

As always, these two were entertaining to watch. Dani was far from bored.

"It's charging and yours is bigger." Lola picked the phone up and flipped it over. "You have a text from Uncle Rob…" Her voice trailed off as she stared at it. "Eww, Dad! He says he's still waiting for new pictures of my hot doctor! Creepy much?"

Dani couldn't decide if she was more disgusted or shocked. She'd go with a combination of the two. She glanced at Lola briefly, and they both turned their gaze toward Paul.

He blinked at them both owlishly. "Who?"

"Uncle Rob!"

"I don't know who that—"

"Your brother? My uncle?" Lola looked at her father as if he had something extra growing out of his head.

Paul laughed nervously. "Oh, you mean Bobby." He turned toward Dani then rolled his eyes and did this weird shimmy with his shoulders that looked more like a seizure than anything. "Rob. Nobody calls him Rob. I got a little confused."

"I call him Rob all the time," Lola screeched. "I wonder if Mom will know who Uncle Rob is?" The last part was said teasingly.

He leaned a little closer to Dani. In reaction, Dani took a step away.

"It's the painkillers," Paul whispered.

"I can hear you, Dad, and I'm not taking anything for the pain anymore. Am I, Dr. Russell?"

"No, you're not." Dani stared at Paul. His face turned bright red.

Paul let out a high-pitched chuckle. Moving quickly, he snatched his phone from his daughter's hand.

Dani continued to meet his gaze. In the past couple minutes, she had gone from shocked and disgusted to somewhat amused. This man was being taken to task by an eleven-year-old.

"Uhm." He cleared his throat. "I think I'm gonna go get coffee." Paul didn't wait for a response. He walked briskly toward the door.

Dani and Lola watched him go. As their gazes met again, Dani pressed her lips together to keep from smiling. "So…still bored?"

Lola shook her head and grinned.

A couple hours later and at Dr. Meda's request, Dani stayed behind after Morning Report.

"Jesus," Dani whispered as she peered at the most recent MRI of her newest patient again. The Wilms' tumor on the boy's kidney was… "That's huge." Her words were superfluous, but she still felt the need to speak them aloud. She minimized the screen and set the iPad down before peering back up at Jacob's treatment team. She and another resident were lucky enough to be asked to be a part of it.

"Yes." Dr. Meda, the attending, put his pen back in his pocket. "Still, Jacob's mother wants to try or rather she wants to believe that chemo will shrink the tumor into nonexistence—"

"Most of the kidney including vital blood vessels have been compromised," Dani said. "He looks to be in stage two, according to his preoperative scans. Jacob's a very lucky kid, and kind of a cursed one too, to be his age with a Wilms' tumor. Chemo and surgery. That's how this works. There's no way around it." Dani looked to Dr. Meda.

"The reminder is unnecessary, Dr. Russell. You're in a room full of doctors, and Sheri, his mother, is aware of this information. Her husband died less than two years ago during what should have been a routine procedure. Her hesitancy regarding surgery is well earned."

Dani glanced at the faces around her. Some nodded in understanding, and others didn't seem affected at all. "Has somebody talked to her? He has an excellent chance at a full recovery."

"As I said, she's very aware. It's been a difficult pill for her to swallow," Dr. Meda reiterated.

"No, I mean really talked to her. Broken the hard parts down and treated her like she's human instead of a possible journal footnote?" Dani winced inwardly, hoping her words didn't sound overly harsh.

The other resident stared at her with wide eyes, and everyone else looked equally as shocked. However, Dr. Meda smiled.

Maybe backtracking a little bit wasn't a bad idea. Dani sucked in a breath. "That came out wrong. I didn't mean—"

"Yes, you did, but that's the main reason why you're here. Medicine isn't your only talent."

Dani sat up straight and blinked. "Oh...oh, you want me to—"

"Talk to Sheri. Treat her like she's human. Break down the hard parts," Dr. Meda repeated. "She doesn't seem very impressed by the rest of us. A fresh face could make all the difference. We'll proceed with chemo, and when the moment comes for surgery, you can help ease her through that reality." He stood, and everyone else did the same.

As the resident and other doctors filed out, Dani waited behind.

"Was there something you wanted to add, Dr. Russell?" Dr. Meda wasn't a tall man, but he had a regal bearing that his perfect diction reinforced.

"Yes, I was wondering if you could give me any insight on Sheri? Anything that might help?"

He nodded. "She's blunt, sometimes brutally so. I thought initially that mimicking her attitude would be effective, but it wasn't. I'm afraid, at this point, a change of tactics by someone she's already met will seem dishonest to her. You and Sheri have that trait in common since you show your fellow residents something similar, but with patients you have compassion, patience, and everything else in abundance."

"I wouldn't say brutal..."

Dr. Meda stared at her pointedly.

Dani stopped talking.

"It's okay. It works for you. Plus, you're cordial to whom you need to be."

She nodded.

"Read Jacob's chart from start to finish. I left several personal notations that may be of help as well."

"No problem."

"Good. I look forward to your overall input on this case."

Dani smiled. This was just what she needed right now—a real challenge.

Now alone, Dani's initial intent was to educate herself by reading everything she could find about Jacob, but in this situation, that felt wrong. Maybe it was a better idea to start with meeting the actual patient.

A few minutes later, Dani stood in front of the open door to Jacob Cook's room. Instead of knocking, she listened and watched. Sheri Cook sat by her son's bedside. She leaned forward, getting as close as possible. Dani couldn't hear what they were saying, but the laughter that followed, no matter how weak it was, warmed her heart. Children really were the most resilient miracles. Sometimes, no matter how much pain or discomfort they were in, they found laughter and tiny pockets of happiness.

Dani rapped her knuckles lightly against the door. As both mother and son turned to look at her, the laughter faded as if Dani was a reminder of where they were and what they had to endure. She stepped forward and glanced around the room.

"I'm Dr. Russell, a senior pediatric resident, and I've just been added to Jacob's treatment team. But…" Dani let her voice trail off as they digested the new information. "Can I just say I like you guys already? Any boy who can sleep in the My Little Pony room and not complain is impressive in my opinion, and the mother who's raising him is obviously the best."

Sheri Cook studied her. It was an odd feeling, kind of like being poked and prodded by hands Dani couldn't see. So instead of fighting it, Dani moved forward and gave Sheri time to examine her further as she turned her gaze toward Jacob.

"Ma says I look good in pink," Jacob informed her. His voice started out strong but softened almost immediately. As expected for a nine-year-old with cancer, he was tiny, fragile.

"And what do you think?" Dani asked.

"It's cool. I like orange too. She thought I was too black to pull it off, but I showed her." Jacob nodded and gave her a wan smile.

Sheri chuckled, and she looked at her son with eyes so full of emotion that Dani found it hard to swallow. She almost stepped away from the intensity.

"Yes, he did. He's shown me a lot of things." Sheri leaned forward and kissed her son's forehead.

"Yeah, she knows how to play GTA V now."

Dani definitely got the impression that what Sheri had learned from him went much deeper than that.

Sheri shook her head. "Let you tell it." She glanced up and held Dani's gaze. Her expression unreadable. Her only tell was the crinkle between her eyes.

Just like with superheroes, Dani'd heard enough about video games to have a working knowledge. GTA V was part of the Grand Theft Auto series. Games full of violent, criminal, and sometimes sexual content. Dani wondered if maybe Sheri was waiting to be judged for allowing her son to play.

Well, she was going to have to wait longer. "I've heard that game has a lot of driving in it. Doesn't that get old?" Dani looked at mother and son for the answer.

"I—"

"No! You don't have to, but you can steal cars, rob people, and do whatever you want." Jacob interrupted his mother. "That's the best part."

"But we know none of that's real and decent folks don't act like that, right?" Sheri looked from her son to Dani and back again.

"Yeah, Ma. I'm not ever gonna be 'bout that."

The best thing for patients and their families was to meet them where they were, whether it was in denial, anger, sadness, or anything else. From what Dani had learned so far, the Cooks seemed hopeful, so that was where she was going to be as well.

"I know he doesn't have a lot of energy right now, but I don't see anything wrong with him playing the games he wants here," Dani said. "We have some, but they're not the most recent ones."

Sheri's eyes widened.

Jacob's smile was wide and bright. "She's all right, Ma. I like her."

Dani grinned. "I'll leave you two to discuss it. I'll be back later." She walked backward toward the door. Sheri's expression settled back into inscrutable, but Dani remained hopeful that she'd made progress even if it was only an inch.

Pasta was supposed to taste better on the second day, but in this particular instance that was not the case. Dani picked up her napkin and got rid of the overly dry mess in her mouth. She bookmarked the medical journal she was reading to prepare for the lecture that was going to be given in Noon Conference and got up to dump the rest of her food in the trash. Whatever they were serving in the cafeteria had to be better than what she'd just thrown away. That's what she got for trying to cook her own food. She was determined to have an early lunch.

Once there, Dani eyed the sandwiches. Chicken salad and croissant seemed to be the most decent choice. Besides, they usually made the kind with grapes and walnuts in it. She grabbed a bag of chips and a bottle of water to go along with it. As she waited to move up in the cashier's line, Dani leaned against the railing and glanced out at the cafeteria. It was bustling just like always, but full of more visitors than hospital personnel.

She was a little surprised to see Rick at a table by himself. Obviously, he had the sense to stay away from the pasta she'd made. Three days had passed since they'd talked on the roof. They'd been cordial since. So much for working things out. Rick being alone was indeed unusual. He had other friends. Just then, Sandra walked up to his table. Dani couldn't hear what was being said, but irritation flashed across Rick's face just as clear as day before Sandra nodded and walked away. Was he isolating himself on purpose? Was he punishing himself?

"Can you move up, please?"

Dani jumped slightly and looked at the woman behind her. "Sorry." She inched forward in line. It was strange to see him like this. Despite his neutrality, Rick was now firmly entrenched in their little melodrama, and it wasn't agreeing with him at all.

For a moment, Dani put herself in his shoes. Stuck between two women he loved like sisters and trying vehemently not to hurt either one of them. Rick looked up. Their gazes caught. His smile was slight, hesitant, and then it disappeared completely.

Somebody needed to do something here. Somebody needed to be the bigger person. It had to be Dani because Becca didn't have it in her. When things got tough, Becca had a tendency to lash out and eventually leave. She had hard evidence of that. Maybe, just maybe, if Dani waited it out, Becca would leave again and things would go back to normal. She glanced at Rick once more. What kind of person would she be if she let Rick get ripped to shreds in the meantime?

Finally at the front of the line, Dani gave her lunch to the cashier to scan. She smiled and agreed to have the contents bagged. A few seconds later, as she neared the exit, Dani cast one last look at Rick. Dani would have loved to join him, but this was a working lunch. She had every intention of talking with him later at home where there were no real time constraints. He'd been by her side for so long, she couldn't remember what it was like without him. Everything that had happened recently hadn't negated any of the past.

Dani filed onto the elevator behind other people and moved to the side since the button to her floor had already been pushed. Forgiving Rick would help him, help them, but he was just a piece in the overall complicated puzzle. She had to go where things were most broken: straight to Becca. Dani pressed a hand to her stomach in an attempt to alleviate the sudden hollowness that invaded her insides. She'd push through it for him, and maybe at the same time, she could get some closure.

Finishing up her final rounds, Dani saved her most difficult case for last. She'd done the obligatory walk-through with the attending and the rest of the team much earlier, so additional visits to patients weren't needed. That didn't keep Dani from doing them despite the extra work. She considered it part of affirming or building rapport.

She stopped at Jacob's partially open door and knocked softly. Seconds later, Sheri stood before her. She didn't look any more welcoming than she did before. Discreetly, Dani looked past her into the dimly lit room.

Sheri moved to the side obstructing her view. "He's sleeping."

Instead of being put off by Sheri's protectiveness, Dani was moved by it. "I know. I promise not to wake him. I'd like to see him and check on some things. I saved him for last. Figured you'd want to talk."

Sheri's eyes widened again as surprise flitted across her face. "Yeah, I do, actually." She stepped out of the doorway completely. After glancing over her shoulder at her sleeping child, she pulled the door closed all the way.

"Listen." She lowered her voice and crossed her arms over her chest. "It's all well and good that my son likes you, but we're not here to be friends. I just want the best for him, so you don't have to pretend for me, Just do your job." Her tone wasn't bitter or full of attitude, just matter of fact.

Dani could respect that. "I hear you."

"Good." Sheri nodded and dropped her arms to the side.

"With that being said, Jacob is not just a rare disease to be studied, zapped, and poked. He's a pretty sick child who needs care, compassion, and hope from all those around him. That's part of the healing process too." Dani paused. "For both of you. You're people, and I'm going to treat you that way. Okay?"

Sheri's mouth opened, closed, and opened again.

"Now, I promise I'll do my best not to wake him." Instead of pushing things further, Dani gave Sheri the reprieve she needed to gather herself.

Sheri stared, but the wrinkle between her eyes was gone. She stepped out of the way.

Dani smiled. Confident that she was on the right track, she basked in the positive. Not just for her, but for Jacob and his mother too. Maybe that feeling would stay with her for the rest of the night. More than likely, she'd need it.

Emmet stopped the police-issued Chevy Impala in front of a ranch-style home right smack dab in the middle of Buckhead. The shrubbery was overgrown, and the grass was mostly waist-high weeds.

"This address isn't on the list of open cases you gave me." Rebecca glanced at Emmet.

He exhaled noisily. "No, this one has been handed over to the Feds. They're not big on giving out info, so I like to check in with the mother at least once a month. Make sure she's in one piece. I'm late. Shoulda stopped by a couple weeks back."

So, the man who played it by the book had a huge soft spot as well. That was something she could get behind. Even though Emmet had only given her the bare bones regarding the situation, it was still enough to figure out. "Human trafficking."

"Yeah, and these guys are good but not very original. Lured girls, aged sixteen to eighteen years old, with the promise of a modeling contract. A shit-load showed up, and they really leaned on the ones who didn't have a lot of support." Emmet shook his head. "You know how it goes. It's been over two years. A couple of them had aunts, uncles, or something. A lot of them have moved away. Who can blame 'em?"

"No one. That's a hard reminder to live with," Rebecca answered.

"Exactly."

"There's no car in the driveway. So…"

"Yeah, I saw that. Probably shoulda called ahead. She's usually home though."

Rebecca looked at him. "You wanna leave a note or somethin'?"

Emmet shook his head. "Nah, I'm gonna go knock anyway. If she's not home, I'll call her tonight." He got out of the car and was back a few minutes later. "Let's go. Nobody's home."

"Okay, why don't you let me drive?"

His eyebrows shot up. "Oh, I'm fine."

"I know, but I'm a little tired of being chauffeured around. No offense."

Emmet's face reddened. "Damn, yeah sorry. It's nothing personal. Even when I'm with one of the guys I usually drive. I didn't mean—"

"Emmet," Rebecca interrupted.

He blinked. "Huh?"

"Shake it off. It wasn't a personal attack."

"Good. We'll figure each other out eventually, huh?"

Instead of answering, Rebecca grunted and opened the passenger side door.

A few seconds later, she pulled away from the curb.

"You're not a big talker, are you? We've been riding together almost a week. I can count on one hand the conversations we've had that weren't case related."

Rebecca cut her eyes at him. "And you are."

"I'm what?"

"A big talker."

"Yeah, I guess so." Emmet's forehead wrinkled.

"Balances things out, then, don't you think?"

He snorted. "No, not at all."

Rebecca bit her lip to keep from smiling.

"Mind if I turn on the radio? I'm a little tired of hearing my own voice."

She did smile this time. "Knock yourself out."

He turned it on and immediately pushed number three out of the five programmed stations. Hip-hop music filled the car.

Rebecca cringed. "No."

"What?" Emmet turned the volume down.

"I said no. Find somethin' else please."

The wrinkle was back on his forehead. "Oh, for real?"

"For real, for real." Rebecca glanced at him to let him know she was serious.

"Okay, then. I can live with that. Rock, country, or alternative?"

"No to country too."

"Yeah, I can't stand it either." Emmet's voice was laced with laughter.

"Good, as long as we understand each other." Rebecca wondered if he was always this easy.

"Okay, let's call it that."

Rebecca merged onto I-75 and ramped up the speed to match everybody else's. By the time she hit her stride, she was going eighty miles an hour. Out of the corner of her eye, Rebecca spied Emmet taking hold of the passenger grab handle. Good for him. He didn't exactly drive like a grandma, but he wasn't much faster either.

Emmet cleared his throat. "Uhm…"

Ignoring him, Rebecca eased into the fast lane. The car in front of her braked. She grumbled under her breath in response. Rebecca moved closer, hoping the driver would get the hint and switch to the other lane. Instead he braked again, making her do the same. "Oh, come the fuck on! There's a special place in hell for people who don't know how to drive!"

"Uh, Rebecca? We're supposed to observe the same traffic—"

"Shhhh!" She held up a hand in front of his face.

Determined, she gripped the steering wheel and changed lanes, intent on passing the asshole in front of her. Rebecca peered out the driver side window as she accelerated, staring at the guy. He mouthed "fuck you" as she flew by him. "Yeah, no thanks. Men who drive like you are cock light!" Even though he couldn't hear a word, Rebecca gained a certain amount of satisfaction.

A startled gasping sound filled the car.

Rebecca glanced at Emmet. His face was red and his lips pressed together in a thin line. But it was the shock and the glaze of fear in his eyes that made her laugh out loud. "What?"

"Jesus Christ! What do you mean, what?" Emmet screeched.

"Oh, you're fine." She waved off his concern.

He glared and reached for the radio. He pushed number three again and turned it up louder.

Rebecca's work day didn't have any incredible highs or devastating lows, but she still felt the need to unwind. She could either go with her melodrama-soaked classic-movie collection or something a lot more badass. Crying wasn't an option, so *Imitation of Life* was out, and there was no way in hell she was in the mood for a love story. Sandra Dee was just shit out of luck.

Peyton rubbed against Rebecca's leg. She glanced down at her. "What?"

She stared and meowed loudly.

"Okay, you don't have to yell." Rebecca bent over to pick up her empty food bowl. Peyton swiped at it, sending it tumbling to the floor.

Rebecca sighed. "Doing stuff like that is counterproductive. I know you know that."

Peyton meowed again and blinked. Those big green eyes and that sweet face made her look so innocent. Before moving to Savannah, Rebecca could've sworn she wasn't a pet person, but loneliness and meeting Peyton at the ASPCA had made her out to be a liar.

"Yeah, you know."

As Rebecca retrieved the bowl from the floor, Peyton nipped at her wrist. "Stop it. I'm going as fast as I can."

This time, the yowl was a lot louder and longer. Her black-tipped tail swished at the same time.

"Jesus." Rebecca filled Peyton's bowl from the dry food bin on the counter and opened the refrigerator to get the wet. "I got all the drama I need right here, yeah?"

Peyton screeched and reared back like she was either going to jump on the counter or on Rebecca's leg. "Don't you dare!"

She stretched instead.

Rebecca put Peyton's food where it belonged on the floor by her water. She'd made her movie decision—badassery all the way. She mentally flipped through her DVD and Blu-Ray collection, concentrating on Samuel L. Jackson. There was just something about that man's presence on the screen that was all attitude, and sometimes he even projected it in real life. By the time he was done with Hollywood, the term "motherfucker" needed to be retired. No one would be able to use it better. Why couldn't he be her uncle or a distant cousin? He'd definitely be someone she'd seek out and get to know.

She reached into the cabinet and pulled out a bag of movie-theatre butter microwave popcorn. That, along with a Coke and a couple of beers, was an easy dinner. As the microwave beeped with finality, Rebecca made her decision: *Jackie Brown*. Couldn't go wrong with Samuel L. Jackson and Pam Grier in the same movie.

Almost an hour later, the ringing of the doorbell irritated and confused her. Peyton, as she always did, scurried away at the sound. Rebecca racked her brain and came to the simplest and most likely explanation. It had to be Rick. She stood and didn't bother to pause the movie. Backing up slowly toward the door, she kept her eyes on the television and started mouthing Ordell's words. He was right: an AK-47 was the best thing to use to kill everyone in the room. Rebecca chuckled. She needed a little levity to prepare to deal with Rick and the whole situation they were wrapped in.

She turned and nearly tripped over her own feet. Through the curtain that covered the glass part of the door, Rebecca saw the outline of a woman. As she got closer, the outline became clearer, illuminated by the light on the porch. Rebecca pulled the curtain aside and was in no way prepared to see a wide-eyed Dani staring back at her.

Rebecca's vision tunneled and all she could see was the light and Dani. Even though the movie blared, she couldn't hear it. Her heart beat so loud that the sound filled her ears. Fear, the first emotion that snaked its way to her belly, was quickly followed by guilt and resignation. Everything Rebecca had done to hurt Dani, everything they'd done to each other, flashed before her. She'd done her part the past few months of their relationship to help change Dani from an open, generous person into someone apparently closed off, wary, and argumentative.

Behind her glasses, Dani's eyes narrowed, and she pressed her lips together. Her whole face seemed to harden. "Open the door, Becca."

Rebecca stood frozen, absorbing the moment slowly through her pores. Visually, Dani had barely changed at all. Her hair, in a messy ponytail, was longer, but it still looked just as dark and thick as it always had. She was as pale as ever, but there were spots of color high on her cheeks seeping downward. The thin line of her lips had reverted to their normal fullness.

"Open the fucking door, Becca!" Dani smacked her hand against the glass.

Those sounds together were enough to yank Rebecca from the weird world of memories she'd visited. She met Dani's gaze and unlocked the door. Dani stormed inside as Rebecca quickly stepped out of the way, but not before she was hit by a familiar scent, Midnight Pomegranate. She savored the smell; it had stayed with her for months after she left.

Rebecca closed the door but stayed near it, putting as much distance between them as possible. Things had never been violent between them, but Rebecca knew that sometimes emotional bombardment could be more painful than a physical blow. She wanted to be as far away as possible when things started to fly.

Dani kept her back to her but her body was angled toward the television where she seemingly stared.

Rebecca cleared her throat. "Sorry, I know that's loud."

"*Jackie Brown?*"

"Yeah."

The exchange was almost polite and totally weird. But, at the same time, it was a testament to the fact that she was in the presence of a person who knew her better than anybody, or at least she used to.

Dani turned.

Rebecca flipped on the light.

Even though the movie blared in the background, the quiet between them became a living, breathing thing.

"I wasn't gonna sit around and wait for you to make an appearance. We both know you don't do personal confrontation until you're about ready to explode."

Just like that, Dani launched the first missile, hitting Rebecca square in the chest, drilling through the other side, and unleashing a tide of anger, resentment, and a dull throbbing pain.

She lashed out accordingly. "First off, don't come at me like that! This is my house. I haven't done a damn thing to you! It's been four years." Rebecca did her best to wrangle her emotions. "I was trying to give you… give us both some time to get used to the idea of me being back here." Each word was uttered through clenched teeth.

"So, it's okay to keep Rick dangling in the middle while you make decisions for everybody?" Dani scoffed and crossed her arms over her chest.

"That's not what I said!" She balled her hands into fists. It was hard to put a cap on her rising temper. So, Rebecca didn't even try.

"It might as well be! First you had him hiding things from me, and now he's just plain miserable."

Before she knew what was happening, Rebecca took a couple steps forward, pulled by feelings she couldn't contain. "Hold up! I didn't have him doin' anythin'. That was his choice."

"Yeah, and it was the only choice he thought he had! You know how he is. He was trying to protect both of us."

"I know that!"

"He shouldn't have been in that position in the first place!"

"His choice," Rebecca spat at her.

"God, are we just gonna talk in donuts?"

"Isn't that what we always did?"

Dani covered her face with her hands and actually growled. Seconds passed before she lowered them. "No, it wasn't."

It had only been five minutes, and Rebecca was already tired. Everything she'd learned about herself, the changes she'd made were instantly forgotten. Right now, she inhabited the body and the mind of the person she'd been years ago. It was her house, but all she wanted to do was leave. "How'd you find me?"

"I never met your aunt, but I did know who she was, remember? Wasn't hard to find the address."

"Fine. So, what do you want, Dani?"

She was met with laughter. Honest to God laughter. Dani's eyes were bright with emotion. "Oh, is my being here inconveniencing you? *You* were the one who left with no warning and moved back with just as much!"

Rebecca huffed. "Whatever." Her response was petty but the only thing available.

Dani's glare was piercing and intense enough to melt plastic. "I didn't come here to rehash everything."

It was sure starting to feel like it. Then again, how could they not? Rebecca pressed her lips together to keep from responding, which didn't work. "Really? I can't tell, goddammit!"

"Yes, really. Somebody has to be the bigger person in all this, and we all know it won't be you. I don't have the time or the patience to stand by while you chew your feelings and figure out what you're gonna spit in my face."

Dani's comment cut deep. Rebecca hated the person she used to be and learning to love who she'd become had been a long, winding road. Still, there was a very thin line between love and hate. "Oh, fuck you! You never had time for me before, so why the fuck would you start now? Because it doesn't matter anymore?"

All the color in Dani's face drained. "I made some mistakes, but I tried. You know I did," she croaked.

Rebecca closed her eyes. It felt like they were in a middle of an argument they'd had a million times before with the same results. Familiar words sat on the tip of her tongue waiting to be spoken, and she lost the battle. "Consistency is fuckin' key." She pointed a finger at Dani, stabbing the air around her with each word.

Dani gasped, and the guilty expression Rebecca had seen over and over in the past made an appearance. After four years, it was shocking to learn that the wounds they'd inflicted on one another could still be so raw and gaping.

Rebecca opened her mouth to apologize.

"Rick…has been a friend to both of us." Dani's voice was thick, ragged. "We live together, and I don't want him to continue feeling torn up about it. He shouldn't have to sneak or hide to spare our feelings. He can be in both our lives. I'll do my best to stay out of your way, and you do the same."

Dani moved toward her, and then she brushed past Rebecca without a word or even a glance. Their shoulders bumped. Rebecca stiffened as a burst of electricity radiated from the area all the way to her fingertips.

The door slammed, and with it came another bout of anger at herself, at the woman who obviously still affected her, and the entire situation.

CHAPTER 7

"Despite what you say, you act like I don't mean anythin' to you!" Becca huffed and crossed her arms over her chest.

"Yeah, that's why I'm standing here being yelled at. It's something I enjoy." Dani rubbed her forehead. She could practically feel her blood pressure rising, and it did nothing to help her headache. They stood in the middle of the living room screaming at each other.

"Please! That has nothin' to do with me. You're just tryin' to make yourself feel better."

"God!" Dani's tone was loud, shrill. Exhaustion set in, making itself comfortable. Dani covered her face with her hands and sank onto the couch behind her. "I'm in medical school." Her voice softened. "I can't just play hooky because you're feeling lonely. It's my last year. I'm trying to fit everything in—"

"I'm not somethin' you just fit in, and you're fucked up for even sayin' that. Rick says you treat your patients like they're dipped in gold and everybody loves you." Becca teased out the words. "That doesn't track. I'm supposed to mean somethin' to you, and look how you're treatin' me."

Dani's chest burned as if someone had actually stabbed her. Anger filled the hole left behind. She balled her hands into tight fists as the ache increased. "You said you understood. I can't just coast through med school. I have to be dedicated. You said—"

"Ohh, here we go." Becca threw her hands in the air and started to pace, her hazel eyes wide and wild. "How many times are you gonna fuckin' say that?"

"Until. You. Hear. Me." Dani's jaw clenched so tight that it felt like she chewed each word before spitting them out.

"You think you're the only person in your class who's in a relationship? Some of them are even married!"

"To other people in the program, for God's sake!" Dani fell back, slamming her head against the back of the couch. She peered up at the ceiling. She couldn't bring herself to look at Becca anymore. Not right now. "They get how consuming it all is. I don't know why you can't."

"You used to at least try. In the past couple months, you've broken just about every promise you made to me, and when was the last time we've fucked? I refuse to even try anymore. You're either too tired or not here. God, sometimes I wish Rick had been sober enough to fuck me at that stupid-ass party. Instead I ended up meeting you. Things would have been way different the other way around."

Dani's mouth fell open. She forgot to breathe. The mental pain that statement caused was the equivalent of a blow to the head. Dani didn't know what to say but words found their way to the surface anyway. "He's in the same class as me!"

"I see him more than I see you. What am I supposed to do, huh? Just sit here and wait?" Becca moved toward her and loomed over her.

"No, do something with yourself. I can't be everything to you, not anymore. It's too goddamned hard!"

Dani woke up gasping. She threw the covers aside and sat up. Pressing a hand to her chest, she willed her heart and respiration rate to slow to normal. Several seconds passed with no improvement.

"Damn it!" Her exclamation didn't make the situation easier. Dani shook her head to clear it, but her mind was overrun, pulsing with thoughts and memories that after all this time shouldn't have mattered.

After her impromptu visit to Becca, Dani had hoped to feel settled, relieved. Instead, inside she churned. Her dream had seemed so real. For a moment, she was trapped in her memories where nothing she did was good enough, and every other word out of Becca's mouth was an accusation or something hateful. The residual pain was sharp, deep, and left an emptiness behind. Dani tried to swallow down the lump forming in her throat. It didn't budge.

The confrontation in her dream had been one of their last. By that time, it had been hard to recall what brought them together in the first place and, when she did, Dani hurt even more. Becca's smoldering intensity had become a thing of the past.

"Stop. Get out of my head," Dani pleaded, and fell backward onto the bed. Becca had been home only a matter of weeks, and she'd already invaded places in Dani's life that should have been locked up tight. "Uhhh!"

Dani sat up again and tried to drag herself away from the past and everything Becca. That was going to be difficult to do from now on for two reasons. One was across the hall. Shared custody seemed like a strange term to use regarding Rick, but it fit. The other was the unresolved emotions that were running rampant inside her. She wished like hell for apathy but it refused to come. Not that she ever had it in the first place.

Squinting, Dani peered at the clock on her nightstand. The red numbers were blurry. She reached out, patting around for her glasses, and found them near the lamp. Dani stared at the clock. It was just past four a.m. She lifted her glasses slightly and rubbed her eyes.

Dani stood and stretched. There was no reason to linger in her bedroom. There was really no reason to stay home. She pulled her door open and walked across the hall to Rick's. Yes, it was early, but she was eager to see him, talk to him, reconnect. She owed him a real apology for her petulance. When it came down to it, she'd do anything to have her best friend back. Dani knocked softly and put her ear to his door. She gave it a few seconds before doing it again.

"Rick?"

No answer. He wasn't a hard sleeper unless he was exhausted. Dani turned the knob, opening his door. She stared into the darkness and then flipped on the light. His bed was empty and unmade. A twinge started in her chest and ended at the pit of her stomach, leaving a brand new pain behind.

Becca. He was at Becca's.

Dani sucked in a breath to ease the feeling as she identified it. Jealousy. Maybe being an adult about all this was easier said than done.

When she finally got to Amery, it was well after five a.m. Dani slammed the door to her decrepit Honda and activated the alarm. Not like anyone would steal it, but still. While weaving her way through the resident parking lot, she fished out her cell phone only to stare at it as she inched closer to the building. She'd tried unsuccessfully to push everything she was feeling away, so maybe letting it all out was the best way to go. Dani slid her thumb across Rick's name and pressed her cell against her ear. It rang three times before he answered.

"Dr. Turn…" Rick paused. "Oh, hey." He sounded surprised.

Dani heard people in the background. A lot of it was muffled but familiar. "Are you at the hospital?"

"Yeah, why?"

"You stayed there all night?" Dani's face heated as shame washed over her.

"Yeah. Oh. You thought…" He sighed. "I think I'm startin' to understand how a kid feels after his parents' divorce."

She wasn't surprised by that statement. Dani'd come to the same conclusion herself. "Look, I'm sorry you're in the middle of all this. I went to talk to her about it. I don't want you to feel disloyal to either one of us."

"I know. She told me."

Involuntarily, Dani gritted her teeth. *I bet she did.* "Atlanta is big. We can all co-exist." Who was she kidding? They'd probably set the city on fire, but maybe it was best to tell Rick what he needed to hear right now.

"You would think." Rick cleared his throat. "So, did things go down like you thought they would?"

"I don't want to talk about it. Why don't you ask her?"

"I did. All I got was a bunch of uh-huhs and enough gruntin' to make her sound like a pig. I think once I see her face to face she'll have somethin' to say."

No, Becca had never been a big talker, but the few words she did speak usually carried weight. "I don't care if you see her, hang out with her, or whatever."

"Hold on." The noise in the background quieted after a few seconds. "Bullshit."

Dani pressed the button for the elevator. She didn't say a word.

"This was easier to handle when she wasn't in town."

"I bet. Look, I'm trying to be the bigger person here. You know Becca won't…" Dani stopped herself before she could go further. "Sorry, sorry."

"She's not the same person she was."

"You could've fooled me."

"Where are you?" Rick asked.

"In the elevator on my way to Peds."

"Come see me first."

"No, I don't wanna do this here. We've said enough for right now. Are you gonna be home tonight?"

"Yeah, I'll be late, but we'll talk then?"

Dani checked the floor number as the elevator dinged. "Yes, we will."

When she got to the Peds wing, most of the rooms were still dark, which wasn't surprising given the hour. Dani stopped at the nurses station, smiling and engaging in small talk with familiar faces, which was a necessary formality. Being on the good side of the nurses in Peds made her days a lot easier. She gathered the needed information from the charge nurse about various patients to better prepare her for the day ahead. By the time she was done, Dani finally had the relief she'd craved earlier as her mind resettled on the challenges in front of her. She belonged to her patients right now, and she'd never felt safer.

As she passed by Jacob's still-dimmed room, Dani paused and pushed the door open a little wider, bringing in some light. Sheri Cook sat on the edge of her rollaway cot. Her hands covered her face. She took a step forward. The need to fix revved through Dani's system.

Sheri looked up then. She rose from the cot and walked quickly toward Dani. "I know this is a hospital, but don't I get some kind of privacy? It's not even light yet. Don't you have a life?" Her tone was bitter, angry, and full of emotion. Dani had no idea what to say. She moved backward, and it gave Sheri just enough room to close the door in Dani's face.

Dani blinked, and for a few seconds, she stared at the closed door. Numbed and shocked by what occurred, she turned and walked with no destination in mind, ending up in the resident lounge.

Moving mindlessly, she poured coffee and sat on one of the couches to drink it. Dani replayed the confrontation over and over in her head, trying to figure out what had rattled her. Slowly, she came to the conclusion that maybe she should've given Sheri some space. The disagreement itself wasn't bothering her. It was what Sheri had said. Did she have a life? Of course she did. She had family she talked to occasionally, and she had friends…a friend. Dani had a life, a very full one.

She was sure of it. Dani did her best to ignore the doubt creeping in.

Alvin smiled slightly as he opened the bottle at his desk and poured the water into a glass. "Here you go."

"Thank you." Mrs. Stern's hand shook as she gulped down the first few swallows.

"You sure you don't want anythin' else? We have coffee, Coke, and some other—"

"No, this is okay."

Rebecca had already hit her Coke quota for this morning, otherwise she'd have one in hand. She scooted her chair closer to Mrs. Stern and angled her body toward her. Alvin did the same.

Mrs. Stern took another drink and held on to the glass, staring into it as she spoke. "I watch *Law & Order: SVU*. Says to wait forty-eight hours, but he didn't come home last night. So, I just…couldn't."

"That's just something they made up for TV. You're doin' the right thing." Alvin said.

"I know I could have just called to make a report, but that didn't seem like enough."

"Any officer or detective would do the same thing we're doing. Sometimes this unit doesn't get involved unless the primary investigation turns up dry, but that doesn't matter. You came to the right place." Rebecca kept her voice soft but conversational.

Mrs. Stern nodded. "Okay. I have a good picture of him. It was just taken a few months back." She licked her lips. "Last time I saw him, he was leaving to get on the school bus."

"What time was that?" Rebecca asked.

"'Bout 6:45 a.m. yesterday."

"Can you give us a description of what he was wearin'?" Rebecca went on.

Mrs. Stern nodded. "His school uniform. Light-blue shirt with a lion crest for Haywood High, khakis, and a black backpack." She drank the rest of her water. "I tried callin' his phone. Had to be 'round thirty times now. It's goin' straight to voicemail. I sent texts too."

"Do you have any reason to believe that Lewis is in danger? Are there any custody issues? Issues with extended family?" Alvin's voice was soft and meant to soothe.

"Lewis is fifteen now, and not a word from that piece of crap. His daddy was long gone before he was even born. His stepfather died a few years back. I got sisters. They love him to death." She picked up the empty water bottle and tore at the label.

"So no calls or texts with ransom demands? Or any kind of threats?"

"No! I don't have any money, and he's a good boy. I can't see nobody wantin' to hurt him, but…" Mrs. Stern looked down at her hands and then back up at them. "He, uh, it's been hard to figure him out lately."

"What do you mean? Can you be more specific?" Rebecca leaned forward.

"He used to tell me everythin', but the past few weeks he's been downright mean."

Rebecca nodded and waited for her to continue.

"Snappin' at me and tellin' me to mind my own business. He *is* my business. You don't know how bad I wanted to snatch him up and knock some sense into him. I did once. Just made things worse. Thought it was drugs, but I know what high looks like. Plus, I never found anythin' in his room."

That didn't necessarily mean anything, but Rebecca chose to remain quiet about it. Instead, she scribbled down everything they'd learned so far in her leatherbound notepad. The conversation was being recorded, but she liked to keep her own notes regardless.

"Did he ever come home bruised or scuffed up? Did he have any…*new* friends?" Alvin asked hesitantly.

Mrs. Stern went rigid. She sat up tall with her shoulders back. "I know where you headed, but no, he never came home beat up. He's no hustler, and he knows better than to sniff around gangs."

"I know questions like that are upsettin'." Rebecca knew they were going to be. Parents liked to think they were aware of everything about their kids. "We didn't mean any disrespect, Mrs. Stern. We just need to cover as many angles as possible."

Glaring, Mrs. Stern huffed. "Right." She paused. "Anyhow, he's been hangin' out with the same group of kids since elementary school, at least he was."

"What do you mean?" Rebecca asked as she wrote some more.

"Haven't seen 'em in a while. About two months, I think. In fact, nobody's been around. He's been goin' to them instead. At least that's what he said. I didn't have reason to think he was lyin'."

"Okay, can we get the names of all his friends? Addresses and phone numbers too if you got 'em. Better include family members in that as well." Rebecca noticed Mrs. Stern's glass was empty. "Do you need another water?"

"No, not right now."

"Names of any places he hung out at or you think he might go to hole up."

Mrs. Stern's eyes widened. "You think he ran away? He didn't have no reason to run away. He could've been in an accident and be lyin' on the side of the road somewhere—"

"Just coverin' all the bases, remember?" Rebecca tried to calm her with the reminder. "We'll make sure to check the local hospitals too."

"Okay, okay." Mrs. Stern took a deep breath. "Maybe I'm just freakin' out about nothin', but he always comes home. Do you think I should wait and see before y'all do all this work?"

Rebecca glanced at Alvin. He opened his mouth to speak but she beat him to it. "Did you check to see if he was at school this mornin'?"

"Yeah, and he wasn't."

"Then what does your gut tell you?" Rebecca asked.

Mrs. Stern met Rebecca's gaze, her forehead creased with worry. "I'll get you all the numbers and addresses you need. I called all his friends. They say they haven't heard from him, but they might talk to y'all." Her eyes glazed over, and seconds later, she was crying.

Rebecca jumped up and grabbed the Kleenex on the opposite end of Alvin's desk.

After taking several tissues, Mrs. Stern wiped her eyes and and pulled out her phone. She stared down at it. "I'm sorry. Can I please use your bathroom?"

Alvin stood. "Sure. Down the hall to the left." He trailed behind Mrs. Stern for a second before turning toward Rebecca. "So that's how it is, huh?"

"What?" Rebecca asked.

"I don't have a problem with you takin' lead on this."

"I'm fine with that, but I wasn't tryin' to step on your toes." Rebecca folded her arms over her chest.

"I'm not like that. It's all good. You've got some experience." Alvin sat in his chair.

"If you say so."

"I just did." Alvin paused. They heard sniffling and it was getting louder. "Okay. Here she comes." Leave it to him to state the obvious.

Rebecca waited until Mrs. Stern was seated before resuming the interview. "It's best if I tell you how this works, especially for a juvenile. We're gonna issue a county-wide alert through e-mail and radio so that everyone local will be on the lookout. Right now, I'm not a hundred percent sure he isn't a runaway."

"I told you. He's not!" Mrs. Stern's eyes were bloodshot, but that didn't keep her from glaring at Rebecca.

"And I heard you." Rebecca held up a placating hand. "But we're not takin' any chances and neither should you. So, I'm gonna put him in NCIC. It's a database that police all over use. If he's spotted, we'll know. We're gonna check with everyone on that list you gave us, including his school, hospitals, everythin'. If it goes deeper than that and we find out he's been taken, we'll follow procedure and get an AMBER Alert issued.

Mrs. Stern nodded and sniffled. "Okay, thank you."

Still wiping her eyes, Mrs. Stern left a few minutes later. Rebecca made some final notations and looked up when Alvin cleared his throat.

"So, whatcha think?"

"Nothin' indicates kidnappin'."

Alvin nodded and scratched at his beard. "He really could be in the wind. Maybe Mom didn't tell us everything, or…"

"Or what?" Rebecca met his gaze.

"We could be dealin' with a mental health case."

Suicide. Rebecca met Alvin's gaze. Some of the signs were there, but it was still a big leap to make without looking further into things. "We'll see."

"Can't rule out the possibility he found himself locked in a nigga moment and ended up in a shit-load of trouble either."

Rebecca cringed. "Don't use that word around me."

Alvin's face scrunched up. "You serious? I said nigga, not nigger. I'm just keepin' things real. Callin' it like I see it. "

"Yeah, I'm doin' the same thing." She hated that word. There was no way to use it in a positive light. It wasn't like he was trying anyway.

His bushy eyebrows shot up. "All right, I hear you."

"Good, I'll put him in the system, and then we can get on with the legwork."

Rebecca pressed her lips together and shook her head as she looked at the dead body of Lewis Stern with a bullet wound to his chest. "Yeah, that's him."

The morgue attendant nodded and covered him with the sheet before closing the drawer. It hadn't taken them long to get a lead. They'd gotten information that there had been a couple of GSWs with fatalities in the area the past twelve hours that matched Lewis's description.

At least he wasn't a John Doe anymore.

"Damn, I hate it when I'm right." Alvin sighed and scratched his beard.

"Maybe, but we don't know the circumstances."

"No, he could have been in the wrong place at the wrong time, but based on what his mother said, he was more than likely into somethin' or about to be."

Still reluctant to agree, Rebecca wanted this young man's life and death to be more than a series of bad decisions. "Let's check with Homicide. I'm sure their hands are full. Obviously they haven't gotten that deep into this case yet, but maybe they could shed some light on this."

"Was just about to suggest that, and I think we should be the ones who break it to Mrs. Stern."

Rebecca grunted. That, she could agree with. "Plus if it's all the same to you, I'm drivin' this time."

Alvin huffed, but it sounded closer to a laugh. "I don't think so."

"Yeah? Why not?" She walked out into the hallway.

"It's my car." Alvin moved in step beside her.

"No, it's police issue."

He shrugged.

"You owe me." Rebecca stared him down.

"For what?

"Bein' an ass."

Alvin laughed out right. "Nothin' new. Might wanna get used to it."

"Not gonna happen. You better get used to *that*." Rebecca stopped and held out her hand.

After turning off the highway, Rebecca passed a few boarded-up houses and blew the horn at some kids playing in the street. Center Hill was a stone's throw from her own home in Grove Park and most of the area was a carbon copy—a mishmash of shitty and decent. For every nice-looking home, there were ten crappy, dilapidated ones. That went for apartment complexes as well.

"Keep an eye out for building G."

"I'm lookin'." Alvin paused. "It looks like some of them are missin' the letters on the side."

"Great. Well, it has to be near F. So look for F."

Rebecca slowed and waited for a group of young men to disperse. A couple of them looked back at the car but continued to block the road.

"Damn kids." Alvin let down his window. "Move, niggas! Don't you see us tryin' to get through?"

"Shut the fuck up, old man!" Laughter exploded from the group.

Rebecca glanced at Alvin. "Yeah, shut up, old man, and watch your damn mouth."

"Sorry, gonna have to get used to it."

"I don't even get how that seemed appropriate to you."

He shrugged. "Like they don't talk like that to each other."

That wasn't the point. Alvin was older and supposedly wiser. It wouldn't kill him to set an example. He had seemed all right at first but now not so much.'

She activated the lights and the siren. The men scattered.

"You talk like this around Mark and Emmet?"

"Yeah, why?" Alvin adjusted his seat belt.

Rebecca shrugged. "Gotta be uncomfortable."

"They never said anythin'."

"I wonder why." She caught his gaze.

Alvin didn't respond, but he looked away.

"There's F." Rebecca pointed.

They both scanned the building next to it.

"Figures it's one of the ones without a letter." Alvin huffed. "Look at this place, this neighborhood. That boy never had a chance. I'm sure we drove past ten drug deals, and those kids blockin' the street had on gang colors."

For several seconds, Rebecca was silent. She pulled into a parking spot in front of what she hoped was building G and turned off the car.

Alvin stared at her. "What did I say now?"

"Nothin'. That's true sometimes, but in this case, we know the boy's name."

Alvin made a sound, and Rebecca wasn't sure if it was in irritation, agreement, or acknowledgement.

"You takin' lead on this too?"

Rebecca met his gaze again. "Yeah, I think I better."

They got out of the car, and instead of looking for a possible elevator, they went for the stairs.

A couple minutes later, they stood outside apartment 367G. Rebecca raised her fist, poised to knock.

"I'm not an asshole. I just call it like it is."

Rebecca glared. "Most of us have a filter."

"Mine went to shit a few years back."

"Now isn't the time to talk about this."

Alvin held up his hands in surrender. "I know."

After taking a deep breath and ignoring the hard twist of her stomach, Rebecca knocked. Even though she'd learned to separate the personal from the professional early on, that didn't mean she wasn't affected. She was human.

"Who is it?"

"APD," Alvin answered.

Mrs. Stern opened the door. For a second, her eyes were wide and full of hope, but only for a second.

Rebecca pulled into her driveway. Sitting quietly for a moment, she embraced the exhaustion rolling through her. That meant she was too tired to think about Dani, in the past or the present. So far, staying busy had been the key. She'd learned years ago that idleness was her enemy, allowing assumptions and suspicions to grow and fester into nasty feelings that were impossible to contain.

Getting out of the car was a minor chore. Rebecca glanced at her house. She'd forgotten to turn on the porch light, and there was no one there to flip it on. There was no one there listening for her car, no one there to greet her, except Peyton.

Lately, the cat wasn't enough.

CHAPTER 8

After pulling up behind Rick's SUV parked on the side of the road, Rebecca got out and joined him under the hood of his car.

"Thanks for comin' to the rescue. Pretty sure my starter just went to shit." Rick shined his flashlight in Rebecca's direction, cutting through the darkness

Rebecca shrugged. She had no idea what a starter looked like or where it was. "Well, while it's wiping its ass, did you call for a tow?"

Rick chuckled. "Yeah."

"Okay, well let's go wait in my car. It's gettin' colder."

He rolled his eyes. "Just barely, and you're only feelin' it 'cause—"

"Before you say it, you know I'm average height." Rebecca walked toward her car.

He followed. "Uh-huh, which is five-foot-four for black women. You're shrinkin'."

Rebecca opened the driver side door and glared at him over the top of the car. "What? I'm not shrinkin'"

"Black women are."

She sat down and glanced at him. "Is that some kind of political commentary?"

"What? That Trump has made you...us smaller?"

"Well, he has to. How else will he keep us down with those tiny hands?"

Rick snorted. "Yeah, yeah, but what's that story with the giant that was taken down by all those little people?"

Rebecca tilted her head as she looked at him. "You mean one of those *Star Wars* movies where they use the rope on that big metal thing that looks like an elephant?"

He reared back slightly. "What? No!" His voice went up a couple octaves. "The one with the white man. It's a story I read in high school, I think."

"Oh, *Gulliver's Travels*?" Rebecca guessed again.

"Yeah, that's it."

"God, let's take a minute and enjoy that imagery. Trump's ass topplin' like a tree with a whole bunch of brown people dancin' around him."

"I know, right?" Rick sighed.

"Mm-hm." Rebecca leaned back against the head rest. "By the way, you still doin' that mentorin' thing?"

"Yeah, when I can. It's mostly teenage boys now, sixteen to eighteen."

"That'll work. They're just about old enough to hold the rope."

Rick laughed. "Great minds…"

"Exactly, but on a lighter note, have you decided if you're gonna do the sports-medicine thing yet?"

"That's not lighter." He groaned and turned to look out the windshield. "I'm leanin' toward it. If I get the right fellowship, my foot will be all up in that door. I already applied early to a few a couple months back. When I'm done, I could get hired on in a private practice and make a shit-load of money."

"Decisions, decisions. Not everybody gets to make money doin' what they enjoy."

"True. I do love what I do."

"You're kinda like Jesus."

Rick glanced at her. His eyes were huge. "Say what now?"

Rebecca laughed. "You know, like a carpenter—you tinker with the framework."

He nodded and smirked. "Okay, I can see it. Like Jesus. I like it."

"Thought you would."

"Thanks for that and thanks for comin'."

"Why wouldn't I?" Rebecca reached out to turn up the heat.

"You coulda been workin'."

"I was actually on my way home when you called."

"Well, damn. Lucky me." Rick put his back against the car door.

"Mmm." Rebecca met his gaze and studied him. The lack of tension in his frame and his teasing were a good sign. "You seem more…you."

Rick shrugged. "I told you, Dani's doin' her best to be okay about this whole thing."

"Yeah." She wanted to believe that, but Rick wasn't there a few days ago when it had looked like smoke was going to come out of Dani's ears.

He narrowed his eyes. "Did you really think all this was gonna be easy?"

Rebecca didn't answer.

"Where do you see things goin' with her?"

She looked at him then. "I don't know."

"Where do you want them to go? And don't say I don't know."

"I..." Rebecca paused to gather her thoughts. "It's hard to reconcile who I am now with the person I was then. I didn't have anythin' but her. No direction. No ambition. Nothin'. So, I put everythin' in her, and lashed out at her when she couldn't do the same."

Rick looked at her silently. Light surrounded them as cars passed by.

"I was wrong to do that, and the guilt..." She shook her head. "I haven't been able to let it go. It's been almost four years, and I wanna make it right. I have to. I've been so fuckin' stuck."

He smiled.

"What?" Rebecca asked.

"Look at you bein' all vulnerable."

"Yeah, well."

"So you want her to forgive you?" Rick pushed on. Thank goodness.

"Yeah, that's part of it, I think, and she's nowhere near bein' able to do that." Rebecca zipped up her jacket.

"Seems like you have to forgive her too."

Rebecca laughed. "I actually thought I already did, but seein' her face to face like that brought it all back."

"Mmm, so then what?" Rick arched a brow and waited.

Glancing away, Rebecca saw in her rear-view mirror a vehicle large enough to be the tow truck closing in on them. "Tow's here."

Rick glared.

The truck drove right past them.

"Well, that must have been embarassin' for you."

Rebecca still refused to look at him.

"You don't know, do you?"

Instead of answering his question, she asked one of her own. "Why didn't you call her to come get you?"

Rick shrugged. "I haven't seen you in a few days. I live with her."

"You think she's home?"

"Don't know."

"Despite her tryin', you don't think she'll have a problem with me just showin' up?" Rebecca asked.

"Do you?"

Rebecca laughed. "Hell, yes."

"You could just drop me off."

"I could." But she wasn't going to do that. Rebecca had to start somewhere, and her last discussion with Dani wasn't exactly a good jumping off point.

Light filled the car again, and this time, a tow truck pulled in front of Rick's SUV.

By the time Rebecca pulled into the parking lot of Rick and Dani's apartment building, her nerves were in tatters. Instinctively, she was tempted to hide it. Old habits and all that came with them. She gripped the steering wheel hard enough to cause discomfort.

Rick patted her thigh. "Either she'll try like she said she would—"

"Or it'll be a shitty good time for all of us, especially since she wants as little contact between us as possible," Rebecca interrupted.

"Yeah, but it's my place too. I'm done sneakin' around and bein' a coward about this. Y'all are gonna have to see each other sometime. No way around it. Might as well start tonight." Rick pointed. "She's home. There's her car."

Releasing a long shaky breath, Rebecca tried to prepare herself for another confrontation. If they kept exploding all over each other, eventually the animosity would have to blow itself out. Hopefully. However, she couldn't be the old Rebecca, full of vitriol and resentment. "You're all I have. The only person who sees me for who I am now."

He squeezed her knee. "I know."

Rebecca chuckled even though there was nothing funny. "I'm sorry. Must be a huge responsibility."

Rick held her gaze. "I wouldn't be here if I didn't think I could handle it. Besides, you're more than worth it." He cleared his throat. "That's why I should apologize to you."

"For what?"

"For gettin' caught up and tellin' Dani I was willin' to cut off my friendship with you."

"Oh yeah, that." The statement still stung. Hell, who was she kidding? It was more than a little scary.

"Yeah…that won't happen again. Promise." He reached out for her hand. "Okay?"

"I'm not goin' anywhere."

She wanted to hug him. So, she did.

Dani scrunched her nose as she peered in the refrigerator. They needed to do some serious grocery shopping. She grabbed the huge pizza box. The contents were probably the only thing fresh enough to eat. After putting the box on the stove, she flipped it open and poked at the rubbery cheese. It didn't look too gross. She picked a piece up and nibbled on the edge.

Tasted fine. Dani took another slice and some paper towel and put everything in the microwave. After opening the refrigerator again, she grabbed a bottle of juice. Dani heard the door open. "Hey, all we have is leftover pizza unless you brought something home."

There was no response.

She closed the door and looked toward the living room. He did bring something home. Dani actually experienced lightheadedness as blood drained from her face. It was a peculiar, tingly feeling. She clutched at the counter as dizziness swept over her. The ball of emotions that slammed into her chest was too tight and compact to unravel. Rick was forgotten. She stared as Becca walked further into the apartment.

"…broke down. Had to call a tow truck. Becca picked me up." Dani barely heard him. His voice was background noise.

Becca looked away and actually stepped back. She practically disappeared behind Rick. Confused and somewhat fascinated by her actions, Dani was unable to tear her gaze away. Becca certainly hadn't been like that a few days ago. Then, she'd been locked and loaded, ready to fire. Maybe it was because Rick was here? That had never stopped them before, especially after things got bad.

"Dani?" Rick snapped his fingers. "Did you hear me?"

"Yeah." She turned her attention to him, glaring at him as the microwave beeped.

"It's my place too." He crossed his arms over his chest and glared right back.

"I know that." Dani spat the words at him as resentment inched its way to the forefront.

"Good—you guys figure it out," Rick said. "I gotta pee, and I refuse to hold it."

Now alone, their eyes met again. Dani let it all seep in. It was going to take some time to get used to the shorter hair. The style made Becca look more mature, and her smoky, intense eyes stood out more than ever.

Becca cleared her throat and started to fidget. She shifted from side to side, and she couldn't decide if her hands needed to be in or out of her pockets. Becca didn't fidget. Suddenly, Dani realized that she'd been staring. Heat rushed to her face. Her reaction irritated her, and Dani wanted nothing more than to lash out at the cause. "What—"

"Can I get somethin' to drink?" Becca looked down at Dani's hands, making her realize she was still holding the bottle of juice.

Dani blinked.

"Or I can leave right now if you want." Becca's voice was soft, yielding.

What the hell was going on? Had they all fallen into the Twilight Zone or something? This had to be an act. Dani wasn't sure what the reasoning was behind it, but she wasn't going to be fooled. She laughed and opened the bottle of juice. "There's water in the sink or the fridge. Take your pick."

"What's funny?" Becca's eyes narrowed, and she pressed her lips together.

That was more like it. Dani knew that expression well. "You pretending. What did you do, take a Xanax on your way over?" She chuckled again.

Becca's face hardened even more. "No, but it's beginnin' to look like… Never mind." She shook her head and moved toward the kitchen. Dani stepped around her and out of her way, giving her a wide berth.

"God, I'm not gonna pounce on you or anythin'," Becca practically growled.

Dani looked at Becca and took a swig of her juice. These kinds of interactions were more like what she was used to. They were honest, and Dani had no intention of perpetuating a lie. Somehow talking to each other like this, especially over the last six months of their relationship, had eclipsed what they used to be. Happy, intense, and in love.

Becca reached for the handle on the refrigerator. "You got any more of those?" She pointed at the bottle in Dani's hand.

"I'm selfish, remember? Why would I share?" It was Cran-Apple anyway. Becca hated anything with apple juice.

"Oh for fuck's sake, are you twel—" Becca sucked in a breath. Then her jaw clenched. She glanced down at the juice in Dani's hand. "I don't like Cran-Apple anyway." She yanked the refrigerator door open. "You got Coke?"

Dani's insides actually burned with the need to ruin whatever game Becca was playing. It couldn't be real. There was no way. "No. You're sure asking for a lot considering you don't live here."

Becca pulled out a water. "No, I'm really not." Her tone was almost conversational. It was maddening.

"Aren't you?" Dani scoffed and stared. She was painfully aware that she was acting like a petulant teenager, but Dani couldn't stop herself. Becca's reactions left her confused, shaken. She sat down at the breakfast bar, hoping the world would right itself. What the hell was Rick doing? No one took that long to pee.

Becca held Dani's gaze for a few seconds and then glanced away. She started fidgeting again, this time with the water bottle. The plastic protested loudly as she crushed it.

Dani brought her hand to her forehead, rubbing it slightly. It was starting to throb. She reached for her juice but saw a fine tremor in her hand. She clenched it into a fist. All the noise Becca made didn't help any. "Will you stop that, please?"

Immediately, Becca did. "I'm sorry."

Dani froze. She couldn't remember the last time she heard those words come out of Becca's mouth. It infuriated her. She balled her hands into even tighter fists. The muscles in her arms contracted painfully.

Becca cleared her throat. "For the other day, I mean. I think I had the right to be upset initially, but after that, things got out of hand."

"Did Rick put you up to this?" Shocked and completely taken aback, Dani said the first thing that came to mind.

"What? No, you know me better than that—or you used to."

Dani wasn't sure how to respond to that. So, she made a noncommittal noise.

Rick came out of his bedroom in a ratty pair of shorts and a T-shirt. "Sorry, I just had to get clean." He smiled sheepishly. "You're both still in one piece, I see."

How...

"Cliché much?" Becca finished Dani's thought for her.

He shrugged. "No, not really. I'm not tryin' to play matchmaker. That would be cliché. I just want you guys to learn to be civil to each other."

Becca shook her head. "Now who's askin' for a lot, huh, Dani?" She set the unopened bottle of water on the counter. "I better go. Call me if you need a ride to the hospital. I can go in early. No big." Becca stepped toward Rick and embraced him.

Like she didn't have a car. Like she wasn't even present. Dani bristled and did her best to squash down her rising jealousy. They weren't kids on the playground vying for attention, but at the moment she sure as hell felt like one.

"Dani, thanks for the water and for listenin'," Becca said.

Instead of responding, Dani drank her juice.

Seconds later, Becca was gone.

Dani sat and stared at the door. Rick was doing the same to her. She felt it. She glanced at him.

His mouth opened and closed.

Dani stood. She had no idea what had just happened, and right now, she didn't want to figure it out.

"You said something about pizza?"

Obviously, he wasn't planning to push, but it didn't matter. Walking past him toward her bedroom, Dani mumbled, "Microwave."

CHAPTER 9

DANI RAPPED HER KNUCKLES AGAINST the open door before walking in. She smiled at what she saw. "Hey there, Scottie. I'm surprised you're still up."

Lynette Biers leaned down and kissed her son on the head. "Me too, but as you saw this morning, his energy level is great. I'll take that as a good thing. He even asked for ice cream. His daddy went to go get it."

"Shhhh! *Gumball's* on!" Scottie's face scrunched up and he turned red. And, for some reason, he had his right forefinger almost knuckle deep in his ear.

His mother chuckled. "God, I wish I could go back to a time when I had no censor button."

"I think we all feel that way a time or two." Dani nodded in Scottie's direction. "How long has he been doing that?" It may have been nothing, but she needed to check. He definitely didn't need any kind of infection.

"What?"

"The ear thing." Dani mouthed.

"Oh, half an hour I think."

"Shhhhh! I'm missing it."

Dani moved closer to the bed.

"Wait. Is he okay?"

"He's looking better, but I just want to be sure." Dani paused. "Okay, Scottie. I'm gonna have to tear you away from *Gumball* for a few minutes."

He turned toward her. Scottie's lips puckered, and he turned even redder then before.

Dani was determined to head this tantrum off at the pass. "I need you to be a big boy and listen. Big boys are the ones who get ice cream."

Scottie turned tear-filled brown eyes toward his mother. She nodded, thankfully. He sniffled and wiped at his face with his free hand. "I can get chocolate?"

"Yup!" Dani reached for the otoscope hanging on the wall by his bed with other medical examination tools.

Lynette picked up her cell phone and typed quickly. A few seconds later, she gave the thumbs up.

Dani sat on the edge of Scottie's bed. "You've got your finger pretty far up in your ear. Does it hurt?"

He shook his head.

"Then why is your finger in there?" Dani kept her voice soft, playful.

"'Cause."

"Because why?"

He pulled his finger out of his ear canal and shoved it toward Dani's nose.

"What's that smell? I like it."

On instinct, Dani reared backward, nearly falling off the bed.

"Scott Biers Jr.!" Lynette's tone was shrill.

Scottie's smile was huge. He laughed like it was the most hilarious thing he'd ever heard. Better than *The Amazing World of Gumball*. Then he plopped his finger in his mouth like it was natural—and for a five-year-old, it most likely was.

"Okay, sorry it took me so long I had to go back for the chocolate. I got him vanilla too. Maybe he can do the swirl thing." Scott Sr. was a little breathless as he walked into his son's room with his hands full.

Dani stood. She glanced from Lynette to Scott Sr.

Her patient's father stopped and looked at them. "What? What did I miss?"

Biting her bottom lip, Dani did her best to keep from laughing. It came out anyway. She tried to rein it in a few seconds later, but she couldn't stop. Obviously, she needed it. Lynette joined in. Maybe they both needed it.

Scott Sr. smiled and shook his head. He sat on the bed. "Hey, big man. You finally took your finger out of your ear, huh?" He paused. "But why's it in your mouth?"

Sleeping at the hospital the past couple nights wasn't unusual. Dani had done it many times before, but the reason behind it was a tad bit aggravating now. Simply put, Dani didn't want another run in with Becca until she was better prepared and possessed a winning hand in whatever game she'd been sucked into. Tipping her head back, Dani allowed the spray from the shower to hit her directly in the face. The water was a step away from cold, and it jolted Dani just enough to pull her out of her thoughts.

Upon exiting her shower stall—one of three—the bustle of the locker room on the other side of the wall greeted her. Some residents laughed, some expressed excitement about upcoming procedures, and others sounded irate. Their voices were clear and loud. Dani dried off quickly and dressed even faster.

Putting her still-damp hair in a ponytail, she exited the bathroom area just as two tired-looking residents came in. They didn't give Dani a second look, and she returned the favor.

She entered the locker room with much the same fanfare. Conversations didn't stop, but the few errant stares were palpable from residents she'd been to medical school with, when she was a different person altogether. She'd learned to ignore them.

They remembered a Dani who was open, fun, talkative, and willing to help, but they didn't matter. She had more important things to do. Standing in front of her own locker, she opened the combination lock with practiced ease. After throwing her toiletries inside, Dani turned and left without a word to anyone.

Dani entered the Peds wing a few minutes later. She paused as she neared the nurses station. Whatever Rick was saying to the nurse had her blushing. He grinned at the nurse as he took a swig from his Starbucks cup. "Hey, morning."

Dani smiled and nodded in the nurse's direction to show that she was included.

"What took you so long? Your coffee is probably cold." Rick moved away from the counter and reached for the other cup that was hidden from view.

"That's okay. I'll nuke it if I have to. Thanks, by the way."

"Uh-huh. Black and nasty, just the way you like it. At least it's the good stuff."

Someone snorted. Dani glanced to the side to see Betty.

"Where's mine?" Betty asked.

Rick shrugged. "Maybe Dani'll share."

"Not likely." Dani took a sip. The coffee was still lukewarm.

Rick took a few steps back. "I'll get you next time, Betty."

"Sure, sure." Betty rolled her eyes and answered the phone.

Rick touched Dani on the arm and tilted his head toward the end of the hall where the elevator was located. As he walked, she fell in step beside him. "Nice to see you in my neck of the woods."

"Yeah, well, I was just checkin' on you." He stopped and studied her for a minute.

"I'm fine."

"Yeah, okay, so you say." Rick started walking slowly.

"I do say. I just need some space."

"You know, I could catch a ride with you. It would make things a lot easier."

Easier for her, yes. God, she wasn't *that* selfish. "We don't always keep the same hours. I don't want you waiting around for me. That would suck."

"Well, my car should be ready by the weekend if that helps." They eased in behind the small crowd gathered at the elevator.

Dani didn't say anything, but it helped. It helped a lot.

The elevator dinged and opened.

"Okay, maybe I'll crash at Becca's tonight so she won't have to get up earlier to get me. Makes the whole situation—"

"Easier," Dani finished for him.

"Yeah, that." Rick eyed her and then stepped into the elevator.

Easy. Dani liked that word, but she was pretty sure it wasn't going to apply to anything in her life for a while.

Dani knocked on the open door and waited for both Sheri and Jacob to look up before she entered. He gave her a tired smile while his mother just watched her. "Morning. You didn't stay up all night playing video games, did you?"

Jacob's forehead wrinkled and he poked out his bottom lip. "No, Ma made me turn it off right in the middle of a mission." He glanced at his mother.

"Sure did." Sheri leaned in and kissed him on the top of his head.

He scowled even harder. It was adorable. "She wanted to make sure you were ready for today," Dani said.

Jacob looked down at his lap. "I know." He paused. "I remember what you and Ma said about it bein' okay to be scared."

"It is." Keeping her eyes on his, Dani nodded and walked closer to the bed. "You remember what it's called?"

"Chemo...chemotherapy?"

Sheri wrapped an arm around Jacob, pulling him close. He leaned into her. "And it's gonna make me feel bad but better at the same time."

Touched by the sight, Dani smiled slightly. "That's right." She cleared her throat and focused her attention on Sheri. "Mrs. Cook, do you have any questions about the drugs being used?"

"No, I don't think so." Sheri met Dani's gaze. Her concern and worry were evident by the crinkle in her brow and the way she held on to her son.

"Ma memorized them. They're hard to pronounce."

"Yes, they are," Dani agreed.

"Show her that you know 'em, Ma."

Dani didn't dare say a word. She stood, waiting.

"It's okay, baby. She doesn't wanna hear me mess all that up." Sheri glanced at Dani and then down at her son.

"Please?" he said. "I bet you don't. You're smart."

Sheri sighed. "Okay, since you're trying, I will too. Dactinomycin and Vincristine." She looked at Dani as she sounded out the last syllable. Her eyebrows were raised in challenge, but there was something else in her eyes too. Dani couldn't identify it.

She smiled in response. "Excellent, and remember they'll be given for five days every two weeks. I want to make sure both of you know what's going on every step of the way. No secrets or surprises. So, if there aren't any questions, I'll be back in a couple hours to get things started."

Jacob pressed his face into his mother's neck. Dani backed away and turned.

"Dr. Russell?"

Dani glanced over her shoulder.

"Can I talk to you outside for a minute?"

Surprised, Dani nodded. Their conversations the past couple days had consisted of Dani giving her medical information. They stepped out in the hall. Dani made sure to give her room to breathe.

"I'm sorry about the other morning." Sheri looked her directly in the eyes. There was no hesitation, no subterfuge. "It wasn't right to take my frustration out on you."

Dani took a step forward. "It's okay."

"Don't placate me." Sheri sighed and looked heavenward.

"I'm not. Just…hear me out." Dani held up a hand, physically asking for patience. "I'm not here to be your friend either. I'm an ally, a resource for both of you. So, if you need someone to yell at, I can take it, and if you need a shoulder to cry on, I hope in time that you see that I can take that too."

Sheri leaned back against the wall and closed her eyes. Seconds ticked by, before she opened them again. That look Dani had seen a few minutes earlier was back, and she was no closer to deciphering it. Sheri took a deep breath and pushed away from the wall. Dani held her gaze, waiting for some kind of response.

Sheri nodded, and that was all Dani needed. She watched quietly as Sheri went back into Jacob's room.

"So, durin' this sleepover, are we gonna do mani-pedis?" Rebecca threw herself on Rick's living room couch.

He snorted as he headed for his kitchen. "I don't know about yours, but my feet are tight." He pulled open the refrigerator. "You want somethin'?"

"No, I'm good, but would you hurry up? By the way, why is it takin' four days for your car to get fixed?"

"I went the cheaper, dirtier route. He had to shop around for the parts. It'll just take me a couple minutes to grab some things. You sure you're okay with me stayin' this long?" He opened a bottle of water and took a swig.

"It's just two nights. You're not movin' in."

"Just checkin', but hey, you gotta promise to keep Peyton in your room. It's creepy to wake up with her starin' at me."

Rebecca laughed. "She only does that to people she likes."

"Musta had a lot of sleepovers to figure that out."

No, there really hadn't been. Rebecca sobered. "Not really. Can you speed it up, please? I really don't wanna be here when Dani comes home."

"Why? You're gonna see her. What's the point in runnin' away?" Rick set his water on the counter and looked at her.

"I'm not runnin' from anythin'. I just need to be prepared for her. I don't know what's gonna come out of her mouth. If I lose my shit, we'll be right back to square one."

Rick hummed in agreement. "Yeah, got it. I'll be right back, then."

As he walked away, Rebecca changed her mind and headed for the kitchen. They had to have Coke this time. It was the South—everybody had Coke. The refrigerator was full to bursting with the ingredients to make a hell of a sandwich and a whole lot of other things. Rebecca shifted and pushed stuff to the side to find what she was looking for. Finally, she found a six pack of Coke in the crisper, surrounded by veggies. Weird place to put it, but who was she to judge? The can sighed as she opened it. She took a long pull and closed the refrigerator.

"Sooo, you live here now?"

Startled, Rebecca stumbled backward, spilling Coke all over her shirt. "Shit!" She ignored Dani's question and headed straight for the paper towels on the counter. She dabbed at her shirt and then bent down to get the mess on the floor. Her heart rammed against her chest. Rebecca took a couple deep breaths to center herself and stood. "Sorry 'bout that. I think I got it all."

"Uh-huh." Dani threw her bag on the couch and moved toward the kitchen.

Rebecca froze. It was like someone infused her muscles with lead, but her eyes, her brain, and her heart worked just fine. She watched helplessly as Dani got closer.

"I don't know what you're playing at, but pretending to be somebody you're not isn't working on me."

Rebecca had to dig deep not to rise to the occasion. She stiffened her spine and threw her shoulders back. Right now, it didn't matter that Dani had a few inches on her. "I'm not—"

"Stop it!" Dani slapped her hand against the counter and glared. Her face was flushed. She moved forward quickly. They were mere inches away from each other.

Rebecca gritted her teeth and took a step back. It wasn't fear that drove her. It was this woman's closeness. For a moment, she doubted her sanity. How could she feel even slightly attracted to Dani when all she saw before her was a tower of resentment? She met Dani's gaze, heavy and piercing enough to burn, and God, she couldn't help but remember the fires they had started together, the laughter, and the way they used to talk.

It had to be more than just memories. Lack of closure? That could be part of it too, but the simplest explanation was probably the best. Rebecca wasn't over her. With the way Dani was acting, was it too late for niceties on her part? At first Rebecca would say yes, but being this pissed off after almost four years had to mean something more. Maybe Dani was stuck too.

"Hey! What the hell…" Rick rushed into the living room. His voice trailed off and his eyes widened. "What's goin' on? I thought I heard—"

"It's fine," Rebecca interrupted.

Dani looked away, breaking their standoff. Her chest heaved like she'd been sprinting, and there was no hiding the redness that still covered her face.

Rick stared at Rebecca, and she stared back. When Rebecca nodded slightly, he switched his gaze to Dani. "You okay?"

She cleared her throat. "Yeah, yeah, I'm fine, but I thought you were staying at—"

"I am…" He pointed at his bag. "Till Saturday mornin'. Had to come get some stuff."

"Oh, okay."

Rick opened his mouth, but nothing came out at first. "So, I'll see you this weekend. We need to make another dent in the DVR." He looked from Dani to Rebecca and back again.

Dani gave him a strained smile. "Sounds good."

"I'm ready if you are, Becca."

Rebecca felt as if she were coming out of a trance. She shook her head to clear it. "Let's go, then." She walked past Dani, and their arms brushed. She could have avoided the contact, but what would be the point? Despite her clothing, tingles shot through Rebecca like a live nerve had been exposed. A loud gasp filled the space around them. It hadn't come from her.

Pausing, Rebecca met Dani's gaze once more. Her mouth had fallen open, and Rebecca was tempted to call her out on it. But, in a matter of seconds, Dani's eyes went from wide to cold and flinty. That was a look she was used to, but there was no hiding what she'd just seen and heard. Regardless of how much she wanted to, Rebecca didn't look back as she followed Rick out the door.

Now alone, Dani pressed a hand to her stomach. The pressure did nothing to untie the knots. Needing something solid to center her, she leaned back against the counter. Dani had to have imagined all that. One minute she'd been teeming with rage, and in the next, she'd been left hovering a step away from arousal.

Dani exhaled noisily. It wasn't her imagination, and she knew it. How could she feel anything? Better yet, why would she allow herself to? She had to admit that while something big had obviously been wrong for their relationship to crash and burn like it had, they'd had plenty of good times as well. Becca used to make her feel like she could conquer the world. It was an incredible feeling being on a pedestal. She was so high up, everything was within reach. That had to be it. Some part of her was pining and in the past. What kind of idiot did that make her?

Dani clenched her hands into fists. She was so pissed at herself, and it was hard to contain. So, she didn't. "What the hell is wrong with me?" She shouted into the empty apartment.

CHAPTER 10

"DAMN IT." DANI GRABBED A butter knife out of the silverware drawer and used it to scrape at a stubborn spot on the counter that wouldn't come clean with just Windex and a towel. When she was done with that area, she hit the stove and the refrigerator again, making sure they were both gleaming.

Despite the cleaning she'd been doing the past two hours, Dani still had energy to burn. She'd woken up that way. She blew out a breath and scanned the kitchen as well as the living room, looking for the tiniest thing out of place. Unfortunately, both areas were spotless.

Her bathroom and bedroom floors could use a good cleaning. What good were hardwood floors if they weren't clean or shiny enough to eat off of? Dani chuckled out loud, but nothing was funny. Things were more pathetic at this point. She reached behind her to redo her ponytail. Too much hair had escaped, leaving tendrils brushing against her face which only increased her level of irritation. There was nothing around her that could keep her attention completely. Dani needed something to not only tire her body but take over her mind as well. Incessant cleaning was a habit easy to fall back on. It wasn't as if the apartment hadn't needed it, but as her hands, arms, and legs worked, Dani's mind was free to do what the hell it wanted, which was to focus on Becca.

Dani grabbed the Swiffer mop and a refill just in case the liquid cleanser ran out before she got done. She stomped toward her bedroom.

Slapping the Swiffer on her bedroom floor, Dani shoved it violently back and forth. She pressed the nozzle to spray more citrus-scented cleanser, but nothing came out. The mop made a humming noise as Dani tried again and again. She shook it in hopes of unclogging it that way, which wasn't at all effective. Dani even removed the cleanser from its housing and checked for an obstruction. There was nothing. She put everything back in place and tried once more.

"Piece of shit!" Dani threw the Swiffer across the room. "Fuck you!"

She was so close to being the doctor she'd always wanted to be. She had trimmed the fat so the only people who understood her drive and goals were present. Why did Becca have to come back? Dani didn't have room in her life for all the things Becca brought with her—memories, confusion, a whole host of emotions, but most of all, need.

Right now, it was that feeling that scared Dani the most. If it was anyone else, she could explain it all away by citing her lack of social life and sexual connections. However, this was Becca, and just like when they'd met years ago, where there was smoke, a fire raged underneath. Dani had no intentions of getting engulfed again. It hurt too damn much.

"Fuck. You." Her voice was a tired whisper. Finding it suddenly hard to breathe, Dani bent forward and tried to take deep, even breaths. She couldn't be here, but the hospital could give her everything she needed. She was scheduled for the graveyard shift tonight, but what did it matter if she showed up three hours earlier?

As Dani reached for the front door, it swung open. Rick walked in, then stopped and stared. "Hey…you're dressed for work."

"Yeah, I can get a lot more done—"

"Uh-huh." He continued to study her.

"'Uh-huh?' What is that supposed to mean?" She gritted her teeth. Dani didn't want to fight with him. He could probably breathe on her wrong right now and put her on the defensive.

Rick shrugged. "Whatever you want it to."

"I don't have time for this." Dani huffed as she moved toward the door.

"Sooo, this is you tryin'?"

Dani stopped and turned around. "I can't do this right now. I can't." Knowing that she was a step away from being overwhelmed, Dani took deep measured breaths.

He crossed his arms over his chest. "It's not just about you, Dani. I wish you could just get out of your own way."

"What is that supposed to mean?"

"It means that we've hardly spent any time together and, when we talk, most of the time I feel like I'm havin' a conversation with a jealous teenager. In case you're wonderin', I'm fine, by the way. Being the referee between you and Becca is all I got goin' on." He layered on the sarcasm, and there was nothing subtle about it.

Dani's mouth fell open. "Oh, fuck you. If this was happening to you, do you think you'd deal with it any better? You think throwing truth bombs is just going to make it all go away?" She slapped her hand repeatedly against her chest. "I'm doing the best I can. I'm sorry I haven't been there for you for the past few weeks, but to be honest I don't even know how to be there for myself right now, so I can't do much for anybody else."

"Well, maybe I need to be the one who transfers and starts all over away from all this." Rick waved his hand almost violently between them.

She sucked in a breath and deflated a little. That was the last thing she expected him to say. "Wait. What?"

Rick looked away. "I didn't mean for it to come out like that. I applied for fellowships at the end of my second year. Some of the interviews nearly kicked my ass. I heard from Northwestern. They're encouragin' me to come and finish out my residency with them."

"I remember you applying. So, you're leaving?" Dani took a step closer to him. His words jolted her toward clarity.

He was right. She had been jealous. A fresh wave of shame crashed into Dani, making her face hot. To make matters even worse, here she was thinking only of herself yet again.

"I don't know. It's not all that unusual for a doctor to do their fellowship somewhere else."

"I know that. I mean you're leaving to finish your residency? Did you even apply for the fellowship at Amery?"

"I don't know if I'm leavin', and yes, I did."

Dani moved closer. Tentatively, she touched his hand. "Does Becca know?"

Rick shook his head and released a shaky breath. "I just got the news myself. I'm a little worried. She hasn't been here long, and she doesn't have anybody else…"

"She wouldn't expect you to put things on hold just because she's ba…" Dani stopped. Would she? She pretty much wanted Dani to do something similar.

"No! She wouldn't, especially now." Rick's eyes were wide.

"Sorry. I just…" Dani tried to swallow down the lump forming in her throat. "Are you really considering this because of what's going on between me and Becca?"

Rick took her hand in his. "No, I was just angry, but I'd be lyin' if I said I'm not thinkin' about it. Amery is the shit, but Northwestern is nothin' to spit at. It would be a challenge to switch gears so late, but that's part of why it's so attractive."

"I get it, and I'm still sorry that you're in the middle of this mess. You really shouldn't be at this point."

Rick nodded. "I kinda agree, but it's my choice. So, I probably shouldn't complain so loud."

Dani looked down at their linked hands and back up at him. "I'm sorry I've been so crappy toward you. I'm proud of you, and whatever you decide."

"It's a big decision so I'm not gonna make it lightly. If I don't go now, there's an option of me joinin' them for my last year."

She swallowed hard as realization smacked her in the face. Just like Becca, Rick was the only person in her corner too, but he didn't need to hear that, not with everything he'd just dropped on her. "It sounds like they really want you."

"I know, right? They're givin' me a couple weeks to decide about this year's residency, so I'm really gonna take the time and think on it."

"Sounds like you have a plan." Suddenly, going to the hospital didn't seem like the answer. Despite the fact they'd started off arguing, Dani needed to be near her best friend, and maybe he needed her too. "I guess I could hold off leaving until we make a dent in the DVR."

Rick smiled.

"So, you wanna do *Law & Order: SVU* or *Grey's Anatomy*?"

Dani stared at him. "How could you even ask that? *Grey's* helped me through some of the worst times."

Rick sat on the couch and reached for the remote. "Yeah, nothin' wrong with worshippin' at the altar of Shonda, for she is wise and all knowin'."

"This is true. Plus, the drama." However, at the moment, the doctors on *Grey's* had nothing on her.

Rick snorted.

Flipping through the channels had become tedious to Rebecca after a few hours. Television couldn't really hold her attention anyway. She couldn't stop her mind from working. Despite Rick's presence, she'd spent the past couple of days going back and forth. Rebecca had reached the same conclusion every time: Dani was still affected by her. The realization gave Rebecca hope. It was a relief to know that she wasn't in the boat alone, and the fact that it wasn't sinking bolstered her even more.

So, the plan remained to stay the course and hope that eventually Dani would see she'd changed, and when that epiphany came, Rebecca would seek forgiveness. Who was she kidding? Some part of her wanted more than that now, or was starting to. The heat behind Dani's touch wasn't just a one-time thing. With each encounter, it was going to be a more powerful shock to her system.

She looked forward to it, but where the hell was her sense of self-preservation?

Rebecca glanced down at Peyton, who'd curled herself into a tight ball right beside Rebecca's thigh. She scratched the cat behind her ear and was immediately rewarded with a purr followed by a stinging bite. "I don't even know why I try."

Peyton had the nerve to purr again and rub herself against Rebecca's leg. "Too late to be nice now." The cat meowed loudly and jumped down. She sashayed away with her tail high in the air, more than likely proud of herself. Peyton stopped at the wicker box spilling over with cat toys. After choosing a fuzzy pink ball, she turned back toward Rebecca.

"Really?" Rebecca rolled her eyes.

Peyton growled as if that were some type of response. When she got close to Rebecca's feet, she dropped the ball and promptly screeched.

"All right. Shit, you just got here." Rebecca bent down and picked up the soft fuzzy ball.

Peyton's eyes widened, and she made a weird chirping sound as the ball sailed across the room. She took off, nearly sliding into the wall. A few seconds later, she brought the ball back and placed it at Rebecca's feet.

"Yeah, let's get this out of your system now so you won't put the damn thing, covered in cat spit on my pillow at three a.m." She snatched up the ball and tossed it toward the other side of the room.

Again, Peyton ran toward it, but before scooping it up in her mouth, she growled and hissed at the toy.

"You just can't be nice for more than a few minutes, can you?" Her words gave her pause and sent her back into her own head for a second. Even with her feeling somewhat hopeful, Dani seemed the opposite.

Rebecca could only account for her own progress, not for Dani's. All the little tidbits Rick had dropped in the past and what she'd seen so far made her wonder if Dani had changed for the worse.

Rebecca groaned out loud. Just like that, doubt crept in. After throwing the ball a few more times, she stood, trying to shake the feeling free. The negativity would do no one any good, least of all her, especially since it left her with a deeper sense of loneliness. She could always call Rick to hang out, but that would be selfish—he needed time with Dani as well, especially now that he might be leaving.

She paused. It'd been a big-ass shock when he dropped that bomb over dinner last night. It was going to take her a while to wrap her head around that news, but she planned to be supportive no matter what he decided. It was all about him and his dream. They'd done the long-distance friendship thing. Instead of four hours, it would be closer to eleven—Rebecca had checked—which wouldn't make a difference at all.

In fact, maybe it was time to branch out. Her previous squad were good people, yet she'd held them at arm's length. Rebecca was cordial, courteous, and loyal when she needed to be. Maybe her new team deserved more of a chance.

CHAPTER 11

REBECCA SET THE BOX OF chocolate croissants, from Amelie's French Bakery and Cafe, on the corner of Emmet's desk. The cafe was a little out of her way, but so worth it. Since she'd made the decision to reach out and blend in the week before, she'd been bringing little morning surprises. Sniffing out decadence, Alvin and Mark got out of their seats and came closer.

"Where's Emmet?"

"You ask too many questions." Mark shooed her away with a wave as he flipped open the box. He groaned and stared at the pastries as if savoring the whole situation. Alvin, on the other hand, scooped up two and licked his fingers as he walked away.

"You're welcome!" Rebecca told his back.

He glanced over his shoulder and gave her a single bob of his head in acknowledgment. The man really could be an asshole, but at least he was honest about it.

Rebecca rolled her eyes.

Mark picked up a napkin and scooped up what had to be the biggest pastry in the box. He smiled and hummed as he tore off a little piece on the end and popped it into his mouth.

"Oh God, that's good," he said. "You've been spoiling us every day the past week or so. What gives?"

Rebecca shrugged. "Just bein' friendly."

"Well, will you stop it? You're gonna make me feel bad." He took another bite. "Do I need to start bringing you a cappuccino or something every morning? Or are you the espresso type?"

She sneered. "Coke will do me just fine."

"Huh, had a feeling you were gonna say that. Let me guess—none of that cherry or vanilla mess for you? Am I right?"

Rebecca grinned. "On the nose."

"Figured. Hey, Lieutenant!" Mark called out in greeting as Benz walked in.

"Strong, it's way too early for you to be so on, but good morning," she said.

"I think you have me confused with Emmet," Mark chimed in.

Benz stopped and gave him the once over. Her lips curled into a smirk. "It's okay. You can admit that he's rubbing off on you."

Alvin let out a bark of laughter.

"Besides," Benz continued, "if you keep eating things like that"—she pointed toward the pastry in his hand—"you'll be trying to tone your arms and legs too, like Emmet."

Alvin laughed again.

Rebecca couldn't help it; she was amused as well. She smiled and shook her head at their exchange.

Mark pointed toward the box on Rebecca's desk. "Chocolate croissants. Rebecca brought 'em. You want one?"

Lieutenant Benz moved toward him. "Oh hell yes. I do. I really do."

"Take two," Rebecca encouraged.

Benz glanced her way and raised a brow. "I see you, Detective Wells." She bared her teeth in that weird smile of hers. "Keep working the room." She scooped up two croissants and walked toward her office like she had all the time in the world.

"Interestin' lady," Rebecca whispered.

"Huh?" Mark shoved more pastry into his mouth.

"Nothin'."

He swallowed and licked his fingers. "Good. So you with me today?"

"Yeah, I'm in."

Mark leaned toward her and dipped his head. The fluorescent light hit his bald spot, making it look shiny. "It's okay. I know you like me best. It'll be our lil secret." He smirked, and his eyes twinkled with amusement.

She had paired herself with him every day last week and had started off this week with more of the same. Rebecca found that his temperament fit hers. He was a straight shooter, right down the center, and so far, Alvin had been a little too much to one side of that same target, and Emmet too much to the other. Not that they weren't good cops. Their closure rates spoke for themselves, but Rebecca had made the decision last week that she'd dabble with them and stick with Mark a majority of the time if she couldn't handle a case alone. "No comment."

He chuckled.

Emmet walked around them and sat down at his desk. "Ugh, I can't eat that." He reached for one anyway and shoved almost half of it in his mouth. Leaning back in his chair, Emmet moaned. "You're gonna make me fat."

Rebecca dropped her eyes down to his pot belly.

His eyes widened as he gave her a horrified look. "What? I work out."

"Arms and chest?" Mark's tone was gleefully teasing.

"Well…" Emmet sputtered. "Legs too! I work out. For real!" He devoured the rest of the croissant and reached for another one.

"How long have we worked together, Em?" Mark tilted his head and stared at him.

"I do! You're not with me twenty-four-seven. There're things about me you don't know."

"Sure, you're right." Mark turned away.

Rebecca sat at her desk across from Emmet, who continued to grumble even as he reached for a third pastry. Good thing she'd scarfed down one when they were still warm and gooey. She raised a brow at Emmet and he looked back sheepishly as he wiped his mouth.

"Thanks for breakfast."

"You're welcome." Pastries, donuts, and biscuits weren't much by any stretch of the imagination, but it was Rebecca's way of settling in and forming rapport with her team. It wasn't anything she hadn't done before, but she had to do better than she did in Savannah, getting past common courtesy and superficial niceties. Rebecca was home now. She planned on staying and putting down roots.

"Okay, Pete, have someone escort her up." Mark hung up his phone, and Rebecca turned to look at him.

"We got somethin'?"

"Yeah, saddle up. A scared mother in tears. They had a hard time understanding everything, but they got the gist. Told them to send her straight to us. We can pull the uniforms in if need be."

This wasn't the first time something like this had happened. It wasn't exactly procedure, but so far no one had gotten on their backs about it. Rebecca nodded. She'd been sifting through active cases, hoping that fresh eyes would shed some light on them. She'd been totally focused the first hour, but then her mind had started to wander to Dani. There was no competition after that point.

Rebecca wanted many things from her, and she'd recently added one more thing to the pile. When they were together, animosity ran rampant, at least on Dani's part, but there was an undercurrent that sizzled as well. Rebecca wasn't ashamed to admit that she wanted it to grow, despite it all. Maybe she was a sucker for pain as long as it had a pleasurable edge to it. She stood and refocused herself. She had to.

"Mrs. Dorset, let me make sure I understand you. Right now, Shane is with a sitter?" Mark asked. His expression was for the most part flat, but his eyes were kind as he talked to Shane's mother.

"Yes, I know it sounds crazy."

"No, we just wanna make sure we have a clear picture of what's goin' on," Rebecca said. "Your ex-husband has threatened to take him. Is that correct?"

Mrs. Dorset closed her eyes and sighed. The sound was heavy with exasperation. She opened her eyes again and stared right at Rebecca. "Many times. I've even caught him trying to pick him up from school last week. Now, I've been getting there extra early just in case. The school wasn't even going to call me because he has joint custody, if you want to call it that. He has every other weekend, but I've stopped that after he said it wasn't enough anymore and made threats. I know I'm violating the court order, but what else am I supposed to do? They don't know him. When he wants something, he goes after it until he gets it." Her tone was pleading as she continued to look at Rebecca.

Rebecca reached out to her, touching her arm in hopes that the connection was soothing. "You're scared, and you're tryin' to be proactive."

Nodding, Mrs. Dorset also started to cry again. "Yes, I'm not making this up. I know him. So please…"

After giving Mrs. Dorset's arm a supportive squeeze, Rebecca peered up and caught Mark's gaze. He shook his head.

"Mrs. Dorset—" Rebecca decided to be the one to break the news.

"No, no! Don't fucking tell me there's nothing you can do!"

Rebecca's stomach tightened in sympathy.

Mark added, "I'm sorry, Mrs.—"

"You don't get to sit here and tell me that I have to wait until he's kidnapped my son to do anything!" Mrs. Dorset jumped up. Her hands were fisted, and Rebecca couldn't blame her one bit for the impulse to use them. The tension in the room was thick and chewy, making it a little harder to deal with, but a kernel of an idea took root in Rebecca's head.

"You violatin' the custody agreement might totally negate this, but do you personally feel threatened or harassed by him?"

Mrs. Dorset laughed, but she wasn't smiling. "The last six months of our marriage and every day since."

"You've pretty much outlined a pattern of behavior, especially if it's hinted at in the divorce or custody proceedings," Mark chimed in. "It could be enough to charge him with stalking, and with a good lawyer, it may be enough to get a restraining order. That's not much, but it's something." He sounded relieved.

"It was brought up during the custody hearing. That's why he got so little time with Shane. He had to get counseling, do some anger management, and in a year there's a possibility of him getting more visitation." Mrs. Dorset sat back down.

God, that was sad to hear. Rebecca wondered what went through some judges' heads sometimes. The truth of the matter was that even if Mrs. Dorset had come to report an actual kidnapping, nine times out of ten it would be looked at as a family issue.

"My lawyer was pathetic. Do you know somebody? I don't have a lot of money…" Mrs. Dorset looked from Mark to Rebecca and back again.

Mark nodded. "Yeah, I might. Let me go get his card. I'll be right back."

The air in the room changed, becoming lighter and breathable.

"Shane was the only good thing to come out of our marriage. A big part of me hates Phillip, but the rest of me can't because he helped to make our son."

Rebecca listened quietly. It wasn't unusual for a parent to tell their life story in this kind of situation.

"That's the main reason I didn't report this right away, but I figured it out. This isn't about me. It's so much bigger than that."

Mrs. Dorset's eyes were watery, but they were also full of hope and relief. Dangerous emotions in this kind of situation, but Rebecca understood. "Nothin' wrong with tryin' to get a handle on all this."

The door to the interrogation room opened. "Sorry it took so long. I gave him a buzz." Mark handed Mrs. Dorset a card. "He's expecting your call."

Dani lifted her hand to knock on Jacob's open door, but seeing his bed empty stopped her. She stepped inside, and the sounds of violent regurgitation pulled her toward the bathroom.

"Uhhh, Ma, I can't stop."

Sheri murmured something, but it was hard to understand. She was on her knees beside Jacob stroking his back.

Though it was an unavoidable byproduct of treatment, Dani's heart went out to both patient and mother. It must be killing Sheri to see Jacob like this. A moment of indecision stopped her cold. She wasn't sure if she should leave or push forward. The moment passed as fast as it came. Dani rapped her knuckles against the bathroom door.

Sheri looked up quickly, and for a second, Dani was privy to her worry and fear. Then it was gone. Her eyes hardened. "The trashcan and that little pan they gave me was full. I had to carry him in here." She spat the words out, making them sound accusatory. "The medicine you prescribed for his stomach stopped working."

Jacob groaned weakly as his mother sat on the floor completely. Sheri scooted back against the wall and pulled him into her arms.

Nausea and vomiting, even with an antiemetic, wasn't unusual, but to say that aloud would sound flippant. "I'm sorry."

Sheri's gaze softened by a few degrees, and she sighed heavily. "No, I'm sorry. It's not your fault."

Her words seeped in, leaving some residual emotions behind that felt a lot like relief. It was good to know that Dani was on steadier ground with Sheri. "Is there anything I can do to help?"

"No, I got this. I'll take care of the hands-on stuff, but is there something else you can give him to help with the puking?"

Dani nodded. "There is. I'll prescribe dexamethasone. It's a steroid which should help with the nausea and keep his appetite stimulated."

"Okay, I hope that works."

"Doc D?" Jacob croaked.

"I'm here." Dani kneeled, lowering herself to his eye level.

"Why I gotta get so sick to get...well?" Jacob's eyes started to droop.

"Why don't you ask her about that later? Let's get you back to bed," his mother said, softly.

It took some doing, but they were able to get him back under the covers.

"I'll put him on some fluids too. I don't want him dehydrated."

Sheri sighed long and heavy. "When they first found the tumor, I was hoping he could do his chemo treatments at home with a nurse. But he needs to be here. Despite everything that hap..." She shook her head and pressed her lips together. "He needs to be here," Sheri whispered again a few seconds later.

Dani was almost afraid to move as if doing so would negate the major breakthrough that had just occurred. Little by little, Sheri was starting to trust her and be more open. The death of her husband was a tragedy. The fear and reluctance to believe in and deal with hospitals or doctors were normal after effects. Dani couldn't imagine the strength it took to overcome it all. She wanted to commend her for it. She wanted to promise that Jacob would be okay, but they both sounded like the beginnings of empty platitudes that Sheri wouldn't react well to.

Instead, Dani nodded and said, "Let me get those orders in so you both can get some rest."

Sheri barely acknowledged the statement. Her eyes were on her son. Dani backed away. She was reluctant to leave. While Jacob's case was pretty straightforward, his mother was the one with layers. Once she got past the initial intensity, there was more underneath lined with a fierceness and she wasn't sure what else. In that way, Sheri reminded Dani of Becca.

A hollow feeling invaded her chest, but it didn't last long as warmth filled her instead as her mind eased toward Becca. Dani backed away slowly and turned toward the door, running from the invasion of emotion. She had other patients to see.

Rebecca rubbed her eyes and leaned back in her desk chair.

"Workin' late, Wells?"

Rebecca opened her eyes to see Alvin walking by. "No, I was about to go. What about you?"

"I got a few things to wrap up," Alvin said. "Gonna be here for a while."

"Need some help?" The question shot out of Rebecca's mouth before she could stop it.

He huffed out a laugh. "I thought we kept things between us real?"

"We do. I was just tryin' to be nice. Knee-jerk reaction."

"I hate those."

Rebecca chuckled and stood. "They do get people in trouble sometimes."

"Sure do. Now, get the hell out. I like havin' the place to myself. Helps me think."

"Don't hurt yourself."

"C'mon, Wells. You can do better than that."

"I got a lot on my mind. In the mornin', I'll look up how to call you an asshole in Chinese."

Alvin laughed. "That was a little better." He paused. "I gotta tell you, havin' that attitude of yours around makes shit in this little room a lot more interestin'." He looked down at the computer keyboard and started typing.

Rebecca stared at him. His words were compliment adjacent, which was probably as close as she was going to get from him.

"Stop lookin' at me. I'm just keepin' it real. Now, go bother somebody else." Alvin didn't so much as glance up.

"I'm bringin' biscuits tomorrow."

"See if they have packets of apple jelly this time," he requested.

"Okay, good night."

"Uh-huh."

Following Alvin's encouragement to go bother someone else, Rebecca entered Rick and Dani's apartment building with determination, but as she got off the elevator onto their floor, she faltered. Everything with Dani was stagnant and in some kind of weird holding pattern. The past week and a half, they'd barely said two words to each other, which was helped by the fact that when Rebecca came over to see Rick, Dani made herself scarce any way she could.

The animosity was still there, but Rebecca hadn't had the chance to stir the pot or even try to empty it completely. As she walked slowly down the hallway, Rebecca decided that taking some initiative really was the best course of action. Hopefully, it worked for Mrs. Dorset and it could work for her as well.

Each step Rebecca took bolstered her. By the time she made it to Dani's door, she had a full head of steam. Without pausing in her momentum, Rebecca knocked.

A few seconds later, Dani opened the door. Initially, her forehead scrunched in irritation, but then her eyes widened in surprise. "Uh, Rick's not—"

"I know he's not here. I saw your car, so I came up. I was wonderin' if we could talk?"

Dani blinked. She opened and closed her mouth several times. Her hair was loose around her shoulders and still damp from an obvious shower. She brought a shaking hand up to her throat, and that's when Rebecca noticed that the dampness extended to her chest as well. There were even distinct wet patches on her T-shirt, making it cling to her skin. Dani's nipples stood at attention, and for a moment, Rebecca's mind went blank. "You, um, showered."

"I try to every day." Dani narrowed her eyes.

An uncomfortable quiet lapsed between them, but for whatever reason Dani wasn't displaying her usual belligerence.

Rebecca took that as a good sign. "Can we?" She held her breath as she waited for an answer. This could still go either way.

Dani dropped her hand to her side.

Rebecca followed the progression, but then she got lost at Dani's neck, staring at her rapidly beating pulse. She sucked in a breath as her heart started to do the same.

"I don't think that's a—"

"Please?" Rebecca interrupted with a whispered plea. She held Dani's gaze. "I let you in. Remember?"

"So have I."

Rebecca shook her head. "No, Rick let me in. There's a difference."

Dani sighed and looked away. Then she stepped aside, giving Rebecca plenty of space to get through, as if she didn't want them to touch.

Rebecca was surprised and relieved at the same time. "Thank you." She headed straight for the couch and sat down.

"You must have caught me at a weak moment."

"There's nothin' weak about you." The words were out of Rebecca's mouth before she could think and reel them back in.

Their gazes met, and Dani's mouth parted slightly. She cleared her throat and remained standing. "What do you want?"

Rebecca's brain scattered. She really didn't think she would get this chance, so she said the first thing to come to mind. "This is your last year of residency."

"I'm aware of that." Dani crossed her arms over her chest.

"You were always so determined and driven, and you have such a big heart. That sucked me in, I used to hope some of it would rub off on me. I guess it did in a way. You know…after I left."

Dani's face hardened. She pressed her lips together and exhaled. "What do you want from me?"

"I know this might be statin' the obvious, but you're still so angry at me."

"Are you kidding me?" Dani laughed and started to pace. "You're damn right I am. Aren't you? That last year, I can't remember a day when you weren't! Don't even get me started on the way you left."

"No, I'm not angry. At least, not really."

Dani stopped and stared. Rebecca stared right back.

"Wh…what?"

"Not like you are," Rebecca clarified. "I'm not the same person I was."

Dani watched her.

Rebecca hadn't come here with some kind of speech prepared. Winging it seemed to be working. So, she continued to go with it. "I think…all that anger you have means somethin'."

"No. No, it doesn't."

"Dani—"

"I said no!" Dani's hands were fisted at her side and her chest heaved. "Why would you even go there? We were miserable together."

Rebecca stood. "Not always."

"Are you serious right now? I doubt we could even be friends, but either way, you need to leave." Her tone was soft but no less guttural.

There was so much more Rebecca wanted to say, and she couldn't help but wonder if she'd get the chance. She nodded and slowly made her way toward the door.

"I'll tell Rick you came by." Dani's voice was wooden, monotone.

Rebecca paused but didn't turn around. "I told you, and I know you heard me. I didn't come for him." Not waiting for a response, she pulled the door open and left.

CHAPTER 12

Dani arched her back, dragging her nipples across the sheets, which only added another layer to her pleasure. She bit into the pillow pressed against her face. She could barely breathe, but it was worth it. So worth it. Even though she was on her knees, Dani spread her legs wider, doing her best to keep her ass in the air. She turned her head and moaned as Becca's hands trailed up the inside of her thighs. This time, her touch was light, barely there, but still electric. Yet again, her fingertips stopped short of Dani's sex, brushing through the wetness that clung to Dani's skin instead.

"Becca." Dani drew the name out into a needy plea. Her body was poised to erupt like a rumbling volcano, and with all the build up to this point, the explosion was going to be magnificent. Her skin felt tight and overstimulated, as if she'd grabbed hold of a live wire, but Dani had no intention of letting go. In fact, she had plans to wrap herself in it. "Touch it…"

Becca released a loud, shaky breath in response, but instead moved her hands back over the curve of Dani's ass.

"Please!" The muscles in Dani's legs quivered in anticipation while the rest of her shook with need. Becca's fingertips went lower still, grasping and parting Dani's cheeks. She held her open. Cool air fluttered against her sex, making her clench desperately at nothingness. Dani whimpered.

Becca groaned.

Ready to beg in earnest, Dani murmured, "Please, Bec—" She didn't get to finish, crying out as Becca slid her fingers inside her. Dani's entire world shrank and centered itself between her legs, and when Becca slumped against her, pressing their naked bodies together from back to front, she cracked open all the way down to the core.

Dani's eyes snapped open. Just like yesterday morning, her hand was already between her legs, working furiously. Seconds later—and in case she wasn't alone in the apartment—she put her other hand over her mouth to keep from crying out as she came. Her body jerked with aftershocks for several minutes. She whimpered each time. It was difficult to catch her breath when her body refused to cooperate. Dani threw her arm over her eyes and waited for the world to become normal again.

Minutes passed. Slowly, Dani took her arm away and stared up at the ceiling, barely seeing it. Her room was dark except for the light filtering in from underneath the bathroom door. Dani lay as still as possible. Suddenly, she laughed, and it wasn't the shy kind either. It was loud, boisterous, and straight from the diaphragm. After having such a powerful release, she was still hungry for more. Her growing frustration left her empty. She covered her mouth with her hand again, getting a whiff of herself, and just like that, the laugh became a sob.

After all the pain, Dani had no business thinking about Becca and reminiscing about how it felt to have all that intoxicating fierceness focused on her. Regardless, her body sure missed it. Maybe the rest of her did too, and that's why Dani had let her in a couple days ago. No. This was insane. "Damn it."

What was going on? What was she doing? This need and everything else she felt should have been firmly behind her, but it wasn't. That knowledge shook her down to her bones and so much deeper.

"Damn it!" She covered her face with her hands. A minute ago, she was worried about Rick hearing her, and now she was practically yelling.

Dani wanted nothing more than to wipe her hands clean of the whole situation. She sobbed harder, knowing that wasn't entirely true. Becca wasn't the same woman from four years ago—that much had become obvious. Dani sensed patience and maturity mingled with her ever-present intensity.

She peered up at the ceiling again. Who did that make her? She'd been far from patient or understanding, and she hadn't even touched on kindness. Did that make her the child in this scenario? She skimmed through her behavior over the past several weeks. Her breathing shallowed. She squeezed her eyes shut.

Just because she was still drawn to Becca. Just because Becca had changed and was within arm's reach didn't mean Dani had to put herself within touching distance. Dani kicked her covers away as anger, familiar as a friend, eased over her. It splayed in all directions, inward at herself and outward toward Becca. While coming home might have been the best thing for Becca, Dani was almost sure that it had been the worst thing for her. The door to their past had been kicked open, and everything behind it was bleeding into the present. Dani was going to try like hell to at least give the illusion that it could be closed and locked again.

She sat up and reached out, moving slowly as if her limbs had turned to stone and patted the nightstand in search of her glasses. Dani's heart raced, and deep inside her, something simmered rapidly close to boiling, leaving her hot, cold, scared, and balanced precariously on the razor's edge.

Rebecca swirled her cup to ensure the Coke inside was as cold as possible. It was an extra-large cup from Popeye's Chicken that she'd kept from the night before and filled to the brim before leaving her house. She took a long pull from her straw and swore she could actually feel the caffeine working through her system.

"Oh yeahhh." Rebecca didn't drink Coke just because it was sweet and tasted like heaven, although those reasons were compelling enough.

She walked into the squad room. Alvin was on the phone while Mark and Emmet each pecked away on their computers. Alvin acknowledged her with a nod, but she got nothing from the others. As she closed in on her desk, Rebecca stopped and stared at the refrigerator pack of Coke and the box emboldened with a Panera Bread logo that had been set on the edge.

Emmet looked up then. "Hey! We haven't even opened it yet. Bear claws. What cop doesn't like bear claws? I wonder, though, did cops start liking donuts because that's what TV cops ate or vice versa? Chicken or the egg? We also seem to have a thing for tacos and hotdogs, but I don't like either."

Rebecca eased into her chair and blinked. "That's a lotta words, and I haven't even finished my Coke yet."

He glanced down at the twelve-pack on her desk. "That should be enough to last the day, right?"

She rolled her eyes. "Funny, but thanks." Rebecca unclipped the holster from her belt and shoved it along with her service weapon inside her top desk drawer before locking it.

Emmet grinned. "It's from all of us, and you're welcome."

She took another long pull from her drink and flashed a smile at him. This whole setup felt good. Shit, maybe even great. Something needed to be to balance out everything else.

"Hey, Rebecca?"

She swiveled her chair in Mark's direction. "Yeah?"

"Mrs. Dorset called that lawyer friend of mine and got herself a restraining order. He's even trying to get them back in court to challenge the custody order."

"Good to hear."

Mark nodded. "Let's consider that one put to bed. I got a lead on one of our open cases. You coming?" He stood and walked toward her.

Rebecca opened the box of bear claws and snagged two in one hand and her Coke in the other. "Let's go. Somebody put that in the fridge for me?" She pointed at the pack of soda with a bear claw.

"I got it," Alvin said from behind her.

She grabbed a napkin, shoved the pastries at Mark, and retrieved her holster and gun from her desk.

Mark tossed her the keys and opened the door on the passenger side of the sedan. "Just don't kill me or anybody else."

"No promises." Rebecca slid into the driver seat and set her drink in the cup holder.

Barely ten minutes later, Rebecca was blaring the horn. "I'm gonna turn on the lights."

Mark laughed. "Aren't we past giving out traffic tickets? Besides, she's going the speed limit."

"It's Atlanta, and everybody knows the speed limit is really eighty-five!"

"On the interstate," Mark reminded her.

Rebecca grumbled.

He laughed again.

"So, how'd you end up in Missing Persons so early in your career?"

Cute. He was trying to distract her and get her to open up at the same time. Rebecca decided to humor him. "It was the only openin', and I took a few courses specializin' in the area."

"Yeah? Nothing more to it than that?"

Out of the corner of her eye, Rebecca saw him staring and waiting.

She snorted. He wasn't even trying to be subtle. Rebecca glanced at Mark. Here was her chance to till the soil and make it just right for cultivating strong, deep roots. She cleared her throat. "My great aunt raised me 'cause nobody else wanted to."

"Ah, so you were kinda lost and she found you."

"Nothin' as simple as that. She took me in, and in her own way, she tried. I pretty much stayed lost until I was ready to find myself."

Mark went quiet. He leaned forward and turned on the radio, putting it on 98.9, better known as 99X. The volume was just right, not overpowering or too soft.

"You got any more questions about the case we're working on?"

Rebecca shook her head. "Nope, I'm clear." She sucked in a breath and released it slowly. It felt good to reach out to someone new, especially since he was making an effort to understand her.

As the hours passed, it became abundantly clear that no matter what Dani did, Becca invaded her thoughts, and to say that she was beyond peeved was a gross understatement. Memories and recent encounters played in her mind like some movie reel and included the way Becca looked at her both then and now, like she could swallow her whole, no matter if they were fighting, fucking, laughing, or doing nothing at all.

Dani had been raised to be confident and driven, but loving Becca and being loved by her made her feel like she could have it all, which had turned out to be a lie.

She slammed the iPad against the counter at the nurses station, hard enough to make some of the people around her jump and others stare. Good thing it had a case. Dani caught the gaze of one of the nurses behind the desk. "I'm taking a break. No pages unless it's an emergency." Time to herself wasn't going to help matters, but it would at least give her a minute to recoup so she didn't start taking things out on the people around her.

The nurse nodded.

Good. Maybe she could grab a snack and head up to the roof.

She walked into the cafeteria. After grabbing a bottle of juice and a couple of other small items, Dani stood in line. It moved slowly which didn't help her nerves any. Needing something to occupy her, she peered out at the sea of tables. The people talking, laughing, and possibly crying, fed into the decibel level.

Dani spotted Rick and Sandra at a table together. He was talking and waving his hands animatedly while she laughed. For some reason, that irked her even more. A few minutes later, she paid for her snacks and headed straight for Rick's table. Maybe talking to him would cheer her up, or at least distract her. Plus, with the possibility of him leaving… Well, she really didn't want to think about that.

As she got closer, Rick looked her way and smiled. Dani wasn't sure if she returned the gesture. It didn't feel like it.

"Hey!"

"Hey, Rick." Dani shifted her eyes to Sandra, but she didn't give her more than that. The smile on Sandra's face faltered, but without further acknowledgment, Dani returned her attention to Rick. "Can I talk to you for a minute?"

With raised eyebrows, Rick's glanced at Dani then at Sandra and back again. "Well, is it somethin' that can wait?"

Dani took a deep breath in an effort to put a cap on her spiraling mood. "Uh, yeah, sure. I'll catch up with you in a bit or I'll see you at home."

"Okay. Sounds good."

She was a few steps from the exit when someone touched the back of her arm. Dani turned around in surprise to see Sandra.

"Okay, I'm not naïve enough to think just because we had sex we'd be glued to the hip. I'm not in your inner circle, but I at least thought we were friendly. Rick told me that you found out that we were a thing a few months back. Is that why you gave me that look and have been ignoring me?"

"What?" Dani was now completely irate. "You're not even *on* my radar, but you're right. It did kind of squick me out to know that me and my best friend had been with the same woman. I wonder how many more people I'm associated with know how good you are with your mouth."

Sandra's face flushed red, and her eyes widened. "Excuse me? Did you just call me a whore?" She shook her head and frowned. "Wow, is this because I'm bi? I've heard enough crap from straight people. I'm not confused. I had sex with you because I liked you."

Dani could see the hurt she caused just as plain as day. She crumbled. Maybe she really was a child. She could be just as petty. "No, oh God, no. That was just me being... I don't even know what to call it anymore. I'm sorry. I didn't mean it."

Sandra huffed and turned, heading back to the table.

Dani met Rick's gaze. His brow was wrinkled either in question or confusion. She wasn't sure which. She mouthed 'sorry' and left.

Had she really said all that? She'd had her moments. A lot of the residents gave her a wide berth for a reason, but parts of her felt off, wrong, while the rest of her sang a different tune altogether. She hated this dissonance, and she placed the blame squarely on Becca's shoulders. As soon as Dani could, she was going to tell Becca where she could get off. It wasn't rational, but it worked for her.

Dani was never more grateful for the boundaries she'd cultivated between her professional and personal life. Despite the emotions boiling inside her, she put a smile on her face as she entered one of her patient's room later to gather information for the attending.

She stopped in the doorway and blinked. Avery Johnson, her seven-year-old leukemia patient, was perched on top of her father's shoulders. Her sister, Mya, was on her mother's. The adults stood against the far wall by the window.

Avery was pale, but her smile was huge. Her younger sister squealed and bucked in excitement.

"Okay, remember, first one to the door wins," Kirk reminded them.

His wife, Beth, nodded and glanced at Dani. "Dr. Russell, you can be our referee."

Avery was extremely sick and yet her family was able to find a moment of lightheartedness and hope. Maybe other doctors would have tried to deter them, citing Avery's dwindling energy level, but not this doctor. The heaviness dissipated from Dani's shoulders. Right then, her problems seemed trivial, even if she suspected the feeling wasn't going to last long. "I'm in. I can record it too, if you want?"

Beth smiled. "Thank you."

CHAPTER 13

Rebecca watched in awe as Peyton rubbed herself all over Mark. To add insult to injury, she purred loudly as well. "What the hell? You have catnip in your pockets or somethin'?"

Mark shrugged. "Pussies love me."

"Oh, my God. Get outta my house. I can't believe you said that out loud." She pointed toward the door but grinned as well.

He laughed. "I meant cats. That's all."

She eyed him up and down. "Uh-huh."

"Seriously. I might be a cop, but I don't have to fit the stereotype and talk like one, do I? Since I have a kid, I try to watch my language or my wife would skin me alive."

"Sounds like a good Southern woman."

"That she is." Dislodging Peyton, he got up off the couch. "Okay, time for me to go."

"You don't want a beer or anythin'? It's the least I can do." Rebecca stood as well.

Mark raised a brow. "You mean you have something besides Coke in your fridge?"

Rebecca snorted. "Occasionally. I may even drink water from time to time. You sure you don't want anythin'?"

"I'm good. I'm no hero. All I did was give you a jump."

"And followed me to the auto parts store and home." Rebecca rolled her eyes slightly.

"I would have done it for anybody. Well, except maybe Emmet, especially if he's getting on my nerves."

"I can definitely understand that. He tries so hard."

"Very." Mark widened his eyes in emphasis.

"Well, thank you for the help and bein' the first visitor to sit on the couch since I took off the plastic." Rebecca walked him toward the door.

He paused. "I'm sorry, what?"

Rebecca chuckled and waved her hand nonchalantly. "It's a cultural thing, I think."

"Okay, if you say so."

A loud, shrieking meow made Rebecca jump.

A second later, Peyton launched herself off the floor and onto Mark's pant leg. He yelped in surprise. "What the fuck!"

So much for him watching his language. Rebecca had to bite the inside of her cheek to hold in her laughter. "I'm so sorry." She had to pull Peyton from Mark's leg. Thanks to her claws, she was stuck on like Velcro. "Did she get skin?"

Peyton scampered away.

He chuckled and craned his head, looking around nervously. "I don't think so. God, she scared me."

"I see that. I guess they really do love you." Rebecca's tone was dripping with sarcasm.

"Yeah, but if they love me like that, I'm gonna have to put them on the scary-as-hell list, right next to clowns."

Rebecca pressed her lips together to keep her laughter at bay once more.

"Go ahead." Mark sighed. "Let's hear it."

She laughed. "You do know clowns make people happy? Right?" Rebecca opened the front door for him.

"They're terrifying, and no one can tell me different." He shrugged then shivered.

"Uh-huh. And on that note, I'll see you in the morning."

Mark stopped at the screen door and glanced over his shoulder. "Shit, I don't know. I may need that beer now."

Rebecca rolled her eyes. "Get outta my house."

He smiled. "Have a good one. Oh, looks like you have company."

She must not have heard him correctly. Rick was working late. Confusion set in and then it transformed into something else completely as she recognized the car parked on the other side of her driveway and the occupant getting out. Rebecca wasn't sure what she felt. Relief, anticipation, hope, or resignation. She settled on a nauseating combination of them all, and her predicament wasn't helped by the look on Dani's face. Like that first night she'd visited, her expression was frozen in determination and her eyes transmitting anger and resentment.

Mark touched her arm, making Rebecca tense up even more. "You okay?" She glanced at him, and he looked back at her with curiosity and concern.

Rebecca turned away. "Uh, yeah. You'd better go."

Mark didn't respond.

Dani slammed her car door and walked toward her quickly. She was in scrubs, and her hair was loose and messy, like she had been raking her hands through it.

Their eyes met.

Yes, Dani looked the same, but there was something different. It wasn't until Dani got closer that Rebecca could feel it—an electricity in the air around them. She swallowed and looked toward the street. It was empty. When had Mark left?

"We need to talk." Dani stopped in front of her, but within arm's length.

She was only a few inches taller than Rebecca, but at the moment, it seemed like a foot. Rebecca didn't like that feeling at all.

"If you came here to fight, we could've done it over the phone. The minute you started up, you woulda been talkin' to dead air, but still..."

Dani's hands fisted at her side. "Why did you have to come back?"

It wasn't just the death of her great aunt that brought her back. So much more was involved. Rebecca sighed. "I had to."

"Well, I'm so glad it's working for you, but I'm a goddamn mess!" Dani's eyes were wild and her face red. "That man, the one who left, does he know what you do to people?"

Rebecca bristled. "What in the black hell are you talkin' about? He's my partner!"

Dani sputtered and tripped over her words. "Okay... Well—"

"And don't come here expectin' me to take responsibility for all the crap in your life in the past four years." Rebecca threw her hands up. "I told you I'm not fightin' with you. If you wanna talk, come inside. I'm not doin' this in my front yard." She grabbed Dani's arm. "C'mon."

Snatching her arm away, Dani's eyes went wide and she gasped for breath.

Rebecca's fingertips tingled as a surge of awareness seeped over her. She looked down at her hand and made a fist. Then she glanced back up at Dani. "I'm not stupid. I know why you're here. At the beginnin', I kinda asked myself the same question that's probably tearin' you up. How can I still want someone who hurt me?" Rebecca moved closer. "You just do. That's the only answer I've been able to come up with." God, it felt good to get at least part of that out. Rebecca was sure at this point that she was far from over Dani, but she kept the last piece to herself for now, fearing it would be too much.

Dani stepped back, but she didn't run or turn away. She crossed her arms over her chest. Seconds later, she stomped toward the house.

Rebecca gave her time before following. When she got to the living room, Dani was pacing in front of the couch. Peyton lay on the loveseat, watching her warily.

Rebecca sat down and waited for the denials and the vitriol.

"I had everything just the way I needed it to be." Dani stopped and looked down at her. "According to you, my career came first, so I made damn sure you were right. You show up, and I'm so…fucking angry all the time."

Rebecca huffed and leaned forward. "I'm not gonna let you blame me. I left you, but you had a hand in that."

Dani started pacing again.

"And don't you think maybe you've been angry all along but it wasn't until you concentrated on real life that you started to feel it?"

"Are you kidding me? Are you the mistress of feelings now?" Dani asked.

"I never said that."

"You might as well."

Rebecca covered her face with her hands then dropped them. "We're not two years old. We can have a normal conversation. We used to have them all the time. There was a time when you were the only person I wanted to talk to, and I remember when we didn't need to talk at all."

They stared at each other. Rebecca saw something come to life in Dani's eyes as they darkened. The fire growing between them generated enough smoke to make it hard to breathe. Dani's chest heaved as if she'd been running, and Rebecca decided to not even try to inhale. What was the point?

"Stop it! Shut up!" Dani closed the distance between them. Her face was still just as flushed, and she seemed to be shaking.

Dani towered over Rebecca, but she didn't feel threatened or slighted. Rebecca was awake and alive. Something was happening here. She had no idea what it was, but it was still happening. Rebecca had a choice to either pull back and leave them dangling over some weird precipice or push forward closer to the other side.

"You're not even gonna try denyin' to my face everythin' that you're feelin'?"

Dani made a sound of sheer frustration. It was somewhere between a groan and a growl.

"I'm sorry I hurt you," Rebecca said softly. Her sudden change in tactic left her wide open and vulnerable to attack, and it would be completely one-sided.

"Stop. Just…stop." Dani's brow furrowed, and her lips trembled.

Rebecca looked up at her, seeing Dani's confusion and fear as plain as day. "No, I can't—"

Lacing a hand through Rebecca's hair, Dani grabbed a handful and pulled back sharply. She crawled on top of her, crushing their lips together.

Rebecca gasped in surprise, then moaned as Dani's tongue slid over hers. Everything around her flashed white then red as a stunning arousal overtook her. There was no gentleness.

Dani kissed her like she was pissed, all hard and heavy like she wanted to leave something behind. Dani kissed her like she was afraid, leaning, then crashing into her as if she needed to be inside and away from her own demons. Most of all, Dani kissed her like she was starving. She whimpered every time their tongues brushed and kept going back for more.

Rebecca opened wide and met her stroke for stroke. She was hungry too, and just as afraid. She wrapped her arms around Dani, sealing their connection, and tried to pull her hips down.

Resisting, Dani knelt in front of her instead, tearing them apart and pushing Rebecca's legs open in the process. Rebecca's chest burned, but she put breathing aside to enjoy the sight before her.

Dani's hair was loose, shaggy, and wild. Her dark eyes peered back at Rebecca with pupils blown wide. Her lips were swollen and wet. Her mouth opened, but she didn't say a word. The moment stretched and pulled taut between them, and it seemed to last forever. Eternity ended a few seconds later, as Dani clawed and tugged at Rebecca's pants.

The urgency made Rebecca moan and scattered her thoughts. She lifted her hips as Dani moved back and yanked her pants down her thighs, dragging Rebecca's underwear too. She had no idea where they ended up, just that she was free of them.

Suddenly, everything stopped.

Dani stared between Rebecca's legs. Her gaze was intense enough to be a touch. Rebecca widened and thrusted toward her. Firmly, Dani pressed her hands against the inside of Rebecca's thighs, opening her even more. Without warning, Dani bent forward and licked into her greedily.

Rebecca cried out.

Dani moaned.

The swipe of Dani's tongue against Rebecca's sex mirrored the anger, the fear, and the hunger of her kisses. She was relentless. Each flick was heavy, deliberate, and designed to pull Rebecca completely from herself. She rolled her hips, arching them forward hard to meet Dani's tongue. But when Dani slipped inside her, Rebecca lost it. "Oh Jesus, fuck!"

Dani's mouth had always been deadly in more ways than one.

Rebecca grabbed hold of Dani's head with both hands and fucked her face, pressing Dani's tongue deeper with each pass.

When Rebecca shattered, she did it with Dani's name on her lips.

After abruptly jerking away from her, Dani crawled into Rebecca's lap.

Rebecca whimpered in protest, needing just a few more seconds to enjoy her orgasm. She tried to wrap her arms around Dani, but her affection was swatted away. Rebecca frowned and was a moment from voicing her indignation when Dani leaned back. She drew Rebecca's gaze downward, where she watched in utter fascination as Dani's hand disappeared inside the pants of her scrubs.

Dani's groan was dirty, raspy, and loud.

Rebecca's sex clenched in empathy. "Let me…" She reached for Dani again, but Dani slapped her away with her free hand. Moments later, Rebecca was more mesmerized by Dani's undulating hips and what she couldn't see. Dani's eyes were closed with her head thrown back and mouth open.

Rebecca's hips arched upward of their own volition. She was more turned on than she had been just a few minutes before. Unable to help herself, she eased her own fingers between her legs and rubbed her clit in tight, hard circles. Dani's emphatic gasp made Rebecca look up. Their gazes locked.

Dani cried out, "Fuck!" She trembled. Her hips jerked and bucked. "Uhhh, fuck."

This time, Rebecca didn't just shatter. She was ripped apart.

Minutes passed, but Rebecca continued to lay there sprawled against the couch with Dani on top of her. She didn't want to move, but she did anyway, tilting her head to the side.

Peyton came into view, still sitting on the loveseat a few feet away. Her glare, complete with ears pasted to her head, could only be described as murderous.

Rebecca snorted. The snort turned into a laugh.

Dani stirred. She pushed hair away from her face. For a second, her expression was clearly satisfied, and then her eyes widened as what looked like fear seeped in. She jumped up and covered her mouth with a hand as she peered down at Rebecca. Her hand shook just as her whole body had done a few minutes ago. Dani turned and ran for the door, and didn't look back.

CHAPTER 14

Talk to me. I kno u want 2.

Dani shoved her cell phone back into the pocket of her scrubs and vehemently pressed the up button on the elevator panel even though it was already illuminated thanks to one of the two people standing beside her.

Whenever her phone beeped or vibrated, she couldn't stop herself from reading the texts, despite the fact Dani knew who they were from. Even after two days, every message Becca sent still made it harder to breathe, and the voice mails caused her chest to hurt, literally.

Her body heated from the inside out with recent memories. It shook her. The need, the desperation, that took hold of her with Becca. It was like everything raw inside her pushed itself to the forefront.

Dani closed her eyes and tried to center herself, but when she did, images flashed past. She moved to the side, not wanting anyone to notice that she was trembling. She took a couple of deep breaths and successfully calmed down. There was no point, no way to deny that Becca still affected her, but she couldn't be a slave to it.

She couldn't.

No matter how good it felt.

Leaving Becca half naked and sprawled on the couch had been impulsive and no doubt hurtful, but she'd had to get out of there because she wasn't at all sure what she would have done next. The way she left should have been enough to end the strange dance they'd been engaged in. Judging by the barrage of phone calls and texts, it hadn't, so she'd decided on another tactic—avoidance.

Dani had been hurt enough, and she had no intention of getting caught in another endless cycle of pain, no matter how much Becca had changed.

Fear overpowered everything else, and being torn apart by the same woman twice didn't seem at all conducive to her sanity.

That one encounter was enough to satiate her need for Becca. It had to be, and given some time and space, the rest of Dani would fall in line. Putting aside her current reaction, Dani tried her best to convince herself that she'd gained a modicum of control. The fact that she could get past her current confusing emotions with deep breathing helped tremendously.

By the time the elevator came, Dani felt almost normal again. The group around her had gotten larger. Dani stepped in and moved to the right, as close to the controls as she could get. The button to her floor had already been pushed. She spotted Sandra. Dani raised her hand to wave and accompanied the gesture with a smile.

Sandra nodded and looked away.

Her response was warranted, but Dani had apologized, and beyond that, she really didn't know what else to do to make amends. Maybe Sandra needed time. Dani wasn't sure since she didn't know her that well. Maybe that was part of the problem? There was nothing she could do about that. Correction: there was nothing she *wanted* to do about that.

Dani glanced up as the elevator dinged for yet another floor. People got off, including Sandra, and people got on. Three more stops until she got to Peds.

Some time later, Dani rounded the corner near Jacob's room. She paused. Sheri stood outside her son's room on the phone. Slowly, Dani moved closer, not wanting to interrupt or intrude, but curiosity got the better of her.

Sheri's features were pinched, and the hand she moved in animated fashion was fisted. "It's cancer, and unfortunately it takes more than a month to treat it." However, except for the slight sarcasm, Sheri's voice tone was modulated and almost pleasant.

Sheri glanced up and caught Dani's gaze, but she didn't wave her away. "Yes, I'll be sure to keep you posted." She hung up by stabbing at her phone and turned to Dani. "That was my boss."

"Oh, I wasn't trying to intrude. I didn't know you—"

"Didn't know what? That I worked? You know all people of color aren't on Medicaid."

Dani held up a hand. "No, that never crossed my mind."

Sheri sighed loudly. "Look, I'm sorry. You didn't deserve that. I'm out on FMLA, and he had the nerve to ask me if Jacob got better sooner whether I'd be back before the twelve weeks were up."

"Oh, he's a bit of a douche." Dani cringed in empathy.

"A bit? Try a whole aisle's worth."

Sensing Sheri's need to talk, Dani pushed further. "What do you do?"

"I'm an associate retail project manager for Paulson's Retail Solutions."

"Oh, nice."

Sheri flashed a grin, but her eyes were sad. "I should be in my boss's position. He has no idea what he's doing. I've been making him look good for a long time despite the fancy college he went to." She sucked in a breath and exhaled shakily. "All the hours that I put in…but the fact he got the promotion didn't matter after Bryan died."

"What are you gonna do when FMLA runs out?" Instead of focusing on her husband's death, Dani concentrated on the more immediate concern.

"I'm not worried about it." Sheri shrugged. "Tom is incompetent, and if they do try to fire me after twelve weeks, I'm pretty confident anybody they hire will run out screaming. They'll beg me to come back. I'll be able to write my own ticket or move on to something better."

"Well played."

Sheri nodded. "I think so. Sometimes I think he tries his best to make me go all angry black woman, but I don't. I'm not the type to mince words, but I know how to be professional. Anyway, I didn't mean to pull you into this."

"It's okay." Dani waved away her concern. "But I do have an update for you. The tumor is still getting smaller. I'm working on determining the reduction rate, which could slow or pick up speed over the course of the chemo, but regardless, his treatment plan remains the same. That means surgery."

"Shrinking? That's good to hear…for the most part." Sheri smiled, and the sadness was gone. "I have a question though."

"Okay?" Dani didn't like the way Sheri had ignored the surgery part of her statement. She wanted to push but decided against it. Maybe actual evidence would eventually soften the blow.

"Why do I see you more often during the day than the rest of his team?"

Dani looked down at her feet then back up again. "I'm not big on rapport with my colleagues, but with patients and families it's a different story. I like spending as much time with them as I can." There were a lot of ways she could have answered the question that probably would have placated, but Dani wanted to be honest.

Sheri stared at her quietly for a few seconds. "Yeah, I have noticed that. When you come in with the doctors who look like they just got out of high school, they give you plenty of space." She shrugged. "But I guess seeing you as much as we do is good for us, I suppose." She stepped away from the wall. "C'mon in. He's been asking about you."

After taking a second to wonder about Sheri's response, Dani refocused as Jacob called out her name.

Rebecca stared at her phone, waiting yet again for a response from Dani. She moved her cell from on top of the desk to under it and stared some more. She already felt pathetic and didn't want anybody else actually seeing her in the act of being, well…pathetic, which was a feeling that didn't fit her now.

Four years ago, when she'd still been begging for the scraps of Dani's attention, Rebecca would have been devastated by her silence. Now, those same emotions hung off her shoulders, misshapen and bulky.

The reemergence of even a sliver of the old Rebecca pissed her off. She'd taken a lot in the past, but she was no doormat then or now. After a ton of texts and a handful of phone calls, Rebecca was tired of being nice. Every time Dani rebuffed her, a tiny piece of Rebecca's patience and understanding fell away. It was like someone was slowly turning up the heat on a pot of water. Her anger sat on simmer. Most of it was aimed at Dani for taking and leaving her half naked and weak. The remainder was self-inflicted.

When Dani crashed into her, Rebecca had been unable to keep herself from drowning in her. The kicker? She'd do it all over again. Having Dani touch her like that after four years might very well be Rebecca's favorite mistake. Damn it all to hell, she wanted her even more now than she had in that moment two days ago, which scared the shit out of her.

The pain she'd suffered through before was a living, breathing thing that could take up residence in the present. She didn't want that, but as if her life was some weird cosmic joke, Rebecca did want Dani. Who the hell did that make her? A glutton for punishment or just fucked up in the head for not being over her?

If they got back together and if things went downhill, would they end up killing each other this time? Dear God, what a way to die. There were so many goddamned questions with no answers, but she had no intention of just letting things go.

Not this time.

She was going to stand her ground.

Rebecca moved her thumbs quickly over the keypad, stabbing at the letters as her emotions got the better of her.

It still happnd no matter how much u ignore me. I'm not goin away Dani.

She knew her text would go unanswered but did get some satisfaction from knowing it had been read.

Someone patted her on the shoulder, making her jump slightly. Rebecca glanced up to see Mark.

He leaned against her desk and crossed his arms over his chest. "Okay, so I know you don't flap your gums every three seconds like Emmet does, but you've been extra quiet the past couple days."

Rebecca shoved her cellphone into her pocket. "I just got a lot goin' on."

"Yeah, well if you stare at the phone any longer, you're gonna go blind. Just saying."

Rebecca met his gaze and deadpanned, "That's masturbation."

He tilted his head and brought his hand to his chin. "With a phone? I suppose if it's on vibrate."

She shook her head. "You need help."

"Every once in a while, yeah, I have to agree with you." Mark stared at her and waited.

Rebecca wasn't sure how much to tell him. Maybe part of her wanted to keep it to herself and make sure it was cemented in memory—every sound, every touch, everything about it.

After the extended silence, Mark stepped away from the desk. "Well, if you wanna talk about it later, let me know." His forehead was wrinkled and his eyes held concern.

"No, sorry. I got stuck in my own head for a minute. I'm havin' woman problems."

He visibly cringed. "Oh, good thing you have insurance."

Rebecca chuckled, which was almost freeing. "No, not that type. Hell, I wish it was that simple."

"Ohhhh!" His eyes widened. "You mean woman…woman problems?"

"Yes, those."

"The lady in your driveway play a part in that?" Mark crossed his arms again.

"She's the star."

"Nice. I like the girl-next-door look too. Mine is blonde though."

Rebecca glared. She couldn't help it. He was getting off-topic.

"I know that's not the point, so don't look at me like that." Mark cleared his throat. "So what's going on?"

She was well on her way to trusting him. Might as well take the last little leap. Maybe he could actually help. "The other night, somethin' huge happened." God, that was the biggest understatement in creation, but Rebecca had no words to really describe it. Her stomach knotted pleasantly.

"Okay."

Rebecca snapped back to the present. "Now, she won't call me back. We have a history, and not all of it's good."

He held up a finger and moved quickly toward the refrigerator and grabbed a Coke. On his way back, Mark took a seat behind his own desk and rolled his chair across the floor toward her. He unscrewed the top of the twenty-ounce bottle and handed it to her. "I think I should be sitting down for this, and you need a tasty beverage. Now, go on. It's just us normal people here right now."

"Okay, so…I've been blowin' up her phone."

Mark grunted and continued to look at her.

"I haven't said anythin' bad," Rebecca added, feeling the need to clarify.

He shrugged. "Maybe she needs some space."

Rebecca shook her head. "I can't. She's already runnin'."

"Has what you're doing helped so far?"

"Well, no."

"Look, I'm not claiming to know a lot about women. I've been married for almost twenty years, but I *do* know that when a woman needs space, give it to her. Things could get worse otherwise. That's common sense. Give her a day or so."

That was some hard advice to take. Rebecca had contemplated giving Dani space in the beginning, but it went against her every instinct to do so. Maybe her instincts on this were too tied up in her own feelings. She took a long swig of her Coke and set it down on her desk. "I don't know, Mark."

"You said you guys have history? Some of it good?" he asked.

"Yeah, when things were good they were really good. My great aunt did what she could, but it was like growin' up in the desert." Rebecca paused, trying to find the right words. "Bein' with Dani was like findin' out the water in front of me wasn't a mirage. It was fuckin' real the whole time."

Mark blinked. "Damn."

"Yeah, I did everythin' I could to keep things steady, but she changed. I changed, and none of it was for the better."

"Well, then after you give her space, remind her of the good stuff." Mark leaned forward. "The bad crap has a way making people forget a lot." He cleared his throat and looked away for a second.

"Sounds like you have some personal experience with that?"

"I said I've been married almost twenty years. Not all of it has been smooth. I'm not all rainbows and unicorns, you know."

She could believe it. No one was.

"You want her back?"

Rebecca took another sip of her drink and licked her lips. "Sometimes. I wanna believe that underneath all the shit, the woman I knew is still there."

Mark smiled. "So that's a yes. You don't have to like them all the time."

"I know that. I'm not new at this." Rebecca scratched at the Coke label, tearing a bit off.

"I get that, but Ms. Girl Next Door is the one who stuck in your craw."

"That's not the best of images."

"Still true."

"I've been with other people since we broke up. Even been in a relationship or two, but I still couldn't get past what I did to her, and vice versa. I thought that was all it was. So yeah, either way, 'stuck' fits the situation."

"It happens, I guess. Let me ask you something?"

"What?"

"What if the person you knew doesn't exist anymore?"

Rebecca shook her head. "All I know right now is that somethin' draws me to her, and it's too strong to just be the past."

They both looked up as Emmet entered the squad room. He sat and looked from Mark to Rebecca and back again. "Why'd you get all quiet? Were you guys talkin' about me?"

"You caught me." Mark grinned. "That's all I do in my free time."

Emmet glared.

Rebecca rolled her eyes. These people were seriously growing on her.

Mark moved his chair back toward his own desk. He fired up his computer and started pecking on the keys.

Rebecca thought about their conversation. He was right, and she had enough common sense to know it.

CHAPTER 15

"So, I've given you enough rope and time to either hang yourself or become an expert at jumping. From what I've seen and heard, you might have graduated to double dutch." Lieutenant Benz shot Rebecca an unflinching look.

Rebecca took the compliment and stored it away, but not before mentally acknowledging the warmth it left behind. "Yeah, things are goin' good." In fact, things at work were going a lot better than she'd thought they would.

Lieutenant Benz raised an eyebrow and nodded. "You still talk too much, I see."

"Worse than Emmet." Rebecca grinned.

The Lieutenant bared her teeth in a smile. "I have to ask this, even though the answer is pretty obvious. Anybody here giving you any trouble?"

Rebecca shook her head. "No. They all bring some good things to the table, but Mark is just more my speed."

"I did notice that you gravitate toward him more, but you'll have to do without him today. Mark took a personal day."

She swallowed down a pang of disappointment. "That's too bad, but I'll make do." Rebecca leaned forward, assuming they were done.

"Good to know. Now, get to work."

Rebecca nodded and stood. She whipped out her cell phone and called Mark on her way back to her desk.

"Yeah?" He answered on the third ring.

"Just checkin' on you."

"Well, whether you want to know or not, I have puke in my hair."

The man was going bald. How on earth did he accomplish that? "Lovely. Should I even ask how that happened?"

Mark chuckled. "It's not mine. My kid's sick. Sheila had something big time going on at work, and the grandparents are out of town. So, I took the day. I got plenty of time off. Might as well use it for a good cause."

"Uhhh, Daddy." His little girl groaning in the background was hard to miss.

Rebecca cringed.

"It's a good place, my bathroom floor. Didn't know it could be so comfy. Thanks for calling. I'll hit you up later?"

"Yeah, take care, and just to let you know, I'm takin' your advice about my woman issues."

"Good. Hope it works out, and just to let *you* know, you're coming over for dinner this weekend. Sheila wants to meet you."

Yeah, she hoped it worked out too. Rebecca swallowed hard, but she didn't hesitate. "I'll be there." She hung up and looked down at her phone. She hadn't sent Dani a text or called her since midday yesterday.

It had been a lot harder than she'd thought, especially since she couldn't stop thinking about her. Yet somehow she did. So far there was still radio silence from Dani's end, but for now she was going to accept it. She sighed and inadvertently glanced in Emmet's direction. He was typing away on his computer.

"Wells?"

Rebecca spun around in her chair to look in Alvin's direction. "What's up?"

"The Dorset case that wasn't really a case?"

That got her attention. "What about it?"

"Mrs. Dorset had one of the beat cops on the scene call us. This just became a case. Mom went to pick the kid up from school and found out the dad snatched him up almost two hours before. It all sounds pretty cut and dried. She called her ex-husband's cell. He answered, threatened her, told her she'd never see the kid again. Plus, she heard her son crying in the background."

"What? They were goin' back to court soon. She was gonna challenge his right to custody. He only had every other weekend, but the guy was stalkin' her." Maybe he thought he was going to lose this time around.

The typing stopped. Rebecca looked in Emmet's direction. Unusually quiet, he just listened.

Alvin shrugged. "It is what it is now."

A sinking feeling settled in Rebecca's gut. "All right, let's do what we can to reel this one in. Let's hope he didn't leave the area yet."

Emmet picked up his phone. "Okay, I'll issue a county-wide alert. I won't even bother with the Georgia Bureau of Investigations since we can confirm it's a parental kidnapping..." He met Rebecca's gaze as his voice trailed off.

"I know. I know GBI may not be able to do anythin'." Rebecca turned back to Alvin. "Did they say he sounded scared?"

If the kid was in danger, they could have gotten a lot more help. GBI didn't intervene in parental kidnapping cases otherwise. That meant no Levi's Call, Georgia's regional version of an AMBER Alert.

Shit.

"No, just that he was crying." He looked down at his desk and fiddled with a notebook. "And that he wanted his mom."

"Double shit," Rebecca said aloud.

"Yeah, so let's dig up what we can on Dad on the fly. The guy doesn't seem too bright. Maybe this will be over before it starts." Alvin stood and peered at Rebecca. "You comin'? I wanna go check his place and hit up his neighbors."

Hell yeah she was.

When they reached the garage, Alvin threw her the keys. As she started the car, he shook his head. "I hate it when family shit gets salty."

She couldn't have said it better herself. Maybe his bluntness would serve them well on this case. Asshole or not, Rebecca was glad to have him.

"If we uncover somethin', you playin' good cop?" Alvin asked.

Rebecca actually smiled. "You playin' the bad damn-near-ambivalent cop?"

Alvin snorted.

Jacob laughed, and Dani smiled at the sound, no matter how weak it was. She didn't let that deter her from whaling on the guy she pulled out of his Mustang. Was it wrong that she was enjoying beating the driver's ass? It was just a video game, after all, but maybe Grand Theft Auto V did have some redeeming value. Hearing sirens, Dani maneuvered her character into the stolen car and drove away. She swerved everywhere, running into things and people. Jacob was hysterical with laughter. Playing this game with him was extremely inappropriate, but who was going to tell?

"Doc D, you suck."

She moved her whole body with the remote. "Yes, I can admit that. You wanna take over for me?"

He nodded, and Dani handed him the controller. The car straightened and began to move like an expert was behind the wheel. "My granny came to visit today. She was my dad's mom."

Really, this kid could be president. How was he able to concentrate on the game and talk at the same time? "If I remember correctly, she comes every week, right?"

"Yeah, but my ma always leaves the room when she's here."

Now, that was something he hadn't told her. "Okay, maybe she just uses that time to take a break every once in a while."

"That's not it. They used to yell at each other a lot. I think they pretend they like each other. I'm not stupid. I like it better when Pawpaw and Memaw come to visit."

She'd heard laughter more than once coming from his room when they stopped in. "Why is that?"

"She's more happy then."

Very astute kid.

Jacob stopped playing and glanced at the door to his room. "Doc D?"

"Hmm?"

"Am I gonna die like my daddy did?"

"No, you're not." Dani met his gaze and didn't blink once. It was a promise she was determined to keep.

Jacob nodded and went back to his video game. "Thank you."

"You're very welcome. It's what doctors are supposed to do."

"Not for that. For stayin' with me while my ma went to go get food. You didn't have to."

No, she didn't, but Dani wanted to. She looked up as Sheri walked back in, carrying a Styrofoam container.

"Thanks," Sheri said.

Dani smiled. "No problem."

"She sucks at GTA, Ma."

Sheri chuckled. "I'm not the best at it either."

"Nooo, you're way better than her," Jacob emphasized.

Dani stood. "And on that note, I'm calling it a night. See you both tomorrow."

"Have a good night, Dr. Russell." Sheri smiled and then opened the container to dig into a huge salad.

After gathering her things, Dani made her way to the elevator. She could've taken the stairs but just didn't have the energy. Maybe she was too exhausted to think. Dani nearly snorted out loud, knowing that wasn't true. Unless she was actively busy and occupied with a patient, Becca invaded her thoughts. She dreaded it and looked forward to it at the same time.

There hadn't been any text or phone calls for over twelve hours. Dani should have been relieved, but instead, she was anxious and wanting. She had started to think there was no escape. Quite a few people were crowded around her when the elevator opened. Some got off, breezing past them to their destination. Dani spotted Rick and Sandra in the back. They stood close to each other and seemed deep in conversation. Dani didn't think twice about taking the spot next to them. Rick looked up, and Dani grinned, encompassing them both in the gesture.

"Hey."

"What's up? You headed home?" Rick asked.

Sandra turned away.

Dani nodded. "I'm wiped."

"I can see that, but you should still join us for a drink. Maybe smooth over whatever's goin' on between the two of you?" He tilted his head toward Sandra.

She huffed and elbowed him.

Dani blinked. Why would she want to do that? She just didn't have the energy to waste on a simple acquaintance, despite the fact they knew each other intimately. "No, thank you."

Rick didn't respond verbally, but his eyes narrowed. They were quiet as people talked around them. Dani was the first of the three of them to step off the elevator when they got to the parking garage. She heard Rick mumble something to Sandra but didn't turn back to see what it was.

"Dani, hold up." He fell into step beside her.

She glanced at him. "You didn't have to change your plans for me. I'm fine."

"I didn't. Told Sandra I'd meet her at Bartaco."

"Oh, then why—"

"So, Sandra's just not worth your time is she?"

God, had he read her mind?

"How long, you think? Until you start treatin' me that way?"

Dani stopped and looked at him. "I would never do that."

Rick paused too. "You pretty much did when Becca first got here." He crossed his arms over his chest.

"That was different, and I thought we were past that."

"We are, but you're harder now and colder."

"Not toward you." Dani took a step toward him. Where was all this coming from? He knew she was having issues right now.

"Sometimes that doesn't matter."

"We're…okay. Right?" Dani tried to keep the panic out of her voice.

"We are up top, but it seems like lately all I've been is a weird cushion between you and Becca. I have my own shit, and I have to figure it out without bein' all wrapped up in y'all." Rick shook his head as he backed away. "I'll see you at home." He turned and walked the opposite way.

She stood there as he weaved his way through a sea of cars. Dani wanted to call out to him, and tell him he was right, but at the same time he was wrong as well. However, mostly, Dani wished she didn't have to think about the situation at all.

Dani jerked awake as her phone chimed loudly. She sucked in a breath and blinked a couple of times. Just as sleep wrapped her in fuzziness again, her phone sounded off once more as a reminder. She groaned and reached out blindly for her glasses. It wasn't the hospital. They wouldn't text her. Dani's thoughts went to Rick. She pushed hair away from her face and put on her glasses. Her breath caught as she read the text.

Ur one of the only ppl who made me feel like I belonged.

It was from Becca. Suddenly, Dani was wide awake. Her heart rammed against her chest, and before she knew what she was doing, Dani answered back.

What are you doing up?

Becca didn't say anything for a long time, and Dani wondered if she was shocked that she'd gotten a response. Not to mention, Becca was being so cordial. She expected anger. It would probably show itself later.

Have a case. Just got home.

Dani closed her eyes as relief, fear, and a whole host of other emotions warred with each other inside her. For the time being, only one came forward as the victor. Need. Dani typed.

Did you find the child?

Not yet. It's a parental kidnapping. Can I call u?

She stared at the words but was suddenly afraid what hearing Becca's voice in real time would do to her.

No.

It took Dani forever to type her answer, but she did, hoping that the word at least solidified some aspect of her resolve.

K.

Then ellipses appeared. Apparently, Becca had more to say.

R u alone?

Dani felt her forehead crinkle. She hadn't heard Rick come in. Was she looking for him?

Yes why?

More ellipses.

Can I come over?

God. Dani released a shaky breath as her stomach tightened. What was she doing?

I have work in the morning. Have to go.

Licking her lips, Dani focused on her phone. She waited several minutes for the ellipses, but they never materialized. The dichotomy between what she did and didn't want clashed. Disappointment tugged at her.

Chapter 16

Dani waited for the latest MRI to load into the imaging system before bringing the scans up on her iPad, then broadcasting them on the surrounding screens for everybody to see. She looked up at her colleagues. Despite what she'd told Sheri—or perhaps because of it—Dani had been looking deeper, and she didn't like the results.

"The tumor has reduced significantly. He has two more treatments left. So it will get even smaller and easier to remove. With the damage done, he'll still need the nephrectomy and additional chemo after to reduce recurrence," she said.

"Yes, I agree," Dr. Meda said. "Adjuvant treatment post-surgery is a must in all cases. How do you think Sheri will respond to such news?" He leaned back in his chair and fiddled with the pen in his hand.

"Not well. She'll be angry with us, which is normal in this kind of situation. More so at me since I'm the one she sees the most, but she'll accept that surgery is the only choice. She knew this from beginning. Now she'll have to deal with it head on."

"You're the face of this team, but they've seen all of us," the other resident, Dr. Luft, chimed in. "I know you like doing your own rounds before and sometime after the structured ones. I'd be more than happy to join you on those too and take some of the heat off you."

Dani shook her head. "No, that would probably have the opposite effect. It's okay. I can handle it, but thank you." She made sure to meet her gaze.

Dr. Luft smiled slightly. "Anything to help."

Looking at them both, Dr. Meda grinned. "Good. Now, do you think, Dr. Russell, that Sheri will need additional mental health support due to the incident with her husband?"

"I don't know yet. If she doesn't talk to me, I don't think she'll talk with anyone."

"Let's wait until we have the scans after the next course of treatment. I want her to be able to see the progression with her own eyes to foster a better understanding. Maybe this will ease some of the prospective tension. Despite any emotional upheaval surgery will cause, Jacob will be better for it, and he has a good chance to go on and lead a healthy life." Dr. Meda looked straight at Dani.

After experiencing firsthand the way Sheri pushed talk of surgery aside, Dani wholeheartedly agreed on waiting. She had already started to mentally prepare herself for the possible fallout. She and Sheri weren't friends, but there was still a growing bond of mutual respect peppered around professional boundaries.

"Dr. Russell, we're going through a couple more cases, and I think it will be beneficial to keep you on this team for the foreseeable future."

God, she loved being able to stay in oncology longer now that it was her last year of residency. A majority of her time could now be spent there thanks to electives and subspecialty rotation. Dani gave Dr. Meda a short nod and refocused her attention to what was to come.

Sometime later, Dani stood as the majority of the team filed out the door. Sensing someone near, she looked up. Dr. Luft smiled at her. "Jacob talks about you a lot. You have great rapport with him."

Shouldn't all doctors in pediatrics be able to successfully deal with children? Dani waited for her to continue.

"Mrs. Cook seems to barely tolerate me. Maybe if I were with you on your next few visits, she'd soften up?" she asked again.

In other words, she wanted to piggyback on her existing relationship with Sheri. So that's probably what she really wanted in the first place. Why not say that? Dani would have respected her more for being honest instead of trying to make it look like she was doing Dani a favor. Dani opened her mouth to answer her, but she could almost hear Rick admonishing her about how she treated people. She pressed her lips together. Something scathing sat on the tip of her tongue and it was ready to go. In that moment, she made a different choice and her decision went deeper than Rick's complaint and became more self-directed. "I'll give it some thought and get back to you."

Dr. Luft's smile got even bigger. "Thanks, I appreciate that." She reached out a hand, but took it back quickly and put it in her pocket instead. Then, after a final nod, she turned and left.

Dr. Meda chuckled. "Well, that was a valiant attempt at throwing Dr. Luft a bone. She does well with children, but struggles with their parents."

Dani was a little shocked that she'd even made the effort. It left a foreign feeling behind that she really couldn't identify. "I only said I'd consider it."

"Yes, well, I'll leave you to your considerations, then, but I think she'd be a lot better if you, as senior resident, were a lot more hands-on with her." Dr. Meda grinned.

Rebecca glanced at Mark as they waited for Mrs. Dorset to open the front door. As she looked back through the window, she saw the other woman approach but she moved slowly, as if something weighed her down. Rebecca imagined that having a child missing would feel like the universe was crashing in on her and bring just as much pain.

The door opened and the walking dead greeted them. Mrs. Dorset was pale, making the dark smudges under her eyes stick out even more. She blinked rapidly as if she hadn't seen the sun for a while and then stared at them with bloodshot eyes. Her hair stuck up in places and she was still in pajamas even though it was afternoon. Her lips trembled as she looked at them. "Did you—?"

"No, we just wanted to check on you and give you an update," Rebecca interrupted.

"You could have done that over the phone!" she yelled.

Mark stepped forward. "Mrs. Dorset—"

"Don't call me that. I hate that man, and I hate that I carry his last name. It's just Gwen." She stepped out of the way. "You might as well come in."

Rebecca was the first to enter. It looked as if someone had tossed the living room and kitchen. She glanced back at Gwen.

She shrugged. "I was looking for information. I thought maybe my ex had left something here that could help. He took care of everything, and I don't know if he had friends outside the few I knew. We never had much money, and I didn't know what he did with what we had…"

Mark picked papers up off the couch and put them on the coffee table before sitting down. "You find anything?"

Gwen shook her head. "I tried calling him, but his phone is either dead or turned off."

"We know," Rebecca added. "But after the last ping we got from one of the cell towers, we at least know he's still in the county."

"Is that supposed to make me feel better?"

It might not have done anything for her, but it gave Rebecca some confidence. "We're doin' everythin' we can."

"No, you're not. Why isn't the FBI or somebody involved?"

Mark leaned forward. "Mrs. Dorset…Gwen, we discussed this. In cases of parental kidnapping with no clear sign that Shane is in danger—"

"He's not a parent!"

"I agree. I have a child of my own, so I can empathize, but our resources are limited. Right now, we're combing a ten-mile radius based on his cell activity. It's gonna take some time. Plus, if he turns his phone back on, we'll have all we need to pinpoint a location."

"You've said all that before. You're not telling me anything new."

"I know it must seem like that, but I do have a question. Do you think he'd take the time to buy a burner phone?" Rebecca asked.

"I don't know. He's not stupid, but he's not a genius either."

Rebecca nodded. "Okay, we're checkin' out the stores where he lived, circulatin' his picture just to keep all our bases covered."

Gwen glanced at Mark. "The lawyer you recommended is trying to get my ex-husband's custody revoked. I know it's not going to happen tomorrow, but if he's able to do it, that makes it real kidnapping, right?"

Real kidnapping. Rebecca didn't get the distinction. It was all kidnapping in her opinion. "Yeah, it would, but this needs to be resolved as soon as possible." They weren't going to be allowed to use extended manpower for a family abduction for much longer. She was surprised they'd gotten the handful of help that they had. Rebecca wasn't sure if that was coming from her cynical side or the realist.

"Gwen, I hate to bug you, but can I have some water?" Mark asked.

She nodded. "Do you need anything, Detective Wells?"

"No, thanks. Not right now."

When they were alone, Rebecca turned to look at Mark and whispered, "Do you think your lawyer friend can really help with the custody issue?"

"That depends on the judge he gets. I'm sure you know how these family cases go. Even if he gets someone willing to listen, none of it's gonna happen quickly."

"Yeah, I just wish it had been possible to do more for her at the beginnin'. She saw it comin' and came to us. That doesn't happen often."

"We did what we could, and things still ended up crappy. I'm gonna see this through as long as I can."

Rebecca met his gaze. "I'm with you on that. You think Benz'll cut us off?"

"She will, sooner or later, especially if something high priority comes in."

She rolled her eyes slightly.

"Yeah, exactly," Mark agreed.

Rebecca looked up as Gwen came back in, giving her the attention she deserved.

"I need some good news," Mark said. "Tell me you have some good news for me? We've barely had time to talk about anything else besides work."

Rebecca cut her eyes at Mark as she made a right turn. "Stop talkin' so fast. You're startin' to sound like Emmet."

Mark scowled. "I know you know what I'm saying."

"I sent her a text this mornin'. Haven't heard back. I don't know, maybe late at night is better, but one time doesn't make a pattern."

"Well, you never know." Mark glanced at her. "Do whatever works."

"I'm not sure if wearin' her down is somethin' I wanna do. If that's what has to happen…" Rebecca didn't finish. She didn't think she had to.

"That's kind of a negative way to look at it."

"Well, I don't believe in sugarcoatin' things." Rebecca turned up the heat. It was a little too cold for her taste.

"No, I would've never guessed that about you," Mark deadpanned.

"Are we best girlfriends or somethin'?"

"No, but I do consider myself a metrosexual." He rubbed the top of his balding head.

Rebecca smiled. "I don't think that means what you think it means."

"Sure it does."

"I'm not gonna argue." Rebecca's tone was playful.

"Good, because we're so off topic."

"I can look it up in the urban dictionary if you don't believe me." Rebecca refused to let it go. She was enjoying herself, and she needed more enjoyment in her life.

"You're driving."

"Voice to text."

"You sure have a lot to say today." Mark looked at her, then out of the passenger window. "Now look who's channeling Emmet." He whispered, but it was still loud enough for her to hear.

"I'm just answerin' your questions."

"If you don't want to talk about your love life, just say so."

"If I didn't, I would have. And doesn't sayin' things like that feel weird comin' out of your mouth?"

Mark glared and enunciated slowly, "Metrosexual." Then he reached out to turn down the heat.

Rebecca smiled.

"Glad I could make *you* feel good," he grumbled.

"Are you still thinkin' about the Dorset case?"

Mark went quiet. "Huh, not really."

"You're welcome."

"Uh-huh. Still thinking about your girl next door?"

Rebecca eased onto the interstate. "If a case can't keep me occupied, then yes, all the time."

"Bet she's having the same issue."

Recalling the night before and the energy between them even over the phone, Rebecca thought so too.

"You got any special requests for dinner on Saturday? I was thinking, if it's nice out, I'd grill some steaks."

"As long as they're seasoned, that works for me. Do I need to bring anythin'?"

"Wait. Why wouldn't they be seasoned? I may not be from the South, but I don't like bland food."

"Good to know. Now, do I need to bring somethin'?"

"Nope. We have plenty adult beverages and sugary stuff for kids, including Coke. Sheila can't wait to meet you, by the way."

Rebecca cleared her throat. "I haven't done this before."

"Done what?"

"Got close to my partner, met his family. You know, the whole nine."

Mark didn't say anything for a few minutes. Rebecca went over what they'd discussed so far, finding nothing obviously offensive. She veered to the right, taking their exit, and when she got to a stop light, Rebecca turned her head. "You've gone quiet."

"Yeah, I figured you needed a break after all that talking." He met her gaze.

Rebecca glared at him this time.

Mark chuckled. "No, but seriously. I heard you. Emmet and Alvin are good guys and good to work with. But, you and me, we're something different... Something better."

She nodded. "Yeah, exactly."

Dani had been in bed less than ten minutes, and she was already falling asleep. Rick had come home and was courteous enough to say goodnight right before she lay down. It was colder tonight, so she piled the bed with an extra blanket. Now, she was snug, warm, and drifting.

Her phone vibrated and danced from the nightstand, but since it didn't continue, Dani knew it was a text. She stared at her phone. It was the only source of illumination in the room. Then the screen went dark again. Dani pushed away her grogginess, and with that, she became more aware of herself. Her heart rate increased, as did her respiration, but the most disturbing thing was the heat that flooded her, followed by an icy chill trickling down her back. Dani burrowed deeper in the covers. However, that didn't stop her phone from sounding off a reminder.

Light flashed in front of her face. Dani reached out for it and then shrank back. She'd listened to Becca's past voice mails and read her texts how many times now? Was she at her weakest when she realized how alone she was? Tired of questioning her strength and confusing feelings, Dani covered her head with the blankets in an attempt to block everything out.

Dani's phone vibrated again. She could hear it even though the sound was muffled. Through the blankets, the light was still bright enough to see. Dani pushed the covers away and reached for her glasses and her phone. This time, she didn't back away.

Remember when we went to NOLA first time together and ended up in French quarter? We were on balcony at Oz?

She read the first text twice before moving to the next one.

Those 2 drunk strippers kept tryin to dance 4 us and one of thm tried to show how flexible she was and fell ovr.

Dani bit her lip as memories rushed over her. It was hard not to smile, but somehow, she managed. Even though she was clearly being baited, Dani typed quickly.

That was at Cafe Lafitte's and you know it.

She found herself staring at ellipses yet again.

Yes it was. Did I wake u up?

Almost. Dani replied.

I didn't think u'd answer. U didn't earlier

Does it matter? Dani typed.

Suppose not.

Why are you doing this?

Dani had to ask even if she didn't like the answer. Maybe it would give her some insight into her own reasoning.

Cuz I want 2.

Shaken by Becca's response, Dani's hand trembled as she fired back.

Why are you acting like things were always good between us?

I didn't forget n e thing.

There were a million things Dani wanted to say to that statement. As she started typing, something else came out.

You're not angry about how I left you the other night?

I'm pissed at u and myself.

You're not acting like it. Why are you texting me?

More ellipses. They disappeared and came back again within a few seconds.

Cuz I want u. No matter what happend wit us I still do.

The words were right there in black and white. There was no taking them back. Mesmerized, Dani stared at them. For a moment, she felt nothing, and in the next, she was bombarded by so much that she couldn't identify it all. Dani drowned in it, and she was afraid that she wouldn't be able to get her head above water any time soon.

The strangest thing was that through it all she was still able to breathe. This woman was most definitely not out of her system. In fact, maybe she had been there the past few years all along, hibernating. The moment was tantamount to emotional whiplash, especially since she'd been denying this very thing.

Dani's fingers hovered over her phone as she tried to figure out what to type. A voice in her head screamed at her to ignore it, but that didn't feel right. Maybe she didn't know what did. New ellipses popped up.

Goodnite. Talk 2 u 2morrow

Not knowing what else to do, Dani's thumbs whisked over the phone's keyboard as she returned the sentiment with one of her own.

Goodnight.

CHAPTER 17

"So let me make sure I got this straight," Rick began. "We've barely hung out the past week, and now that I have a few hours free on a Saturday, you're ditchin' me? Even though I brought Coke?" He hoisted up the six pack of twenty-ounce bottles and jiggled it slightly in Rebecca's face.

"Thanks for the Coke. I can never have too many, but pretty much, yeah."

"I was gonna offer to watch *A Summer Place* with you. I need somethin' to wash my brain. Went to the three-dollar movie with Jason earlier to see *All Eyez on Me*. It couldn't touch *Soul Plane*, but we still shoulda stuck to reading the reviews first like we usually do."

"You played basketball after, huh?" Rebecca eyed his outfit. Nike shorts and a tank that was still damp as hell.

"Yeah, why?"

"Y'all win?" Rebecca grinned.

Rick narrowed his eyes at her. "Shut up."

"Uh-huh. How is Jason?"

"Same old, some old. He asked about you. Wanted to know if you were 'down for whatever.'" Rick smirked.

"No, just no. Anyway, sounds like your mornin' was full. Aren't you happy I actually *have* plans?"

Rick threw himself on the couch. "Plans? Is that like a curse word or somethin'?" Suddenly, he sat up and turned to her. "Are you tryin' to tell me you have a date?"

Rebecca snorted. "No. I'm goin' for an early dinner at my partner's house."

"That could be a date."

"No, he's a he."

"It could still be a date." Rick set the Coke on the coffee table.

"Well, it's not. I'm meetin' his wife and kid."

Rick blinked. "Wait. So, you and your partner are friends?"

"Tryin' to be." Rebecca cleared her throat. All this sounded and felt weird coming out of her mouth.

He smiled. "I can get down with that. It's a good thing for you."

Rebecca sat beside him. "I think so too. I'm sure Dani would love to have you all to herself."

Rick's forehead scrunched, and he ran a hand over his bald head. "She's at the hospital workin' a double, but otherwise, ehh, maybe."

"What's wrong?"

He shrugged. "I'm not sure how much I should say."

Yes, Rebecca was suffering from that same disease. She wanted to tell him everything but didn't want to drag him right back in the middle of her and Dani's situation. "If it's not just her crap and it's affectin' you, go for it."

"That's what I said." Rick shook his head and sighed. "The way she treats people just…"

"What do you mean?" Rebecca asked.

"It's not as bad as how she acts around you."

"Okayyy."

"Besides her patients, she has a handful of people at the hospital, me included, that she actually talks to. She walks around like everybody else stinks."

"What? It's that bad?" Rebecca's voice went up an octave. She found that hard to believe. "I know you said before that she didn't have a lot of friends, but I can't see her bein' cold like that to people."

"Why not? You experienced it firsthand."

Remembering all the heat they'd generated, Rebecca swallowed. "I hurt her."

"That's no excuse, especially since that cold-shoulder shit has gotten worse."

Rebecca's stomach clenched. "Are you tryin' to say that it's my fault?"

"I'm just sayin' that she doesn't get a pass to treat people any kind of way because she's hurt."

She stared at him for a few seconds, and he looked back, unfazed, letting her see everything. A tiny trickle of fear eased its way inside her, displacing a bit of the hope she'd fostered. No matter how many steps Dani had taken backward, Rebecca had to believe that, in her core, fundamentally some of the Dani she knew was still in there. She just had to get to know the new shell that surrounded her. "You're right." Rebecca paused. "Are you two okay?"

Rick shrugged. "Sometimes, but then I see the way she is toward people, and I'm not sure I wanna be associated with it. I mean, some of them are my friends, people I care about."

"I get it. Have you tried talkin' to her about it?"

"Well, yeah, but she doesn't listen all the time or let it seep in. I think I'm gonna have to do more showin' than tellin'…with everythin'."

"What do you mean?"

He released a long breath. "I've been tryin' to step out of y'alls mess. This week has actually been easy, but here I am wrapped in it again. Didn't take much. I guess it's gonna take some time."

"I'm sorry. I wasn't tryin' to—"

"I know. You didn't know."

Rebecca looked at him. "Do what you need to do. I don't blame you. I'll do my best to hold you to it. There's a million other things we can talk about." He didn't need to know about the hate sex and that they'd been texting no matter how much she needed help to figure things out.

"Yeah, for real."

For several seconds, they were quiet. Rick snorted.

What the hell? They both had more going on in their lives besides Dani, even if at times it didn't feel like it. Giving Rick a breather might be harder than Rebecca thought.

A phone chirped.

"That's me." Rick leaned back and reached into his pocket. He pressed a couple buttons. "Good thing I brought my clothes. I'm gonna use one of your bathrooms to get a shower. Sandra switched with someone to get off early. I have to go pick her up for our…thing. Guess it doesn't matter if I move it up a few hours." He stood.

"Your thing? And what's with Sandra? That name sounds familiar."

Rick laughed. "I think I mentioned her about six months back. We had a situationship."

"Okay yeah, I remember, but what's this *thing*?" Rebecca was curious as hell.

"It's a date. I'm tryin' to do somethin' special. Surprise her a little bit and do somethin' different besides hemmin' her up in one of the on-call rooms.'"

"Oh, it's like that?"

He shrugged again. "I don't know. I told her about Northwestern, and she's still interested. So, we'll see." Rick walked toward the door. "I'm gonna go grab my stuff."

"Okay." Something brushed against Rebecca's ankle, she looked down to see Peyton. "Where were you hidin'?"

Peyton meowed. Then she hissed and ran away when Rebecca tried to pick her up. "Fine. It's not like I needed a hug or anythin'."

Dani could have left the hospital a couple of hours ago. Correction. Should have left, but she hadn't. What was the point?

As she walked toward the nurses station, Dani paused when she saw Sandra had joined them. She wasn't a consistent visitor, but she obviously had friends all over the hospital. Dani did her best to be polite and not listen or interrupt the conversation between Sandra and the charge nurse, Jennifer. However, she couldn't help but overhear.

"What are you doing on this floor? Looking all fancy too," Jennifer said.

"Since Hope and the others were busy, I'm picking with you and Nat while I wait on my ride," Sandra answered.

"Wait...is something wrong with your car? Nat's off in thirty. She can give you a ride."

"I'm sure she can, but this ride is special. He's already on his way." Dani could hear the smile in Sandra's voice.

Jennifer chuckled and it sounded decidedly dirty.

Dani had heard enough. Obviously, they were going to pretend like she wasn't even here. She cleared her throat.

Jennifer looked Dani's way. "Yes, Dr. Russell?"

"I'm missing labs."

"Can you be more specific?" Even though Jennifer's voice was even, there was a spark of something in her eyes. Maybe irritation?

Dani bit her tongue and swallowed down her equally irritable response. "Yes, Stevens and Roper."

"Oh, they should be in the system. I got the paperwork some time ago."

"They're not. Can I see the hard copy, please?"

Jennifer turned away.

Dani glanced toward Sandra only to see her staring. Their eyes met, but for some reason, Dani had to look away.

"Cab's here."

Hearing Rick's voice wasn't a surprise to Dani. She'd already assumed that he was Sandra's ride.

Jennifer handed Dani the paperwork. "She's not going if she has to pay."

"No comment." Rick grinned.

It wasn't the best of ideas to have such a suggestive conversation out in the open in the middle of the day. Dani frowned but looked on.

Sandra moved toward Rick. "You could have just texted. I would have met you outside."

"No biggie." He shrugged as he looked down at her. Rick's smile was big and warm.

Waiting for some kind of greeting or acknowledgment, Dani stood in front of the nurses station with a collection of papers crumpling in her hand. The longer Rick took, the more it stung, and she was suddenly in total agreement with her best friend. Things were not right between them, no matter how many apologies they'd extended to each other.

Finally, he looked her way. "Hey, havin' a good one?"

Small talk? He was trying to engage her in small talk like they didn't know each other at all. "So far, so good." Dani wasn't sure why she played along.

Someone called Sandra's name, and she turned. Sandra touched Rick's arm. "Give me a sec." Her hand trailed downward, grasping his lightly before trying to pull away.

Rick held on. "Hurry." Then he let her go.

The look she gave him was full of affection, as was his.

Dani's mouth fell open, and her whole body deflated like someone had siphoned the air out of her. Rick cared about Sandra or he was starting to. Dani's stomach pitted as hollowness filled it, leaving her heavy and with a horrible, sinking feeling. No wonder he was upset with her. Guilt weighed her down even more. God, she needed to do something. She moved toward him. "Can I talk to you for a second?"

He looked at her. His eyes flitted this way and that as if studying her. "I don't wanna be about drama right now, and you look full of it," Rick whispered.

She stepped closer. "Please?"

Rick glanced away as he nodded. "Give me a minute then lead the way." He stepped around her and toward Sandra. Rick put his hand on her back and leaned forward to whisper something in her ear. Sandra glanced at Dani then back at Rick and nodded.

The pit in her stomach deepened, becoming a cavern. Dani headed toward the lounge and hoped that it was empty and that Rick had followed. The room was occupied. Three residents looked up at her when she opened the door.

"Leave." A couple seconds later, she added, "Please."

After they left, Dani turned around.

Rick watched her carefully. "What's goin' on?"

Dani crossed her arms over her chest, but the position wasn't comfortable, so she let them dangle at her side, which wasn't much better. She settled on putting her hands in her pockets. "I'm sorry. I didn't know."

"What are you talkin' about?"

"Sandra… The things I said." She took a step toward him.

Rick's eyes widened slightly. Then he huffed. "Why are you apologizin' to me? I still don't get it."

"You care about her. I would've never—"

"Treated her like shit?"

Dani pressed her lips together and glanced away.

"What? She's not a nobody to you anymore?"

Rick's words burned. Dani crossed her arms over her chest again for protection. She didn't know how to respond to his question.

"Let me ask you somethin' that's probably easier for you to answer. Are you sorry you were crappy to her as a person or are you sorry because you were crappy to her as someone I might care about?"

Hadn't he just asked her that? "I'm not sure. Does it matter? It's not like I knew anything was going on between you two again."

"Yeah, well, it's new, and maybe different this time." It was Rick's turn to look away.

"Why didn't you tell me?"

"Somethin's off between us, and you're not yourself. It just didn't feel right to share."

Was that why she hadn't told him about what happened between her and Becca? Dani wished it were that easy. She tried to clear her head. Here she was thinking about herself. A wave of shame washed over her. "I'm so sorry. I didn't mean...I didn't know..." She looked down at her Clarks. "Have I really been that bad?" Her voice was weak, shaky.

Rick wrapped his arms around her. She stiffened slightly and then melted into him, pressing her face against his chest. Dani hugged him back as tightly as she dared because she dreaded his answer. Still, she was ready to hear it and maybe listen this time.

"Yeah, you have."

Trying not to cry, Dani squeezed her eyes shut. "I wasn't trying to be." It felt like she was repeating herself. "God, you must be close to hating me."

"No, never that, but I don't like you much right now." Rick kissed the top of her head. She could have sworn he'd said those exact same words a few weeks back.

"It's like you're getting' pre-revenge or somethin', but nobody's out to get you."

"I know that." She looked up at him.

Rick didn't seem convinced. His eyes were sad.

"I do," Dani repeated, but even she didn't sound sure. She'd never set out to hurt anybody. She'd been trying to protect herself. Things had been so clear before. Now, it was obvious she had no idea what she was doing.

"I hope so."

She did too. "Will you explain to Sandra? I don't know if she'll understand." Dani paused. "I don't know if I do."

Rick shook his head. "That's not for me to do."

"I don't know what to say to her. I've already apologized." Dani didn't even try to get rid of the pleading sound in her voice.

"Well, when you figure it out, you'll know what to say, I guess."

"That's not very helpful." His lack of assistance was frustrating.

Rick's grin was crooked. "Sorry, I don't think I can be much help to you with this." His expression sobered.

Dani nodded. "Are we—"

"Don't ask that, because you know we're not, but at least it's all out in the open now."

"I'm sorry." Dani couldn't seem to stop saying that.

"I know, but you gotta show it too. You can't keep doin' the same thing over and over."

Dani nodded and tried to step back. Rick wouldn't let her. He pulled her into another full-body hug. She couldn't breathe, but surrounded by him, she was okay with that. What was she going to do if he actually left? Dani closed her eyes. She had to start making his career opportunity about him.

"I better go." Rick kissed the top of her head again.

"Okay."

Even after he'd left, Dani stood in the middle of the lounge. Part of her wanted to blame Becca for all this, but she couldn't. This was on her, and she had no idea what to do with it.

Rebecca parked behind Mark's SUV in his driveway. She held onto the steering wheel and took a calming breath as she looked out at the ranch-style home with the picture-perfect wraparound porch and white picket fence. It was like something out of a sitcom. She expected to see a prefabricated family on the porch laughing together and sipping iced tea.

There was a dream she used to have where an unknown family welcomed her with open arms. It hadn't taken her long to understand it was never coming true. Instead, she'd learned that family could be anyone.

The front door opened, and Mark stepped out. He waved at her, and Rebecca waved back. However, she didn't move. He came to her. She lowered the driver side window as he leaned down. With soft, concerned eyes, he gazed at her for a moment. "Take all the time you need. You want some company?"

"Yeah, sure." Rebecca nodded.

He jogged to the other side.

They sat in silence for a few minutes.

"How'd you know?"

Mark turned to her and smiled slightly. "You're not that hard to read once you let somebody in."

"Is that a fact?" Rebecca met his gaze.

"It most certainly is."

"Well, good thing I chose you. Emmet woulda blabbed all my secrets."

Mark chuckled. "You could be right about that."

"I don't know what Alvin would've done."

"Stared at you in silent judgment daily?"

Rebecca laughed outright. "No, he'd say what he had to in my face too."

"Probably."

She looked down at herself and brushed a hand over her shirt. Rebecca assumed that a button down and jeans were the appropriate thing to wear. "Is this okay?"

"Whatever makes you comfortable."

Rebecca nodded. "Okay, we can't just sit out here. I'm ready."

"Good. Okay, now, just to let you know, children are like dogs." His eyebrows shot up, as did his inflection. "They jump all over you, then get bored when they realize you're not as interesting as they thought."

She threw her head back and laughed. "Thanks for lettin' me know. Let's do this."

Mark smiled and clapped his hands together. "All right, let's get our steak on. I hope you like ribeye."

Rebecca opened the door. "It's my favorite cut."

"As it should be."

"When I came back, the box was empty and Emmet was gone."

Sheila dropped her fork and leaned back in her chair. She tossed blonde hair out of her face. "Wait. He ate four éclairs that quickly?"

"Uh, gross," Millie said. "I don't like that creamy stuff that squirts out." Her expression was as disgusted as a ten-year-old's could get. Her nose was crinkled and her lips pursed.

"Oh my God, baby, I could kiss you right now!" Mark leaned over and wrapped his arms around his daughter. "Say that again in a few years."

"Dad! You're bein' weird."

Rebecca glanced at Sheila, who hid her smile behind a napkin, but the amused glint in her brown eyes couldn't be missed.

"I think Emmet only works out his arms and legs."

Mark grinned at his wife. "That's what I said!"

Sheila laughed and shook her head.

Rebecca scooped up the last bit of her baked potato and groaned as she ate it. She was full, overly so. The steak had been seasoned just right, and the baked potato along with corn on the cob finished things off properly. The smell of smoldering charcoal still lingered around them despite the wide-open space of the backyard. The sun was on full blast, shooting the temperature to the high sixties. Rebecca knew a good time when she was having it, and this was a good time. It brought up memories of Dani and Rick, the way it had been when they were close, laughing and always there for each other.

"You want more Coke, Rebecca?" Sheila asked.

She glanced at her glass. It was indeed empty. "Yeah, but I'll get it. Anybody else want anythin'?" Rebecca stood.

"Can I get some more Sprite?" Millie handed Rebecca her cup.

"No problem."

Mark held up his beer. It was still half full. "I'm good."

"Nothin' for me either." Sheila held up her wine glass, which was almost empty, but it wasn't her first.

Rebecca didn't linger in the kitchen. Everything was easy to find. When she stepped back out of the open French doors into the backyard, she paused and looked out at Mark and his family. He had his arms back around Millie, but this time, she hugged him too. Sheila sipped the last bit her wine as she watched them.

Just then, Mark glanced up. He tilted his head slightly and mouthed, "You okay?"

She nodded. She missed her family, and no matter how long it took, she planned to get it back intact whether Rick was leaving or not.

Rebecca smiled. Mark smiled back.

She'd get it back even if it had a few additions.

Readjusting the scarf around her head, Rebecca stared at her bedroom ceiling illuminated by the lamp she still had on. Peyton jumped up near the foot of the bed. She smiled as the cat climbed her like a tree and plopped down on Rebecca's chest. Not satisfied with the position, Peyton purred loudly as she turned this way and that before kneading Rebecca's stomach and settling down.

"I really don't want your ass in my face."

Peyton ignored her.

"I swear you're only sweet to me at night because I give off a lot of body heat."

The cat didn't even twitch. Rebecca chuckled and stroked Peyton's torso before finding her spot on the ceiling again. Sleep wouldn't come. Too much had happened, and she was still trying to digest it all. Plus her fingers practically itched to pick up her phone. Somehow, the late-night texting had become habit, even though they hadn't been doing it long. Rebecca was wary of wearing out her tentative welcome, especially in light of what Rick had said about Dani. She should play it safe, wait, and give them both some breathing room. But damn it to hell, she really didn't want to.

Rebecca sat up, and Peyton meowed in protest. "Sorry, but there's another lady I need to talk to." She grabbed her phone. Dani was still at the hospital. Maybe she wasn't busy. Rebecca would just have to take that chance. She unlocked her phone and was tempted to bring up yet another shared memory, but a nagging feeling in her gut told her not to. Instead, she revisited her conversation with Rick and knew what to say almost immediately.

Are u ok?

After a few minutes, Rebecca finally saw evidence that Dani was about to respond. Then the ellipses disappeared as if Dani were hesitating and searching to find the right words. Suddenly, they were back.

I don't know.

There's really no inbetwn. Rebecca replied.

I don't know anything right now. I don't know if I should be talking to you. I don't know if Rick will ever look at me the same. I don't know what I'm doing anymore.

Rebecca blinked. She didn't expect such an explosion of words and emotion. Something had shaken Dani up, and Rebecca had no idea if it was a good or bad thing. With that in mind, she chose her words carefully.

Maybe concentrate on what you do kno.

I know I probably shouldn't be laying all this on you.

Y not?

Because what are we and what are we doing?

Tryin to find some evn ground. Rebecca responded quickly. She had a feeling that hesitation would've had fed into Dani's current state of mind and made her back away.

I don't know if that's possible.

Rebecca fired right back She didn't believe that for a second.

Bullshit. When I first got here u wanted to chew my face off.

How do you know I still don't?

I don't like u all the time either, remember?

You don't know me.

I want 2. Rebecca typed.

A few seconds later, Dani responded.

I can't do this with you right now. I'm at work, and I need to be able to focus.

Rebecca was losing her. She had to do something.

Don't go yet I don't mind changin the subject

Ok fine.

Rebecca's thumbs moved quickly, and a little bit of her heart leaked out with each word she typed.

I had dinner with my partner and his Hallmark card family 2day. It was hard at first to evn get out of the car but he helped me get it 2gether. I laughed hard and I haven't done that in a while. They're good ppl and they opened their home to me. Not many ppl have done that because I haven't given them the chance. I wanna be able to take more chances like that.

Minutes ticked by without a word, and finally Rebecca saw that Dani was typing again.

You've changed. I knew that already. The second time we talked I could tell. You want to hear a joke? It's a cosmic one.

Ok???

I feel like we've had some sort of role reversal. I've closed off and you've opened up.

Rebecca stared at the words for a second before giving her reply.

It doesn't have 2 be that way.

I'm not sure what way it has to be, but I have rounds. I need to go.

Ok.

Rebecca waited even though the conversation was obviously over. She wasn't ready for it to end. The need to call and hear Dani's voice was near overwhelming, but she resisted, knowing somehow that it would be going too far right now. She had come out of their discussion with a better understanding. The wall around Dani was higher and thicker than she'd thought it was. She'd do her best to chisel away at it, but in the end, Dani had to want to let her in.

CHAPTER 18

LADEN. THAT WAS THE ONLY word Dani could think of to describe her current situation. The air around her was thick, viscous, and she struggled to move through it. Mentally drained, she was well on her way to being that way physically as well. She'd churned through the past couple days just to get to the end of them in hopes that her brain would turn off and her emotions along with it.

No such luck. Apparently, the shame she carried around didn't believe in taking a break. So, she couldn't either. The images on her iPad started to blur. Dani blinked, trying to bring everything back in focus. It took more time than she would have liked, but she didn't dare complain.

She had hurt people. She wondered how many: she had been in a state of faux oblivion for quite a while, given that deep down, Dani knew what she was doing. She'd created a buffer between herself and everybody else, and it had numbed her, making things extremely easy.

"Dr. Russell!"

Dani jumped at the sound of her name. She looked up, and Betty peered back at her. "Yes?"

Betty continued to study her, along with a couple other nurses in the vicinity. Dani got the distinct impression that Betty had tried to get her attention more than once.

"Did you need somethin'? You've just been standin' there for ten minutes."

She cleared her throat. "I was trying to make sure all my labs have been uploaded before starting rounds."

Betty glanced down at the iPad just as it went dark, as though she knew Dani wasn't being truthful. "Well, if somethin' doesn't show up, let me know."

Dani stepped back, but Betty held her gaze. Her mouth opened as if she had more to say or ask, but Betty closed it quickly. Dani had always been nice to her. They'd laughed and joked, but maybe that had more to do with practicality. It wouldn't make sense to alienate the Peds charge nurse. Dani would never get anything done. God, how pathetic was she?

Using her elbows, Betty leaned forward on the desk. "Are you okay?" she whispered, and reached out touching Dani's arm.

Dani moved away almost immediately. Even though she must have looked like she was falling apart, she didn't deserve Betty's concern. "Sorry, yes, just tired."

"Okay, then, if you're sure."

"I am. I should probably get some coffee and grab a sandwich or something. That might help a bit. I don't remember eating this morning."

"Mmm." Betty eyed her. "Good idea. You might wanna get down there. Around twelve-thirty, those lines take forever to move up."

Her stomach growled, turning the lie she'd just told into a truth. Her face heated. A short trip to the cafeteria really was in order, especially since she hadn't brought anything from home. Hypoglycemia wasn't on her list of things to experience today. "Do you want anything?" Dani tried her best to sound chipper, but she wasn't sure if she succeeded. She even cracked a smile.

"No, just see to yourself."

"I'll be back in a few, then."

In the cafeteria, Dani kept her head down as much as possible. As she got in line to pay for her chicken salad croissant, someone touched her arm. Startled, she jerked away.

"Hey! It's just me. I've been wavin' at you tryin' to get your attention since you walked in here."

Dani glanced up at Rick. "Sorry, I was in a hurry."

Rick frowned. "Jesus, you could trip over all the baggage under your eyes. Have you slept since the last time I saw you?"

She shrugged and tried to move away.

His hand closed around her elbow, stopping her. "Dani?" Rick's voice was full of concern.

"I didn't think you were talking to me."

"Ah, well, I thought you'd need space after airin' things out like that."

"It's been two days." Dani looked down at his hand, hoping her words didn't sound accusatory.

Instead of dropping it, Rick moved closer. "I've been stayin' at Sandra's, and like I said, I wasn't ignorin' you."

"It f-felt like it." There was nothing Dani could do to hide the emotion in her voice.

"Christ, Dani, no matter what's goin' on with us, we're still friends. I wouldn't just cut you off like that. I'm sorry. I figured you'd call if you really needed me."

Dani tried to swallow down the lump in her throat. "Things have never been this bad between us. I wasn't sure."

"Well, now you are. You hear me?"

She nodded.

Rick shook his head and leaned in. "You look like shit." He pulled her to the side, out of line. and toward a quieter corner. His face was creased with worry. "I'm not sorry about what I said."

"I don't think you should be. At least I listened. I'm not sure what I should do next. Send out a newsletter apologizing to everybody I've come in contact with the past few years?"

He squeezed her hand. "I don't know. I guess you'll figure it out."

"I hope so." Dani squeezed back. "I didn't mean to invite you to my pity party."

"Yeah, well, cancel that shit, then."

"You're right. I probably need to." Dani needed to change the subject not just for her, but for Rick too. "How are things with Sandra?"

Rick's eyes widened a little bit. "Uhm, good so far. Look, you don't have to change—"

"Yes, I do."

"Okay, well, I'm gonna change it again."

"I don't want you worried about me."

"I can't help that. It is what it is. Besides, this is about you, not you and Becca." Rick shrugged.

Dani sighed. "Fine. I'm scared. It's like I've become my evil twin or something. Maybe this is who I am now."

"Bullshit. I don't believe that."

"But I don't know how to be anyone else."

"God, I can't believe I'm about to say this, but remember how Becca used to be? If she can do it…" Rick watched her carefully as if expecting her to blow up at the mention of Becca's name.

Yes, Dani recalled quite a bit. There had been no in between with Becca—she was either happy or pissed. It was rather strange having this conversation after the last one she had with Becca. She wasn't sure what to feel at the moment, so she went with what she knew. "You're talking like she's your hero or something."

Rick stared at her, and Dani looked away as embarrassment and shame washed over her. "Sorry."

"Yeah, apology accepted, but you know what I'm tryin' to say."

Too bad Becca hadn't started all that while they were together. Dani quickly stepped away from that line of thinking. It wouldn't do her any good. "Yes, I do."

"Look, trust me when I say I'm not tryin' to push you guys together, but who else do you know who's been through shit like that?"

For a moment, Dani stiffened and stared at him. Did he know something? When he didn't say anything else, something like relief settled over her. "I don't know about that." She wasn't ready to go that deep with Becca. At least, she didn't think so, and if she was, it would be kind of hard since Dani had been ignoring Becca for the past couple days.

"Yeah, me either, but I guess it's somethin' to think about." Rick pulled her into a one-arm hug. "I know I said it earlier, but you really do look exhausted."

No, she was closer to bone weary and debilitated. Dani leaned into him, grateful that she had someone so solid to fall back on.

Even though she had a lot on her plate, Dani had to brush it all aside in order to be the doctor, the person her patients needed her to be. She had rounds, so, somehow, she laughed, she reassured, and she was present in the moment for them just as she'd always been. At least that hadn't changed. Despite the heavy news she was going to have to relay soon, Dani smiled as she knocked on the doorjamb to Jacob's room. They both looked toward her as she walked in. Jacob blinked at her sleepily. Sheri nodded.

"He just woke up."

"Then I have great timing."

"Most definitely. Even though it's his last, he's not looking forward to the next treatment. I can understand that, but I've been trying to give him a pep talk."

"That stuff they put in me makes me so tired." Jacob crossed his arms over his chest and turned away from her.

Dani looked down at him. "Remember what I told you about that?"

Jacob nodded. "Yeah."

"What did I say?"

He finally met her gaze. "The medicine kills the bad stuff and some of the good stuff. That's why I get so tired."

"The whole thing sucks, I know, but you've come this far. I know you have a lot left in you. You're not the type of kid to give up, are you?"

He smiled slightly. "Nope."

Dani bent down and whispered, "Can I tell you a secret?"

Jacob's smile widened as he glanced between his mother and Dani.

Sheri rolled her eyes, but she tried and failed not to grin.

"You're sick, so you're allowed to complain, but adults do it way more even for something small like a splinter."

Sheri snorted.

"Doc D, that was corny." Jacob laughed.

Dani chuckled. "I know, right?"

Jacob's eyes widened. "Ma, you almost let me forget. Can I show her?"

"Yeah, baby. Hold on." Sheri smiled, but there was a sadness in her eyes.

Quietly, Dani stepped back and waited.

"My dad was bald. Ma said I look like him more than ever now that I am too."

Sheri retrieved her cell from her bag. After punching a few buttons, she gave it to her son. It only took him a few seconds to find what he wanted. He held up the phone. "See?"

Dani looked at the picture of father and son. "Yes, you do."

Jacob's smile was so big and radiant. "I don't care if it ever grows back. Can I take the medicine today?"

The resilience of children sometimes left her breathless, and this time was no exception. "No…but keep that attitude."

"I will."

She believed him too. "Is it okay if I hug you?"

He nodded, and his smile didn't dim one bit. Dani held him loosely, but Jacob had no such compunction. He squeezed her hard.

"I'm sorry if I'm being corny again," Dani said as she pulled away.

"It's okay. Ma's like that sometimes too."

Sheri put her hand over her mouth. Her eyes were wide and tear-filled, but they were also bright.

Day after day, Dani bore witness to kids getting through some of the most horrible things and still smiling even if the prognosis wasn't good. If they could do that, she could try to put a foot forward a millimeter or two. Although it took several minutes for Dani to work up a full head of steam, she did her best to not let it dissipate. "I hear you and Dr. Luft get along really well."

"Yeah, she's funny, but she's scared of Ma." Jacob rolled his eyes.

Dani glanced at Sheri. "Scared or not, what do you think?"

"She looks like she's twelve. That's what I think." Sheri shrugged.

"Yes, she does. Jacob only has one more treatment left. I think he needs as much consistent support as we can all give him. So, I'm going to include Dr. Luft during my additional rounds from now on." Dani paused. "If that's okay."

Sheri stared at her and then gave her a slow nod. "If you think it's a good idea, I'll deal with it."

"Startin' tomorrow?" Jacob asked. He was practically bouncing.

"Yes, starting tomorrow."

Minutes later, Dani left Jacob's room and headed to see her next patient. If Dani could bottle the sense of peace, confidence, and the all-around general high she got at the hospital and take it everywhere, her life would be golden. Inevitably, as she walked, Dani's thoughts strayed to Becca, and there was nothing she could do that staunch the tide.

Their situation was truly ironic. Was there a time when Becca had felt this out of sorts and pent up? Maybe she really was the beacon of change that Rick had suggested. Dani had seen it, felt it, tasted it for herself. So far, Becca had been the one to reach out, leaving herself open and vulnerable.

Dani wasn't sure if she could do that. She wasn't sure if she wanted to. Right now, her only goal was to make it through the day with the little light she'd found intact.

Rebecca glanced up and away from her computer as Alvin stopped at her desk, snatching a pastry out of the box. Expecting him to move on, she was surprised when he hovered. "What are you workin' on?" he asked.

"Dorset case." They didn't have anything new, but it sure as hell couldn't hurt to comb over everything in case a piece of information was missed.

Alvin sighed.

She really wasn't in the mood for him today, but she did her best to shake her attitude loose. The baggage didn't belong to him. "What?"

He shrugged. "You know my view on that. Once we figured out the kid wasn't in danger…"

"Shane. His name is Shane."

"Yeah, I know that, but he's with his father." Alvin took a bite out of a not-so-fresh cake donut.

"Who is an abuser and a stalker." Rebecca spun around in her chair to look at him. She felt Emmet's and Mark's gazes on them too.

"But he never did anything to hurt the kid…Shane."

"So in your mind that makes it okay?" She glared at him.

He glared right back. "All I'm saying is that there's a reason the GBI and other agencies don't get involved in stuff like this. Hell, it's even hard to get a judge on board."

"I know that," Rebecca practically growled. Alvin's school of thinking wasn't unusual. That didn't mean she had to accept it. "But that kid is scared, and he's not where he wants to be. That much we know. All in all, I guess it's a good thing it's not your case, then."

Alvin nodded. "Yeah, but it won't be yours for much longer either. Benz is only gonna give you so much leeway." His tone was matter of fact and so was his expression.

She knew this already. Rebecca glanced at Mark and could see that he did as well. "Thanks for the PSA." Alvin just had to be that guy. The one who could look at a puzzle piece and tell it wouldn't fit and had to inform everybody else, even as they tried to wiggle it in. Rebecca could appreciate that guy at times, but not today.

He finished his donut and walked back to his desk.

There were a couple other cases she'd been working. Rebecca pulled them up. She'd go back to the Dorset case with fresher eyes in a bit. Minutes ticked by, but they seemed to drag on forever. Rebecca kept glancing at the clock on her computer. She was teetering toward distracted, and as a result, she reached for her cell phone.

No response from Dani. Rebecca wasn't surprised. It had been a couple days. When she'd first realized she was being ignored, Rebecca racked her brain, going through their conversations to see if she'd said something to scare her away. It hadn't taken long for her to realize she couldn't think that way. So, she kept texting anyway despite her own growing belligerence, and every time she hit send, Rebecca left herself dangling and vulnerable, which wasn't the easiest thing in the world. But one of them had to. Why not her?

Rebecca was by no means fearless in this. The possibility of the whole situation tanking was very real, and despite the little shards of pain she experienced when Dani ignored her or said something less than stellar, Rebecca pushed on and forward with the hope that, in the end, it would all be worth it. With all that in mind, she penned her next text.

Wanna kno y I became a cop? At first I didn't even know y, but I figured out I needed discipline and direction, something u had plenty of. Started to go into military but didn't want to end up overseas somewhere. Goin to the academy helped me get my house in order.

Not waiting for a reply she knew she wasn't going to get, Rebecca put her phone away. She offered Dani these little tidbits to give her a chance to get to know her as she was now in the hope that eventually Dani would do the same.

Her cell phone rang and Rebecca's heart jumped to her throat. It settled a bit when she saw it was Gwen Dorset. "Is everythin' okay?"

"He called me." Gwen was out of breath. A horn blared in the background.

"Who called you?" Rebecca sat up as a sinking feeling settled in her guts. "Gwen, where are you?"

"That motherfucking ex-husband of mine called. Who do you think? It wasn't from his phone. I almost didn't answer."

"Okay, tell me everythin', includin' where you are."

"He wants to be a family again. He said if I came to him, he'd do right by me and Shane."

Rebecca stood and snapped her fingers in Mark's direction. She mouthed the word 'trace.' "I know you wanna believe him."

"I'm not stupid! He's not going to stop until somebody does it for him."

Mark twirled his finger in the air, encouraging Rebecca to extend the call. She set the phone down and put it on speaker. "Listen to me. You have every right to be upset, but the best way to help Shane is for you to be thinkin' clearly."

"I am! I won't go back to him. I won't, but what kind of life would Shane have if he's scared all the time, thinking his dad is gonna snatch him?"

"Gwen, all you have to do is give us his location and this all ends."

"No, it doesn't. You're not going to do anything to him."

"He committed a crime."

"You and your partner told me that nobody cares because he's with his father. Probation won't be enough to keep him away. I'll take care of him myself."

"Then who is Shane gonna have left when you're arrested?"

Gwen went silent for a few seconds. "He has family." She was crying. "People who love him. They'll treat him right. They'll raise him right."

"That's your job." Rebecca said the first thing that came to mind.

"This is my job too."

The line went dead.

"Gwen?" Rebecca asked just to be sure. "Shit." She looked at Mark.

"We got it. She didn't turn her phone off, so we'll be able to get a better fix on her final location."

"She wants us there," Alvin chimed in.

Rebecca agreed. Maybe she'd have a second chance to talk her or the ex-husband down. "Call for backup."

When Rebecca and Mark arrived on the scene, blue lights flashed and bounced off each other, giving the late afternoon an eerie glow. Neighbors stood on their porches watching. A few were even bold enough to move to the edge of their lawns. Rebecca parked and jumped out of the car, not waiting for Mark. Even though it was on a lanyard around her neck, she held up her badge for the other police to see.

Rebecca stopped and cursed under her breath as one of the uniformed officers wrapped a blanket around Shane's shoulders. She grabbed the closest cop. "What's goin' on?"

"She brought the kid out and went back in. He was barely awake."

"Who's in charge?"

The officer pointed toward the police cars and the cops standing to the side. "Ask for Sergeant Pike."

"You should call her."

Rebecca turned to look at Mark. "That's the plan. I wanna let Pike know what I'm doin' first."

Mark nodded. "Lead the way."

Less than a minute later, Rebecca dialed Gwen's number. She was no hostage negotiator, but they were willing to give her a shot based on prior knowledge. She only had one chance because this had become a probable hostage situation.

"Yes?" Gwen answered on the second ring.

"Shane is safe, but he's scared." Rebecca hadn't talked to the boy, but she wasn't above using him for leverage.

"Help! She has a gun. This bitch is crazy!" a man yelled in the background.

Rebecca closed her eyes. This had just gone from a probable hostage situation to a bonafide one. "Gwen, this is serious. Your son is gonna read about all this on the Internet one day. Is this what you want him to know about you? About his father? How do you think that'll affect him?"

She paused and took a deep breath. "This might not be the same, but my mom died when I was pretty young. I don't really remember her, but I know one day she was here and then she was gone. I have…had family, and nobody wanted me. My great aunt took me in, and she did her best. I'm forever grateful for it, but when it came down to it, she wasn't my mother."

Gwen sobbed. "I—" She screamed. There was another loud cry and the line disconnected.

"Dammit! I think he went after her."

A single gunshot resonated.

Rebecca redialed Gwen's number.

"Move in from the back!" Pike barked.

"H-hello?"

"Wait! I got her on the phone!" Rebecca yelled.

"Stand down," Pike ordered.

"Gwen, are you okay?"

"Yes, it was an accident. The gun went off—"

"Is he alive?" Rebecca swallowed.

"Yes, it hit him in the leg."

Thank God. "Gwen—"

"I'm coming out."

Rebecca wanted to shout for joy. While the whole thing hadn't worked out ideally, no one died, and that was the most important thing. "Okay, good. I'll let 'em know." She ended the call and turned to Pike. "She's comin' out. Paramedics need to go in. He's hurt but alive."

Pike nodded.

Someone put a hand on Rebecca's shoulder. She looked up to see Mark. He smiled at her, and she smiled back.

Less than a minute later, Gwen came out of the house with her hands held high.

Rebecca stared up at her special patch of ceiling. Dead to the world, Peyton was cuddled up next to her on the other side of the pillow.

Too wired to sleep, Rebecca thought it best to at least lie down and rest even though she left the bedside lamp on. There was still no word from Dani. She swallowed down the little pinprick of pain and reached for her phone anyway.

You're a doctor and u help ppl. U get them well and even save their lives. Another reason I became a cop was I wanted 2 know what that felt like. I wanted 2 have an impact on lives, a good impact. For a while u were my purpose. U were everything to me. It took me a long time to realize that expectin that from somebody wasn't right. I'm sorry I did it 2 you. I have purpose now. It's bigger than me. Is that what it feels like for u?

She put her phone back on the nightstand and became reacquainted with her ceiling. Rebecca was startled awake by a loud beep. She didn't even remember falling asleep. She sat up and reached for her phone. The time stared back at her—2:36 a.m.—and underneath it was a text.

Yes.

Rebecca smiled and unlocked her phone. She pressed the text app, but before she could reply, something stopped her. She didn't want to tempt fate. Dani was listening, and for tonight, that was enough.

CHAPTER 19

Rebecca walked beside Rick down the hall toward his apartment. "I've been back for a while, so I know you have Coke and food, especially since you're invitin' me over to hang. Thanks by the way. It's been a long week, and it's just Wednesday."

Rick smirked and shrugged. "No prob, and no promises. I haven't been home a lot lately."

She bumped him with her shoulder, but he was big enough to absorb the impact. "Look at you. She must really be somethin' to hold your attention like this."

He elbowed her back, and Rebecca stumbled. She glared at Rick.

"What? You started it and yeah, probably."

"Yeah probably…oh, you mean Sandra." Rebecca sang her name as if she were in grade school.

"Yes, I mean Sandra. I think you two should meet soon."

Rebecca stopped and looked up at him. "Damn."

Rick grabbed her arm, practically dragging her. "C'mon, and just so you know, Dani's home."

"I know. I saw her car." Her tone softened.

Rick paused and met her gaze. His eyes narrowed as he studied her. "Is somethin'…scratch that. I'm not sure I wanna know."

"Okay, consider it scratched." Rebecca moved ahead of him, but she could feel him watching.

They reached the door to his apartment. Rick tried the knob and then whipped his keys out of his pocket.

As they entered, Dani came out of the kitchen. "Look Ma, I brought home a stray." Rick grinned, and Dani smiled back. A second later, when she looked at Rebecca, her expression turned unreadable.

Rick made a sound in the back of his throat. It was somewhere in between a snort and a grunt. "I'm goin' to go hit the shower. I trust y'all won't kill each other."

"We'll be fine." Rebecca shooed him away with her hand, but her gaze remained on Dani.

Rick made that sound again, and then, they were alone. The last time Rebecca had seen Dani she'd been writhing on top of her. Her stomach knotted as her body remembered too. For just a second, she couldn't breathe. "Hey."

Dani's eyes darkened, and another telltale sign that she was far from unaffected was the fact that her nipples were standing at attention. That could have been explained away by the fact that Dani wasn't wearing a bra, but, Rebecca liked her explanation better. Dani went back into the kitchen. "Hey," she called over her shoulder. "Coke?"

There was no animosity in her words or her tone, and the anger that usually surrounded Dani was absent. Maybe this visit wouldn't end up being awkward.

Rebecca smiled slightly and followed her. "I'll get it."

Dani turned quickly. "Uh, no, but you can go back into the living room." She crossed her arms over her chest.

"But, I'm already in here."

"And you can just as easily be back out there." Dani pointed toward the couch.

They were an arm's length away from each other. A light bulb went on for Rebecca and she took a step closer.

Dani moved back.

"What are you doin'?" Rebecca's heart took a dive.

"Is it so wrong that I don't want you near me?" Dani's face was flushed. "Why?"

"I don't know what this is. I can't trust it, and I don't know if I can trust you. Plus, I have too much going on…" Dani's voice trailed off and she shook her head.

"Do I still taste the same, Dani?"

The air around them immediately increased in density and heat. Rebecca savored the ache left behind. Dani's eyes widened and her chest heaved. "Stop…just stop. You can't just say things like that and bulldoze yourself into my life. But anything to get what you want, right? So much for all those 'changes.'" Dani clawed at the air and she actually looked somewhat gleeful while doing it.

Rebecca pointed at her. "You—" She pressed her lips together and took in a deep breath through her nose. Dani did need some bulldozing, but she also needed subtlety. "I'm sorry. I just wanted to get a rise outta you."

"Well, you got what you wanted. Do you want your Coke or not?"

"I do."

Dani turned and opened the refrigerator.

"I thought our conversations would be different after all the textin'." Rebecca watched as Dani paused and stiffened. "But you've been so quiet lately."

"I told you. I have a lot going on."

"I miss it. To me it was more like you whisperin' in my ear at night."

The back of Dani's neck reddened and her shoulders rose and fell as if she were struggling to breathe.

Rebecca moved closer. "Maybe I can help or I can listen, if that's what you need."

Dani spun around. "What did Rick tell you?" The anger that had been missing was more than present now. Dani's face was flushed and her eyes were accusing.

"What? Nothin'. What are you talkin' about?" Rebecca held her hands up and stumbled back.

"Just because you're supposedly a brand new person doesn't make you an expert. I don't know who you think—"

"No, you're right. It doesn't, and I never claimed to be."

Dani's mouth snapped closed. Her shoulders sagged and she looked away. She suddenly seemed more embarrassed than angry. What the hell was Rebecca missing?

The sound of Rick's laughter made them both turn toward it. He walked into the living room with his phone pressed to his ear. He eyed them and looked heavenward before sitting down on the couch. Intent on giving Dani some room, Rebecca went to sit beside him.

Dani wanted nothing more than to go to her room and dive underneath the covers. Wasn't that what people did when they were ashamed? Hide their faces. She was, indeed, getting tired of feeling this way, so Dani made a concerted effort to fight against it. Besides, it was stupid and juvenile to be jealous and resentful of Becca because she'd turned over a new leaf, especially when Dani had deeper things to be resentful for. That didn't stop those emotions from surfacing, however.

To add more to the already overwhelming mess her life had become, seeing Becca shook her; being close to Becca floored her, and having her address the perplexing situation between them nearly made her come apart at the seams. Yet, somehow, instead of retreating to some place safe, Dani headed into the living room with a huge bowl of microwave popcorn and a couple of Cokes.

Rick looked at her curiously when she shoved the bowl in his hands and sat down beside him, opposite Becca. He gave her a slight nod. She didn't return the gesture, but for some reason, his encouragement made things easier.

"We're gonna need more than this, especially since the cupboard is bare." Rick held up the bowl. "Pizza or Chinese?" He glanced at Dani then Becca and back again.

"I'm not picky."

"Chinese," Dani answered just as Becca responded.

"Chinese it is, then. Call our order in, Dani. Since Becca is a guest, she gets to pick what we're gonna watch."

"She's not—" Dani started to argue.

"She doesn't live in this apartment, so that makes her a guest."

Dani closed her mouth. He had a point. Having left her phone in the kitchen, she grabbed Rick's. Conveniently enough, he had the restaurant they usually ordered from labeled 'Chinese.'

Becca leaned forward and glanced at Dani. "You have a menu lyin' around?"

"I know what you like."

Their eyes met. Dani's stomach fluttered. She looked away. "Kung Pao Chicken, extra spicy with veggie lo mein."

"Yeah, that's right." Becca eased back against the couch and turned to Rick. "What's on the DVR?"

"*Law & Order: SVU*?"

"God no. Not right now."

"*Grey's, Lucifer*?" he continued.

"No."

Rick named a few more shows as Dani dialed the restaurant and put their order in for delivery.

"I saw *Unbreakable* in the three-dollar bin at Walmart last week and thought of you. It's somewhere in that mess of DVDs." He pointed to the haphazard collection stacked on top of the cable box.

Becca nodded. "Jackson as a villain. He needs to make more of those."

Dani nearly rolled her eyes.

"I've seen this one a few times, and I still can't get over his hair. Black is beautiful and all that, but my man just needs to be bald in all his movies." Rick shook his head, and he sounded so indignant.

Becca snorted, but it was quickly followed by full-blown laughter. "It's worse than the jheri curl in *Pulp Fiction*."

Being next to them like this was like watching old home movies. Becca had even eaten half Rick's egg roll just like she used to. An ache formed in Dani's chest. She tried to push it down, but wasn't that part of the problem? Her stuffing her feelings? "This is weird." The words fell out of her mouth.

"Good weird or bad weird?" Rick asked.

Dani tried to choose her words carefully. "Not bad, just… I don't know."

Rick smiled. "Yeah, I kinda miss it too."

The ache got bigger. "I didn't say I—"

"Semantics," Rick interrupted.

"Well, I'm not uncomfortable at all," Becca chimed in.

Dani glanced at her.

Becca cleared her throat. "Okay, yeah, maybe I am a little."

Rick chuckled.

"How is that funny?" Becca glared at him.

"Shonda Rhimes should write our story." Rick laughed even harder.

"Oh God." Dani couldn't stop the smile that snuck up on her.

"All we need"—Becca joined in on the hilarity—"all we need is a baby."

Rick doubled over.

Dani glanced at Becca but found that she couldn't look away. Becca smiled at her, and Dani's world tilted a little bit. The temptation to run was impossible to resist. Dani stood and grabbed their plates. Instead of giving in completely and heading toward her bedroom, she went to the kitchen. Progress. That had to be some kind of progress.

She put the plates in the sink and wasn't at all surprised to see Rick standing behind her. "You okay?" He kept his voice low.

"I think so. It was just too much for a second. I don't want to get caught up in the past. That's part of the problem."

"That's understandable, but I guess I see it a little bit differently. That was us gettin' used to us...you know, like we are now." He opened the refrigerator and took out two more Cokes.

"Yeah, maybe." Dani nodded. He could actually be right.

Rick looked over his shoulder as he walked out of the kitchen. "Hurry up. I wanna talk to both of you."

When Dani sat back down, Rick and Becca were laughing. She didn't want to interrupt, so she waited.

A few seconds later, Rick clapped his hands, "Okay, so I have some news."

Dani glanced at Becca. Her eyes were wide, and Dani wondered if she looked as anxious. "I'm...we're listening."

"I'm gonna show Northwestern how it's done!" Rick's smile was huge.

Sucking in a surprised breath, Dani did her best to smile back. She was happy for him, but still.

Rick looked at Dani and then at Becca. "Y'all don't have to look so constipated. I'm not goin' till next year. I don't wanna plop down in the middle of the year and play catch up."

Dani leaned on his shoulder. "You're going to kick ass."

"No doubt. What about Sandra?" Becca asked.

"I'm gonna be doin' the long-distance-friend thing with y'all, so I'm gonna try the long-distance-relationship thing too. So does she."

"Well, good, but I'm tellin' you now, I'm not comin' to visit durin' winter. You can keep all that snow."

Rick chuckled.

No matter what position she tried, Dani couldn't sleep. Her thoughts chased each other around in her head, and she couldn't make them stop. Her night felt incomplete. Dani knew what would settle her, but her rational, practical side fought against it. Her other half reminded her about the baby steps she'd been trying to take toward change. She was tired and wanted it all to go away, allowing one of the voices to get louder. Dani sat up and reached out in the dark for her glasses. She flipped on a bedside lamp and picked up her cell phone.

It was early yet, just after eleven. For the most part, Becca had a tendency to wait until after one a.m. to text her. Before she could talk herself out of it, Dani typed a text.

I'm sorry about what I said about your effort to change. You have obviously worked hard at it.

Minutes passed, but Dani did her best to wait patiently.

Thank u but I really don't understand what made u so mad.

Dani read the text a couple times and contemplated her reply.

It's complicated and hard to explain.

Ok. We can talk about something else if u want. Im just glad to hear from u.

Becca's response wasn't what she'd expected. There was a time when Becca had been predictable in her demands and her anger, but Dani was constantly surprised by this version of her. She racked her brain for something to say but came up dry.

Like what?

I have cat pics.

Dani chuckled but sobered quickly, looking around the room as if someone was watching.

I'm sure you do but I don't want to see them. I still can't believe you're a cat person.

I can't either, but it is now a fact. Peyton owns me. I don't know maybe she could tell how lonely I was.

The ache Dani experienced earlier came back.

How, or better, why do you do that?

What?

Just put yourself out there. Did you forget who you were talking to?

Dani watched the ellipses appear, disappear, and come back again.

No, I know I'm talkin to u and yes doin it is scary.

Then why? I don't understand.

Because I let myself feel a lot more than scared these days.

She stared at Becca's response, letting it seep into her, and before she knew it, she was half way through typing back. *How did you...* Dani stopped and studied her words. She wanted to know Becca's secret, and she wanted it for herself. Yet, she was afraid to ask. She took a deep breath and finished the text. *How did you do it?*

U sure u want to know?

Yes. Dani wrote quickly before she lost her nerve.

The ellipses blinked at her for several seconds, and Dani looked forward to Becca's response.

When I left and found somewhere to settle I tried therapy for a while. I really wanted it to work but it was hard finding the right therapist or maybe I just wasn't comfortable with myself. Not sure but I did learn a lot from them. I was at rock bottom. Hell I couldn't even stand myself, but I got tired of always feeling angry. It was like that was all I felt. Took a while but once I found something 2 like about myself, it went frm there.

Becca's words were both illuminating and heartbreaking.

That must have been hard.

Very. Is it okay that I ask you why u wanted to know?

Yes, I guess. Dani answered.

I'm asking. Becca added a smiley face emoji.

I'm not the same person I was. I don't like her. Nobody likes her. Dani typed out the words in a rush.

I find that hard to believe.

I'm not a nice person. I haven't been for a while. I don't want to be her anymore.

There, it was out. It was almost like she'd screamed the words out loud. She'd said something similar before, but now, Dani meant it more than ever.

I'm sure Rick will b behind u all the way.

He will be. He is.

Good. Becca wrote back.

I don't want to confuse things between us and I don't want to lead you on. But, can you help?

Dani couldn't believe what she'd just asked. The whole thing was more than likely Rick's influence. She was okay with that especially now more than ever. There went the ellipses again. Her heartbeat accelerated, and she studied the screen as if she were looking at an MRI.

Can I call?

Dani swallowed. *Yes.*

Her cell rang. Becca's name flashed. Dani exhaled shakily and pressed the speaker icon. "Hello?"

"Hey. You sure about this?"

"No, but I have to do something." Dani cringed. "I didn't mean—"

"I know what you meant, but like you said, I'm no expert. I'm not sure how—"

"The past few minutes was a start." Dani pressed the phone to her ear, waiting for a response.

It wasn't long until she got one. "Okay…okay, I hope I can help."

CHAPTER 20

"TGIF, GODDAMMIT." ALVIN PRACTICALLY THREW himself into his seat.

Rebecca swiveled her chair to look at him. "Why are you thankin' God when it's your weekend to work?"

Alvin glared at her, but then he smirked. "You just had to shit on my parade, huh?"

She winked. "That's what I'm here for."

"I actually don't mind working weekends," Emmet said.

Rebecca glanced at him. "Well, good, you can take mine next time I'm up, and I can go eat steak at Mark's."

"Damn right you can." Mark chuckled. "Good steak too. Like being at Ruth's Chris Steakhouse."

"Is that right? Next time I want asparagus with hollandaise, and it better be kick ass." Rebecca leaned back in her chair and smiled.

Mark waved her comment away. "I'm sure Sheila has a recipe."

"Uh-huh, all right, Ruthy."

He grinned at her. "Since I got your attention, can I talk to you for a minute in the back?"

Curious. "Yeah, I guess." Rebecca stood.

"If I walk back there and y'all are makin' out, I quit." Alvin's lips were pursed, and his nose was crinkled in disgust.

"Let's do it now, then." Mark grabbed at Rebecca, but she laughed and swatted him away.

"I would, but I like your wife," Rebecca said. "Plus, I'm sure it wouldn't bother him since he lives off making people deliberately uncomfortable."

"I am damn good at that." Alvin smiled proudly.

Rebecca rolled her eyes as she followed Mark to the back toward the interrogation rooms. She stopped in the hallway and leaned against the wall. "What's up?"

Mark shrugged. "Just checking in with you."

She tilted her head as she looked at him. "Why?"

"Dorset case. You weren't able to sleep at first."

"Oh yeah, I've never been front and center like that. I coulda tanked the whole thing. I know she's gonna do some time, but her douchey ex will too. Maybe her lawyer can plead it out somehow."

"But you didn't. I didn't know you were worried about all that. You sure you're okay?"

Rebecca nodded. "Yeah, I'm sleepin' good now. I even hung out and had a little fun with Rick. Dani was there too. How about you?" She looked at him closely.

"It affected me more than I thought it would. Brought back some bad memories of when me and Sheila were talking about divorce. I remember being scared out of my mind of losing her and Millie too, especially since I'm a cop. I talked to Sheila about it. That helped. She actually told me to leave you alone about the whole thing and let you come to me. You know… because you're a woman and it would be offensive."

She stared at him. "I don't work like that."

Mark threw up his hands. "I know, that's what I told her. Anyway, things with your ex still awkward?"

"It's only been two days since I last saw her. You should at least give me four to work my magic."

He laughed.

Rebecca smiled. "At least we're talkin' on the phone…kinda. One minute it's like pullin' teeth and the next it's not. I just listen even when there's dead air."

"Well, that's better than nothing."

She shook her head. "I don't know. I feel like she needs more than that. This is important to her, and I don't want to do anythin' to screw that up." This went past her trying to make an impression or bringing them closer.

"I'm not sure what you're saying, but tell her that. I think she'd appreciate it. Anybody would."

"Yeah, maybe." Rebecca met his gaze.

"Should we kiss now in case Alvin's watching?" Mark stepped away from the wall.

Rebecca slapped him on the shoulder. "You're so not my type."

As Dani stepped off the elevator, she muttered to herself to stay the course. She had to do this. Moreso, she needed to do this not just for Rick, but because Sandra deserved better. So, here she was, walking down the hall of the third floor, instead of getting a snack in the cafeteria. She may not be able to make amends with everyone she'd offended, but Sandra was an important start.

Dani was hesitant and a little fearful because the situation was completely out of her control. She'd been up half the night trying to figure out what to say. Becca had been on the phone with her for some of it. She listened and encouraged, which only helped minutely. Dani was frustrated then, and she was frustrated now. She still had no idea how to really approach this situation. She slowed her gait and tried her best to literally shake out the tension. Dani whispered to herself again before stopping in front of the nurses station.

Sandra talked and laughed with a fellow nurse. She laughed a lot. Dani envied that, and—hindsight being what it was—maybe that's why she was intimate with her, to be close to a light like that. "Can I help you with something?"

Dani glanced at the nurse standing front and center. She was so focused on the matter at hand, she hadn't even noticed her. "Um, yes. I just need to speak to Sandra for a few minutes."

At the sound of her name, Sandra looked up. Other nurses glanced Dani's way as well. Sandra stared at her. The laughter was gone, replaced by a wrinkled brow. Slowly, she moved forward and around the desk until she was in front of Dani. There were a million eyes on them, making her skin burn. "Can we go somewhere more private?"

"If I say the on-call room, will you give me a second to appreciate the irony?" Sandra's question was soaked in sarcasm, but her expression was unreadable.

Dani was confused for a moment, and then it came to her. Sandra had once offered to drag her into an on-call room for a repeat performance.

Blood rushed to her face. "Okay, if it helps, but I'd rather the lounge." Dani headed back down the hall.

She reached for the door, only to have it open as two people filed out. They nodded and smiled. Dani returned the gesture. Too antsy to sit down, she stood in the middle of the room.

Sandra entered, crossed her arms over her chest, and raised her eyebrows as she looked at Dani.

Dani cleared her throat. "I've already apologized…" No, no that wasn't right. She sounded like she was on the defensive. "I mean, it's come to my attention…"

Her voice trailed off again. She hadn't been forced to do this: Dani wanted to. This whole thing was personal, and she needed to treat it as such. "I'm sorry for insulting your sexuality. It's no excuse, but I was in an awful place. I lashed out at you, and you didn't deserve any of it. Even though I never thought of you as a friend, you were a part of a group of nurses I'd decided to try to be friendly with to make things easier for me as a doctor at the hospital. I don't usually go around sleeping with people I work with, but I enjoyed the attention you gave me. No one deserves to be treated that way. I never thought about your feelings in all this. I'm sorry for that too." She did her best to look Sandra in the eyes.

"Rick put you up to this, didn't he?" Sandra huffed.

"No, he didn't."

Sandra studied her. "It didn't take me that long to figure out you were fake."

That stung. Dani braced herself and swallowed down the response waiting on the tip of her tongue.

"But I can tell that wasn't a fake apology."

"It wasn't."

"I don't know you, Dani, and you don't know me. Rick is your best friend, so if I want things to work with him…" Sandra dropped her arms to her side. "But don't expect us to be all cookies and cream by tomorrow."

Dani nodded. She didn't expect them to become fast friends. Cordiality was the best she could hope for.

"I'm gonna get back to work now." Sandra had already turned her back on Dani.

"Okay."

When she was alone, Dani sat down. That was harder than she'd thought it would be, but she had done it without crumbling. It was an accomplishment either way.

Rebecca got in her car and pulled on the seat belt, but instead of putting the key in the ignition, she whipped out her phone. For some reason, tonight she needed to know her destination beforehand. Rebecca dialed Dani's number.

"Hello?" Slightly out of breath, she answered on the third ring.

"Were you busy?" Rebecca started preparing herself to be shot down.

"No, I'm home. I was getting out of the shower when I heard my phone ringing."

"Oh." Rebecca blanked for a minute, wondering about Dani's curves with four more years of maturity attached. From what she'd seen so far, she'd really grown into them.

"Hello?"

"Sorry, got distracted. Is it okay that I come over? There's somethin' I wanna talk to you about."

Dani went silent.

Rebecca took the phone away from her ear to make sure they were still connected.

"We're talking right now."

"I know but I think it'll have a bigger impact…the right impact if we're face to face."

"Becca…"

"It's important, and, if it helps, it has nothin' to do with us."

"There is no us," Dani shot back quickly—too quickly.

"If you say so. Is that a yes?" Rebecca stared out the windshield. She waved back at Mark as he got into his SUV.

"You can't stay long. I have an early morning."

"I won't—I just got off work myself, so no partyin' for me tonight."

"Okay, then." Dani sounded overall unaffected.

"Okay, see you soon."

Dani hung up. Rebecca sighed and started her car. There'd been a thaw between them, but it was only a few inches deep. More than anything, she wanted to get to the molten core.

Twenty minutes later, Rebecca stood outside Dani and Rick's apartment door. She didn't see Rick's car. They would be alone. Rebecca was filled with anticipation and dread simultaneously. She wanted to be near her, but at times Dani, especially this Dani, could be unpredictable. Rebecca reminded herself she was playing the long game, and in the end the payout could be huge.

She knocked. Seconds later, Dani opened it and stepped out of the doorway, giving her a wide berth. Rebecca smiled anyway. She was sure that the pull between them was partly responsible for the way Dani shied away from contact. No way she was the only one who felt something so electric. As Rebecca walked past her, she caught Dani's eyes, and the flare of heat between them made her feel like she was sweating on the inside.

Dani held her gaze for a few seconds before looking away, but not before her eyes darkened.

Rebecca's stomach clenched, but she wasn't here for that. Still, she loved that feeling, and right now, it was palpable enough to reach out and touch. She headed for the couch but paused when she spied the bottle of Coke and a glass of ice on the coffee table. The gesture actually made Rebecca's heart speed up. "Oh, thanks."

Dani rolled her eyes. "It's not a kidney or anything."

"Might as well be." Rebecca laughed and sat down. She wasn't surprised when Dani sat at the other end. She opened and poured some Coke into the glass. Unable to wait, she drank at least half of it.

"It really must be serious."

"What? Why?" Rebecca asked.

Dani gestured toward the glass in Rebecca's hand. "You almost drank it all."

Was it wrong that her knowing that warmed her inside? "Yeah, it is. I just don't want you to take it the wrong way. I've been givin' it some thought."

"Okay, so what is *it*?"

"I don't wanna be the one who keeps you down."

Dani's forehead wrinkled. "What do you mean?"

"What you're goin' through. It's serious, and I don't wanna tell you the wrong thing. I want you to get where you're tryin' to go."

Her eyes widened in supposed understanding. Dani jumped up. "If you didn't want to help—"

Rebecca got up too. She reached out snagging Dani by the arm. God, the spark started at her fingertips, and within seconds Rebecca's whole arm was tingling.

Dani looked down at her hand. She didn't try to pull away. Her lips parted as they stared at each other.

The living room got hotter, smaller, and tighter. How long until things exploded between them again, no matter how much Dani tried to deny that there was a fire at all? Rebecca had patience, but it wasn't biblical. She mentally switched gears again, which was hard as hell. Rebecca stepped toward Dani. "Hear me out."

Dani licked her lips and nodded. Reluctantly, Rebecca let her go. They sat back down closer than they were before, within arm's length. "I'm not sayin' I don't wanna help. I do, and I wanna do it right. Maybe if I had kept at it, I would've found the right therapist and dealt with things sooner. You work at a hospital. I think you should take advantage of that. You can consider me back-up or a cheerleader if that's what you need."

She stared at Rebecca like she had three heads. Dani's mouth fell open, and she flushed red. "Do you…" She sucked in a breath. "So you think I'm that messed up that I need a therapist?"

Rebecca wasn't going to sugarcoat this, and she wasn't going to let Dani make her the bad guy. "It has nothin' to do with bein' messed up. I think it's more about feelin' overwhelmed and needin' somebody to help break things down. Do you feel that way?" She put the decision squarely in Dani's lap.

Dani looked away and swallowed loud enough for Rebecca to hear. When she met Rebecca's gaze again, Dani's eyes were glassy and soft. "Yes."

"Then just think about it." Dani's hand was only a few inches from hers, and Rebecca wanted so much to touch her again. She didn't fight it. As she curled her fingers around Dani's hand, Rebecca expected her to jerk away, but to her surprise, Dani gasped and squeezed. When Dani pulled away several seconds later, Rebecca felt like she'd run a marathon and won.

CHAPTER 21

DANI STUDIED JACOB'S MOST RECENT MRI. "I was hoping to see something different."

"I'm sure we all were. It would have been a miracle if chemo had yielded the results she wanted." Dr. Meda looked around the room. Everyone nodded.

Her gaze fell back to her iPad. "I should probably do the talking to Sheri." Dani quickly glanced up at Dr. Meda. She wasn't trying to offend or take over as head of the team.

He nodded and smiled. "I agree. I'll provide any additional support that's needed, especially if Sheri has more in-depth questions."

Dani glanced back down at her iPad. She felt jittery. Her heart raced, and it was difficult to keep still, as if someone had injected her with adrenaline. She recognized her anxiety for what it was. Had she crossed a boundary with this family? That explanation didn't seem plausible. Dani cared, just like she always did, that this case was more than likely going to have a positive outcome. There was no need to obsess.

Dani's screen blurred as another surge of worry grabbed hold of her. Maybe the screwed-up part of her life was starting to seep through. Patients needed her compassion, her confidence, and, when necessary, some aspect of vulnerability. She didn't want to build a wall shutting them out as well because of her fear of getting hurt.

There was a knock at the conference room door. Dr. Meda got up and escorted Sheri inside. "Good afternoon." Sheri greeted the room, but she caught Dani's gaze and smiled.

As best she could, Dani smiled back and waved her over to the empty seat beside her. Once Sheri was seated, Dani put the iPad on the table between them.

"What you're looking at...what we're all looking at is a collection of scans showing how Jacob's tumor has responded to chemotherapy." With a stylus, Dani pointed at and enlarged the section of the image that showed the tumor. "This is before treatment began."

Sheri exhaled noisily.

Dani went through each image slowly.

"It shrank." Sheri clapped her hands together and smiled.

"It did, just as we discussed," Dani agreed. Someone cleared their throat. Others shifted in their seats. The sound seemed almost cacophonous. "The last two images are what I want you to see." Dani did the same thing she'd done before: enlarge and point.

"But...but it's still there." Sheri's voice shook.

"Yes, but it *did* shrink."

"No...no, no, no. This can't be right." Sheri shook her head. Her chest heaved.

"I'm sorry, but it is." Dani kept her voice soft.

Sheri's eyes were wide. Her lips pursed. She looked both angry and horrified.

"He has to have surgery to remove the remainder of the tumor. His treatment plan has never changed." Dani held Sheri's gaze.

"Can't he just have radiation or whatever?" Sheri asked.

Dani expected that question. She glanced at Dr. Meda.

"No, radiation at this point will do more harm to his body than good," Dr. Meda said. "As discussed throughout his treatment here, the only plausible course of action is surgery followed by an additional cycle of chemotherapy to reduce recidivism. His prognosis is very good, Sheri. I promise you."

Sheri's breathing was loud, raspy. She stared at Dr. Meda, and Dani wondered whether she was really seeing him. Going with her instincts, Dani touched Sheri's arm. It felt as if her skin was vibrating, but she didn't pull away. "I know you're worried, but this hospital has a high surgical success rate."

"That doesn't matter. There's always a chance that something could go...wrong." Sheri's voice was husky, thick.

"That's true too, but what's the alternative?" Dani wasn't going to lie to her. "I know this is hard, but you'll make the right decision."

Sheri stood up almost turning over her chair in the process. "I don't wanna hear anymore."

Seeing Sheri's distress, Dani stood as well. She wasn't sure why. "Sheri—"

"Stop talking! Right now, I feel like you lied to me." Sheri stood inches away from her, pointing a finger in Dani's face.

Breathless, like she'd been punched in the gut, Dani stepped out of the way as Sheri left the conference room.

"Give her time everyone. She'll consent to the surgery." Dr. Meda addressed the team. Most stated their agreement, and then almost everyone stood to leave. Dr. Meda remained, and Dani stood in the same spot, as if frozen,.

"You were expecting her anger. Were you not?"

Dani blinked at him.

Dr. Meda got up and walked toward her. "Dr. Russell…Dani, you seem shaken by all this. If you'd like to talk—"

She held up a hand, stopping his approach. "No, I can't do this right now." Without another word, Dani left.

As she walked briskly down the hall, Dani did her best to push down the shock, the anxiety, and the throbbing ache, but they refused to budge. Needing some space away from everything, Dani tried the on-call rooms. The first one was locked, but the second one wasn't. She locked the door behind her and leaned against it. Frantic, Dani fished for her phone. Without thought, she dialed Becca's number. It rang five times and then went to voicemail. "Dammit!"

Rick had to answer. He had to unless he was in surgery.

"Hey, what's up?"

"I—I need you." Dani's voice shook.

"Dani, what's wrong?" Rick's tone went from laid-back to urgent.

"Just please? Peds' second on-call room."

"I'm comin'."

She hung up. Dani wanted to be angry at Becca for not being there, but she didn't have it in her. Plus the rational part of her screamed at her for thinking it. Becca had a job, and she was also right: Dani needed someone to help her sift through her emotions and everything coming at her.

For the umpteenth time, Rebecca called Dani, but there was no answer. "What the hell?"

A million scenarios ran through her mind. They ranged from something terrible to even worse, and Rebecca had missed it all because she'd been working. She'd texted as soon as she could, with no response. Rebecca had even tried Rick a couple times but somehow convinced herself he was just in surgery. The fact that Dani had called in the middle of the day had to be significant.

Rebecca paced in front of her couch. Peyton watched her quietly from the love seat. "I should probably just go over there or maybe even to the hospital." She glanced at Peyton as if she were about to spout all sorts of wisdom, but the cat only yawned.

Peyton was right. She needed to get a hold of herself. Where the hell was this anxiety coming from? More than likely that little voice that told her Dani had halted everything because she hadn't been there for her, which was beyond fucking stupid. Dani was trying to change the way she responded to things, not stay on the same old behaviors. There was a simple explanation for all of this.

Finally, Rebecca's phone chirped. She accepted the call immediately.

"Did…something happen for you to call and text me that many times?" Dani asked.

Softly exhaling in relief, Rebecca sat down beside Peyton. "Well, you don't usually call me, so I assumed…"

"This day felt like it took a year to end. I put my phone on silent and concentrated on work. I forgot to turn the ringer back on."

"But you're okay, then?" Rebecca leaned back into the cushion.

"Kind of? I guess? I'm just leaving the hospital." Dani paused. "Can I come over? It's out of the way, but still…" She spoke in a rush, and her voice cracked with emotion at the end.

Rebecca sat up. "Now you're scarin' me."

"I think I scared myself. It's hard talking to you sometimes after everything, but since you're trying, I should too."

Whoa. She hadn't expected any of that, and to hear it sent Rebecca soaring. "Yeah, you can come over."

"Okay, thank you."

"See you soon." Rebecca hung up. She stared down at her phone and did the same to the far wall. That person on the phone had been more like the Dani she knew, and Rebecca hoped she'd get to see a lot more of her sometime soon.

She scanned the living room anxiously, making sure everything was in place. If there was one thing instilled in her growing up, it was that the rest of the house could be a damn mess, but the living room always needed to be spotless.

Rebecca smiled as she thought of her aunt. She scratched Peyton behind the ears and stood, willing her nerves away. Maybe she and Dani were well on their way to being friendly, which was a huge step in the right direction, even though she hoped to go much further.

Twenty minutes later, Rebecca opened the door. Having come directly from work, Dani was still in scrubs. Her ponytail swished from side to side as she walked in. "Hey, thanks again for doing this."

"Like I'd say no."

Dani turned to look at her. "You might."

"No…I wouldn't have." Rebecca met her gaze. Dani looked away, but not before Rebecca saw something in her eyes that kept her hopeful. "You want anythin'? I have cran-grape juice; no apple though."

"No, I'm good." Dani sat down on the couch.

Giving her some space, Rebecca went to the end closest to Peyton. She glanced down at the empty cushion between them, which seemed to invite Dani to do the same. Their gazes met again like they had a choice. Peyton jumped on the couch between them. She glared up at Dani.

Dani jerked back in surprise. "Uh, it's a 'she,' right?"

Rebecca nodded.

"She looks like she's about to pounce."

"Yeah, she always does. If she's curious enough to bother lookin' at you like that, she likes you."

"I find that hard to believe. The first time I came here there was a lot of screaming. The second time—"

"There was lots of comin'?"

Dani reddened.

Rebecca held up her hands. "Sorry, bad joke." She had the feeling that she needed to push past it fast. "Mark is the only one she goes crazy over."

"Is that someone you're…" Dani's eyes widened slightly, and her face was still flushed.

"No…God no." How could she even ask that after she'd let Dani let her tear her apart in the best way possible? "He's one of the guys from my squad."

Dani continued to look at her.

"He reminds me of Rick a little." When the words left her mouth, Rebecca realized she wasn't helping herself any. "It's not like that. He's married and has a great family. God, Rick asked me the same thing."

Looking down at her hands, Dani murmured, "I just realized that I don't know much about what's going on with you. That makes it so one-sided. I'm such a selfish asshole."

Rebecca didn't correct her. She stayed quiet and waited.

"Tell me about them."

"Are you sure?" Rebecca took note of how Dani still looked so flustered. "Don't feel obligated to—"

"I don't. I really want to know." Dani maintained eye contact, and the sincerity was there.

Rebecca nodded and started talking. By the time she stopped, Dani was at least smiling. It was bright enough to make her want to reach out and touch it.

"Sounds like a weird mini version of *The Breakfast Club*."

"How so?" Rebecca chuckled at the reference.

Dani shrugged. "You know. The asshole, the intense one, the insightful one…"

"Which one am I?" Rebecca wasn't afraid in the least to ask. She had a feeling she already knew the answer.

"I'd say you can be a combination of them all."

Rebecca felt her mouth drop open. She was actually shocked, but Dani's words also made her wary for some reason. "Why'd you wanna come over?"

Dani looked down at her hands again. "Um, I had a really bad day or, at least, part of one. I'm so scared that the crap in my personal life will start to bleed over, if it hasn't already. That's why I called, and when you didn't answer, I wanted to be mad at you. I even wanted it to be your fault." She glanced back up at Rebecca. "But it's not. I was able to get Rick. By that time, I'd already decided that you were right, so I made an appointment with a therapist at the hospital."

Speechless. Rebecca was totally speechless.

"I know I could've said all that over the phone, but it didn't feel right. I'm doing my best to figure out what feels good and go with it, and this was one of those things. So, thank you."

"I… You're welcome." Rebecca couldn't look away. They stared at each other long enough for it to become uncomfortable, but Rebecca loved the crackle of heat between them. She was tempted—so tempted—to say something about it. She stopped herself, knowing that right now, it wasn't appropriate.

Dani stood. "I should probably go."

Rebecca pressed her lips together to keep from protesting. She followed Dani to the door instead. Rebecca pulled it open for her. "Do you want someone there at therapy for moral support, at least the first time?"

"No, I should probably do this on my own."

Their eyes met again for the millionth time in less than thirty minutes. Rebecca nodded. "Okay." Dani's mouth opened like she had more to say. Her gaze was dark, intense. With one last look, she turned away and left.

CHAPTER 22

DESPITE OTHER RESIDENTS COMING IN and out, Dani sat in the lounge at a table covered with medical reference books. Some were open, and some she hadn't even cracked yet. Using her iPad, she got herself up to date with new cases that Dr. Meda's team were overseeing. She tried to pump up her level of excitement for the challenge of a patient with Ewing sarcoma and one with rhabdomyosarcoma. Dani was indeed looking forward to working with new families, new personalities, and different diagnoses, but at the moment, it was hard to concentrate.

Every other thought was of Becca, and the situation would have been more manageable if those thoughts were the soft, fleeting kind. Instead, Dani's mind settled heavily on the fact that when Becca was in the room, Dani hardly looked away.

To add to matters, keeping physical distance between them was a must. She couldn't trust herself otherwise. With every nice thing Becca did and with every giving gesture, she felt herself weakening and believing. Dani knew what that look in Becca's eyes meant. She'd seen it at least a thousand times when they were together. Becca hadn't hid it then, and she wasn't trying now.

Dani didn't understand how there was room inside her to feel any of this with all that was going on with her personally. The timing and her feelings made little sense. It all had to be just physical because the alternative made Dani's head spin. Reaching for another book off the pile, Dani did her best to renew her focus on the task at hand.

Exiting a patient's room, Dani walked toward yet another—her last two, to be exact. Dr. Luft leaned against the wall outside Jacob's room.

She muttered to herself and fidgeted. When she saw Dani, she walked toward her. "Since I haven't been doing well with them and with everything going on, I figured it would be best to wait on you. I'm not good with confrontation."

"I get it. I do, but your first mistake is thinking of this as a confrontation. It's not. We all want the same thing here. Eventually, you're going to have to learn to deal with a wide range of emotions coming from parents and patients alike." Dani kept her voice soft when she really wanted to tell her she was in the wrong profession. Even though she expected a cold shoulder the equivalent of Antarctica, Dani walked into Jacob's room without hesitation.

Jacob turned toward her in such an exhausted state he could barely keep his eyes open. His smile was tremulous at best. Yet it was still there. "Doc D."

Dani grinned and greeted him in return. "Hang in there. It's almost over."

Sheri stood next to him on the opposite side, watching. Dani hoped she took the words to heart as well. By the time she finished with a physical examination, Jacob had fallen asleep.

She glanced at Sheri, and sure enough, her face was twisted in anger. "Can we pull you away for a minute?"

Sheri didn't nod or speak. She walked quickly toward the door. Dani followed her with Dr. Luft trailing behind.

Before she had a chance to open her mouth, Dr. Luft began. "We, um, just wanted to check to see if you've made a decision yet about Jacob's surgery."

"Do you have any questions about it at all?" Dani cut in. "Maybe I can help smooth over some fears." She pressed her iPad to her chest and waited for a response.

Sheri crossed her arms in front of her. She didn't even look at Dani, which stung, but not as much as it had a few days ago. Sheri only had eyes for Dr. Luft, and her gaze was full of challenge. "When I'm ready to talk about it, I will."

Dr. Luft stepped forward. "I know this is hard—"

Even though she was impressed by Dr. Luft's sudden bravado, Dani wrapped a hand around her arm and hoped she would follow her cue. Sheri had made herself clear. "Let it go."

She nodded, and they both watched as Sheri went back into her son's room.

"You called it. She's very upset with you."

"I know, but she has time to work through it and figure things out." Dani was Jacob's first line of defense, and to Sheri, Dani had let her down.

Dani left Dr. Luft and made her way back down the hall. She was surprised to see Rick standing at the nurses station when she passed. "Hey, what are you doing here?" Dani smiled as Rick turned.

"Shhh, don't tell anybody. Playin' hooky. You got a sec?"

"Sure. Walk with me. Is everything okay?" She glanced at him as they made their way down the hall.

"Same old, same old for me. I actually came to check on you. Thought a text would be a little impersonal, considerin'."

Dani stopped completely. "Wait. Are you talking about my therapy appointment without really talking about it?"

"Slick, huh?" He rubbed his hands together.

"Yes, so smooth." Dani rolled her eyes.

Rick chuckled. "Seriously though, this is a big deal."

"I'm not backing out if that's what you think." Dani couldn't stop the sudden surge of defensiveness.

"Wasn't thinkin' that at all. Just thought I'd be here for moral support. I hear that's what friends do."

Embarrassed by her misplaced display of emotions, Dani looked away. "It is what they do. I'm sorry for jumping down your throat."

"Don't sweat it. I got you." Rick threw an arm over her shoulder.

Even though they were nowhere near where they'd been a couple months back, things felt promising. Maybe they were becoming something better. He definitely stood behind her, even when they were in two different places.

"Thanks." Dani hesitated, wondering how much she should share. "You, uh, were right about Becca. She was actually the one who suggested therapy."

"It's good to know that I know what I'm talkin' 'bout sometimes." Rick smiled.

"I know you're trying to be Switzerland for your own sake, but I figured you'd want to know." It was difficult not to say more, but she'd be selfish if she didn't.

Rick opened his mouth and closed it a couple times as if he was trying to figure out what to say. "Nah, more like Cleveland. Nothin' ever happens in Cleveland."

Well, that wasn't true at all. Dani glanced at Rick. He grinned crookedly. She rolled her eyes. "You really think you're funny."

Rick nodded. "I do. Sandra thinks so too." His eyes lit up.

It was good to see him happy. It was even better to know that, as friends, she and Rick were on the mend. "She has to say that."

He bumped her with a shoulder, making her stumble slightly. "Whatever. I'm proud of you, by the way."

Dani smiled. Maybe she was a little proud of herself too.

Trying to settle back into old and better habits, Dani took the stairs up to the twelfth floor. When she got to the tenth, she stopped and leaned against the wall. Not because she was tired, but to gather herself. She was fifteen minutes away from ripping herself open and letting all the ugliness spill out. There was good stuff too, but in the past couple months, that had seemed few and far between. She had to do this. No more running. No more hiding. She was a good doctor, and she wanted to be a good person again too.

Dani shoved her hands in her scrub pockets and took a deep breath. She bumped against her phone. Pulling it out, Dani glanced at it to see two missed calls from Becca, one in the last five minutes. Maybe she thought a text was impersonal too. Becca had left a voicemail, but Dani decided that calling her back would be better.

"Hey, I was just—"

"I'm fine. I promise," Dani cut in.

"It's almost time, huh?"

"It is."

"I was worried. I didn't want you to think I forgot. This is a big deal."

The warmth that seeped into her was very hard to ignore. "Rick beat you to the punch. He came to see me about an hour ago."

"Dirty bastard." There was laughter in Becca's voice.

Dani smiled too, and God, it felt incredible and freeing. When was the last time something had felt that way? Her thoughts shifted and landed on Becca with her head thrown back, blown pupils, and crying out. Dani pushed away from the wall as her stomach hit the concrete. "Um, it's almost time. I'd better…"

"Wait. I just wanted to say that you can do this. It's weird at first to spill your guts to a stranger, but if she's right for you, I bet it gets easier."

"Becca." Dani didn't mean for her voice to be so soft, but it was hard not to at this point.

"Yeah?" Becca sounded so hopeful.

"Thank you."

"You're welcome. Call me later or somethin' and let me know how it went?"

"Okay, I will."

"Good luck." Becca hung up, but Dani kept the phone pressed to her ear.

Rebecca put her phone back in the little cubby between the driver and passenger seat, then completely refocused on driving.

"Look at you, all glowy and lit up like a Christmas tree." Mark laughed.

"Shut up." Rebecca cut her eyes at him.

"You don't scare me. You never have, even though I know you can probably kick my ass no matter how little you are."

He sounded more and more like Rick every day, but Rick with a twist. "It's good to know you're aware."

"I am. I totally am." He paused. "Sooo, things seem like they're getting better between you and your ex."

"They're gettin' somethin'. I'm just takin' things as they come."

"The thing that broke you up still an issue?"

Rebecca went quiet. It took her a minute to figure out how to answer his question. "I don't know. She hasn't really taken responsibility for her part in things. I do know that much."

"That don't bother you?"

"Sometimes, yeah. It scares me too, but apparently not enough to stay away from her. At least right now."

Mark's only response was a light hum.

"Sayin' all that out loud makes me sound pathetic." Rebecca glanced at him.

He shook his head. "No, it doesn't. Makes you hopeful and a bit stupid."

Caught off guard by his response, Rebecca laughed. "I like that a lot better than pathetic."

"Bet you do. You love her?"

Rebecca didn't hesitate. "I could again if she lets me."

"Hope she catches on to that."

"Me too." Rebecca changed lanes when she saw their exit up ahead. Speaking out to him and to the universe made things more real somehow.

"Good talk." Mark was smiling; she could tell. His cell rang, and he answered it right away. "Detective Strong."

Rebecca did her best not to eavesdrop, but it was hard with him being so close.

"Yeah, thanks for the update." He hung up. "Damn, that's at least semi-good news."

"What?"

"The DA is willing to plead out the Dorset case, and with the whole mess making the news, Steve, that lawyer I told her about, found a judge that will listen about the whole custody situation. Hopefully, they won't completely yank parental rights away from Gwen. She's like the poster child for mitigating circumstances."

"Hope not. What's the plea?" Rebecca asked.

"Aggravated assault, but Steve stressed that it was in done in prevention of crime and the DA accepted that. She'll get a couple years' probation since she doesn't have a record." Mark sounded relieved.

"Good. Sometimes shit really does work out."

Dani pulled in behind Becca's car and turned off the ignition. She hadn't called or anything to see if this was okay, and she wasn't sure what had made her come here instead of going straight home. Was it just because she wanted to share news about her first therapy appointment? Was it because she wanted to see Becca? More than likely a combination of both, with a little bit of this and that thrown in, to guide her. Regardless, Dani was determined to see it through. If Becca didn't want Dani in her home, she'd leave, but deep down, she knew she wasn't going to be turned away. She pocketed her keys and got out of her car.

When she got to the screen door, Dani could hear and see distorted black-and-white images from the television. She let herself into the porch area and rang the doorbell. The sound stopped, and the people on TV ceased all movement as well. Seconds later, Becca opened the door. She frowned. "Everythin' okay?"

Dani nodded and smiled. "Yes, I hope I'm not bothering you."

"No. Got home early, so I'm watchin' a movie to pass the time. I was hopin' to hear from you, but this works too." Becca stepped behind the door, giving Dani plenty of space to come in.

Dani took off her jacket and laid it over the back of the couch. She glanced at the TV and back at Becca. She knew the movie well. "*The Children's Hour*. Ugh. I still don't get how you can stomach that movie. It was probably the onset of the dead lesbian trope."

"I know, I know, but it's like a train wreck that, once I put it on, I can't stop watchin'. If you're stayin' for a while, we can watch somethin' else if you want?" Becca brushed by Dani on her way back to the couch, bringing heat with her but leaving a shiver of awareness behind.

"No, this is fine." Dani sat down. Becca did too, leaving the habitual cushion between them. Dani expected the movie to play again, but it remained on pause. She looked at Becca only to find her gaze already on her.

Dani didn't even try to turn away. The living room expanded, but the world shrank to include just the two of them. Dani forgot herself for a moment, and words just dribbled out of her mouth. "Where's the cat?"

Becca tilted her head, studying her as if she had trouble understanding. "Uh, I'm sure she heard the doorbell. Give her a couple minutes to come be nosey."

Silence stretched between them, but Dani's gaze didn't waver. She nearly came out of her skin when Peyton jumped up on the cushion between them. Becca chuckled. Dani took that moment to breathe. "You can take the movie off pause, if you want."

Becca scratched Peyton behind the ears, causing her to purr loudly, and when she trailed her hand down her back, the cat arched into the touch.

Dani was mesmerized. Becca said something, but she wasn't sure what it was. "I'm sorry. What?"

"I said I changed my mind. I don't want to keep watchin'." Becca smiled, and it seemed to get bigger by the end of the sentence. "And I asked you how your appointment went."

She'd missed all that? "Oh, it was…different."

"Is that good or bad?"

"Well, she was smiling so hard at first it started to freak me out."

Becca blinked and then she laughed so loud that Peyton ran away. Dani bit her bottom lip to keep from smiling. "I asked her to stop. She did. Then she laughed and apologized."

"You're makin' that up."

Dani put a hand over her chest. "Swear to God, I'm not."

"Well, that's startin' things off with a bang."

"I know. I really think she did it on purpose to see if I'd say anything."

"It worked."

"Yes. It all just took off after that." Dani shrugged.

"So, you like her?"

"I think so. She told me to call her by her first name, Patti, and for some reason, I can't think her name without putting Peppermint in front of it."

Becca threw her head back and laughed even harder.

It wasn't like Dani hadn't seen her do that hundreds, maybe thousands, of times before, but *this* time held her attention unlike any other. Becca's hazel eyes were bright with amusement, and her nose scrunched at the top as she continued to chuckle.

"I can't remember the last time we talked like this."

"I can," Becca said softly.

The moment seeped into Dani, dribbling slowly like molasses. It was scary but not overwhelmingly so. Still, she let it push her forward, and Dani continued to talk. By the time she stopped, the DVD had reverted back to the main menu.

"I should probably go." Dani scooted forward and stood. Becca did as well. She moved to the other side of the coffee table, letting Dani go by first.

Dani opened the door and stepped out onto the porch. She turned toward Becca.

"You know, everythin' you said coulda been relayed through a phone call." Becca crossed her arms over her chest and rocked back and forth as a nice gust of wind came along, but her gaze was soft, watchful.

"I didn't want to, and thank you." Without thought, Dani stepped closer and pressed her lips against Becca's cheek.

Moving quickly, Becca turned her head, bringing their lips dangerously close.

Everything stopped for Dani and then flared back to life within seconds. She was floating away, needing something to hold on to, so Dani grabbed Becca's shirt at the bottom, balling it into her fist.

Becca's chest heaved, and it was then that Dani realized that the only sound was their ragged breathing.

Heat pooled into her stomach and flashed outward. Dani's body developed a mind of its own. Yanking Becca by the shirt, she pulled her closer.

Becca sucked in a deep breath, and it quivered coming out. "Uh, you should probably go."

Dani watched as each word fell from Becca's lips, but she was confused by their meaning. She wanted them close like this, straining and needy. Didn't she?

Becca's eyes were nearly black, and her heart was beating hard enough to make the artery in her neck pulse.

Dani was tempted to just take like she had before, but Becca stepped away. Her expression was pinched as if she were in pain. Dani's confidence wavered, and her fear went up a few notches. She dropped her hand and moved back, looking down at her feet.

"No." Becca grabbed her hand. "Don't disappear on me like that. I wanna be sure you're not ridin' some type of high after everythin' that happened today, and that you wanted to kiss *me* and not the person you knew four years ago."

"Okay." Dani nodded. The rejection still stung, even though part of her understood the reasoning behind it.

Becca squeezed her hand before letting go. "I don't think you'll ever know how…hard that was." She still sounded shaken.

Maybe. Maybe not. "I better go." Dani turned to do just that.

"Dani?"

She stopped and glanced over her shoulder at Becca. "It's okay."

Nothing was okay at the moment, but it would have to be.

CHAPTER 23

REBECCA'S PHONE VIBRATED ON HER desk. She finished the sentence on the report she was typing before flipping it over. There was a text from Dani waiting for her. It surprised Rebecca, pleasantly so, that even after what had happened two days back, Dani still accepted her calls and texts as well as did the same in return.

She didn't regret pulling away but had expected the fallout to stink things up a lot more than it did. There was some awkwardness between them that resulted in extended silences and shorter calls. They hadn't really talked about what happened yet, but Rebecca had no intention of letting that fly. She'd given Dani some space, but Rebecca wasn't going to let things fester. Was she scared that the conversation would set them back? Yeah, she was, but that was fixable. An implosion later on? Maybe not so much.

Sandra talked to me today.

She unlocked her phone to text back.

Rick's Sandra?

Yes. We had a falling out but it was my fault.

So that's what Rick meant when he said Dani had hurt people that he cared about.

Sounds like things r going in the right direction then.

I'm glad. I think he really likes her.

Me too. Rebecca wrote back.

It was strange at first knowing we had sex with the same woman.

Rebecca blinked then stared at the text. It was like she was in a car that screeched to stop at a red light, and while she waited, jealousy wiggled its way inside.

We weren't seeing her at the same time.

Rebecca rolled her eyes. She was only human, but she was totally being ridiculous as well. *Ok.*

That's been the highlight of my day so far. How about you? Dani asked.

Talking to u is mine. Rebecca typed out. She stared at her phone. No ellipses to hint that Dani was responding. Maybe Dani was doing the exact same thing she was, looking down at her cell and trying to figure out what to say next.

Finally, three little dots appeared.

Lunch is over for me. I have some charting to catch up on.

Disappointment had a taste to it similar to burnt food. Rebecca had learned that a while back. Sadly, she was accustomed to it, but she didn't want to be.

K. Talk later?

I'll call you when I get home.

Rebecca put her phone face down on her desk. Hopeful and a tad stupid. Mark's words had stuck with her. Right now, she was settling for scraps because Dani had a lot going on. But how was that different from how things used to be? Rebecca knew what she wanted—Dani, and another chance for them to get things right. Rebecca hadn't done a damn thing to make that crystal clear, which was a total fuck up on her part. The scariest thing was that she had no idea what Dani wanted and wondered if Dani even knew.

Rebecca's stomach twisted and left a heavy feeling behind. Despite being terrified of Dani's response, Rebecca had to push forward and hope that Dani had changed enough, or was willing to, so history wouldn't repeat itself. First, Dani had to admit she'd had a hand in it all. Rebecca stared at her computer screen as whatever was on it turned into an indecipherable mess.

Mark touched her shoulder as he breezed past. Rebecca stiffened even though she didn't mean to. His chair creaked as he sat down. "You okay?"

No, she wasn't. Rebecca didn't answer him.

"Becca?"

Rebecca's head snapped up. She met his gaze but didn't correct him for what he'd done to her name. It just sounded right coming from him. "Yeah?"

"You need to talk or something? We pretty much have the place to ourselves."

She did need to talk, but not to him. There was nothing Mark could say or do. "No, not right now."

He looked at her a beat longer, before nodding and turning away.

Dani opened the refrigerator door and scanned the contents. She reached for a container of leftover pasta she'd enjoyed at lunch earlier. It was good enough for dinner as well. The apartment was quiet and felt drab like it always did when Rick wasn't there. However, for some reason, Dani experienced an extra pang of loneliness tonight in his absence. Maybe she missed him more now that things were settling between them.

Maybe being inside her own head wasn't the best place to be and she needed a familiar face around. Her day had flown by, and, except for Sandra smiling and joking with her about Rick, it had been pretty uneventful. So, it seemed her night was going to be more of the same.

All she had to do was pick up the phone. Becca could make her laugh, make her want, make her need. Dani put the container in the microwave and opened the drawer to get a plastic fork. She hadn't called her yet because every time she talked with her, Becca's rejection was front and center. She understood the reasoning behind it, but that didn't mean she liked it. This whole thing between them had the potential to become ultra-complicated.

The basest part of her wanted to keep things simple because the thought of them being anything else petrified her. If that were the case, what had they been doing lately? Why had she allowed things to go so far? *Like I have a choice*. Dani shut the voice in her head down. It wasn't helping at all.

The microwave dinged. Dani used a dish towel to remove the container. She tested the heat level of her food and then slammed the microwave closed. She'd just stepped out of the kitchen and into the living room when someone knocked at the door. Dani set her food down on the table and stood there. Her heartbeat quickened. It could have been one of the neighbors, but Dani knew better. Regardless, she asked, "Who is it?"

"It's me."

Dani had already taken a few steps toward the door before she realized it.

"Dani?"

"I'm coming." She walked closer and unlocked the door before pulling it open.

Becca stood there. Her jaw was set and her eyes intense and determined. Dani's stomach clenched. Becca was always at her best when she had something to prove.

Dani stepped out of the way, letting her in.

"I know I shoulda called, but we need to talk."

Dani had a feeling her food was going to be cold by the time she got to it. "Okay." She didn't ask if something was wrong because clearly there was. "Coke?"

Becca nodded. "Please." Instead of sitting, she followed Dani into the kitchen. "Sorry for interrupting dinner. It smells good, but this is important."

Becca's gaze might as well have been a touch. It carried that much weight.

Dani nodded, and for the second time in ten minutes, she opened the refrigerator. "This is about the other night?"

"Yes." Becca's voice was soft, and it sounded closer than it had been a few seconds ago. Dani grabbed a Coke and turned to see Becca only a few inches away. She couldn't breathe right with Becca this close, so in order for them to have a rational conversation, Dani stepped to the side, toward the cabinet, intent on getting a glass and a second to gather herself.

"Don't run away from me." Becca grabbed her arm. Her voice shook slightly.

Dani didn't even have the chance to reach up. She set the Coke on the counter and swung around. "I was about to get you a glass." She swallowed and tried to ignore the way Becca's touch left her feeling scorched. "I wasn't running." Dani met her gaze.

Becca looked like some kind of war raged inside her. Her expression remained dark, focused. Becca's mouth was open, and her lips trembled as if she had something profound to say but it wouldn't come out.

"I'm listening," Dani whispered.

Becca slowly moved closer. Dani shuffled backward. Her back hit the counter.

"Dani, I…" Becca paused and glanced at her lips. Her breathing stuttered.

Dani gripped at the edge of the counter. There was only a little space between them, but it felt as if Becca was already deep inside her.

"I really don't think you have any idea how hard it was to turn you away two days ago or how hard it is now."

Why fight it? Maybe whatever was between them would finally burn itself out and they'd be free. "It doesn't have to be."

Becca gasped, and in that moment, time slowed. Dani was outside herself watching as Becca crashed into her, but when their lips touched, she slammed back into her body, whimpering as Becca's tongue tangled with her own. Becca pinned Dani against the counter. Her hands were frantic, pulling at Dani's T shirt.

When Becca finally touched skin, she shuddered. Dani arched into the caress, inching up her torso, chasing the heat left behind. Her nipples tingled and hardened in preparation. Becca knew exactly what she was doing. Dani's breasts were ultra-sensitive, so when Becca's fingertips actually skimmed the area, Dani, even with an abundance of self knowledge, was nowhere near ready for the results.

She cried out.

Becca moaned. Both sounds were muffled by their kiss.

Dani gripped hard at Becca's shoulders. That floating feeling was back, and she wanted to make sure she had a tether. When Becca's hands slid over her breasts, grasping and kneading, Dani was cleaved in two and exposed like an unprotected nerve. Each caress left her burning, raw.

She tore away from the kiss and whimpered brokenly, realizing that she couldn't catch her breath. Becca plucked at Dani's nipples as her lips trailed over her neck, and each flash of pleasure caused a corresponding pull between Dani's legs, leaving her swollen and slick.

As Dani's shirt was pushed up, Becca's mouth moved downward, grazing Dani's left nipple before covering it completely and sucking at her like she'd been dying from thirst.

"Fuck!" Dani cried out.

Becca groaned and took her in deeper, flicking and swirling her tongue before adding teeth to the mix.

Wanting to watch herself being devoured, Dani dipped her head only to see nearly her entire breast in Becca's mouth. She closed her eyes, but there was no darkness, just flashes of light behind her eyelids. Heat more powerful than before rolled through her, pooled low, and pushed itself outward. She couldn't press her thighs together with Becca between them, so her hips undulated helplessly. Her sex clenched, and without a doubt, Dani knew that just having Becca's mouth on her breast was going to be enough to pave the way for orgasm.

It wouldn't be the first time.

For some reason, that acknowledgment tipped the scales as fear climbed on too. The added vulnerability made Dani even more afraid, but she didn't want this to end. It just needed to happen her way. She wrapped a hand in Becca's hair and yanked her away. Dani's body cried out in protest. It was almost a physical pain, but most importantly, the fear abated.

Becca's eyes were lidded and her mouth swollen. She looked drunk, pliable. Perfect.

Dani brought their lips together once more, but Becca's hands continued to map her torso, spreading fire. When fingers closed in on her breasts again, Dani slapped them away and turned the tables, flipping their positions.

Refusing to give up, Becca slid her hands down the back of Dani's sweatpants, palming her ass roughly. Dani moaned and almost gave in again. It took some doing, but she was able to regain control. Dani pressed Becca's hands against the counter, silently demanding that they stay. She gazed down at Becca. Her pupils were blown. She blinked rapidly and struggled to breathe.

"Wha...what are you doin'? I need to—" Becca's voice was husky.

Dani tried to quiet her with a heated kiss. She bit into Becca's bottom lip and swiped it with her tongue. "Let me..."

Becca whimpered. Yet again, she wrapped her arms around Dani as if they belonged there and found skin. Her touch was firm, demanding, and a bit desperate.

Dani wanted to drown in it, but instead she pushed Becca away, pressing her hands back against the countertop.

Becca's expression changed from aroused to confused. "Dani?"

"Shhhh."

"No...no," Becca responded.

Dani swallowed as she looked down at her. Becca's eyes had cleared.

"That night on my couch, it wasn't just because you needed me so much, was it?"

Dani tried to step away, but Becca wouldn't let her, grabbing both her arms.

"You won't let me touch you." Becca whispered the words as if she couldn't believe them.

Unable to hold eye contact, Dani dropped her gaze. She didn't know what to say.

"What kind of shit is that? Look at me."

Dani did as she was told.

"How is that even okay to you?" Becca's eyes were wide and filled with anger, hurt, and disbelief.

"I..." Dani paused to clear her throat.

"Is this because I left? Because I hurt you?"

She tried to look down.

"Don't do that. Look at me, please."

Dani did.

"You gave up on us," Becca said. "You know you did. There was no reason to stay. I couldn't do it all by myself."

Tears burned Dani's eyes.

"You stopped listenin', stopped tryin' to find balance for us. I wasn't important to you anymore. I know my part in all that, the way I acted, but I'm not the bad guy here. We both were." Becca's tone wasn't cruel, scathing, or even angry, but it was matter of fact.

Dani shook her head. Guilt crept up on her. "No, that's—"

"Yes," Becca interrupted. "Yes, and if you can't accept that, how do I know the same thing won't happen again?" Becca put a hand over her own mouth but pulled it away a few seconds later. "I've been avoidin' that question, but I can't anymore. I don't want just a quick fuck from you. I wanna see where all these feelings lead. I know that's stupid and dangerous, but I can't help it." Becca's lips trembled as she smiled, and her eyes were full of sadness.

Hearing those words caused an almost unbearable warmth to filter through Dani like the sun was shining directly on her, but at the same time, a chill remained, working its way through as well.

"I'm not sure what you want from me," Becca continued. "I don't think you are either, but to be fair you have to figure it out. I may have been an asshole four years ago, but after everythin' that's happened these past couple months, don't you think I deserve more? I actually believe we both do."

"Becca…" Dani closed her mouth. Everything inside her was jumbled up, and she didn't want the wrong thing to get out, making the situation worse.

"I should go. I said what I came here to say. I didn't mean for anythin' else to happen. I just got kinda lost…in you." Becca let go of Dani's arms. Then she reached for the edges of Dani's T-shirt and pulled it down over her bare stomach. It was that sweet gesture that finally made Dani's tears fall. She had fought so hard at first to keep Becca out of her life, and now the thought of her leaving again made her hollow.

Dani wiped at her face. "I'm sorry. I didn't… You can't just—"

"I'm not goin' anywhere, Dani," Becca said. "I'm home. I don't know what I can be to you, but I do know I can't be this, not with the way things are." She waved a hand between them at the obvious closeness.

Not knowing what else to do, Dani moved back.

Becca eased past her. As she exited the kitchen and walked into the living room, Becca glanced over her shoulder. "I'll text you later, okay?"

Dani bit her bottom lip and nodded. There were so many feelings that she couldn't decipher them all. She wanted to call out to Becca. She wanted to let her go. She wanted her arms around her. She wanted to feel safe and unafraid, but in the end, Dani just stood there. When the door closed, she was even lonelier than before.

At least Becca was going to text.

CHAPTER 24

REBECCA WAS GOING TO DO her best to fake it until she made it where Dani was concerned. In a short time, she had gotten used to so much all over again—Dani's touch, her laugh, her voice, and so much more, but she had no choice. She had to take a step back so that Dani could figure out if she could move forward. But Becca couldn't, wouldn't, cut her out completely. They were beyond that and nowhere near the kids they'd been four years ago.

On the surface, doing this seemed noble, but there was finally a bit of self preservation involved as well, despite the bravado that had gotten her this far. She leaned back in her chair and put her hands on her head. This whole thing had been keeping her up at night. Not calling Dani had been more difficult than she'd thought it would be, but nothing about this situation was simple.

Alvin stopped at her desk, snatching a pastry out of the nearly empty box that always seemed to be sitting there.

She could feel him looking at her. "What?"

"Are you pouting because your boy is off today? It kinda looks like it."

"How would you know? We're not *that* close."

He shrugged. "All women look the same doin' it. It's easy to spot, with the bottom lip all poked out and the sad-puppy expression."

Rebecca glared at him.

Alvin smiled. "What?"

"That wasn't the least bit sexist at all."

"No, it wasn't." He nodded in agreement.

"Uh-huh. Go tell Benz that, then. See what she thinks about it."

Alvin pursed his lips. "Nah, that's okay."

"That's what I thought."

"You still have the sad dog eyes, just to let you know."

"Well, again, thank you so much."

"I'm not Iyanla, so I'm not about fixing your life."

Rebecca huffed. This was getting better by the second. "Good, leave Iyanla on the Oprah Winfrey Network where she belongs, and this is when I say you're bein' an asshole."

"I know, but hear me out. I got a case. You want in on it? Might help you get your mind off of whatever." Alvin crossed his arms over his chest.

She eyed him. "Emmet turned you down, didn't he?"

"In the hallway, thirty seconds ago. He said he wasn't up for me today. I mean, I can work this by myself…"

Rebecca laughed. "What do you have?"

"Don't know everythin' yet. Got a call from downstairs that they're kickin' up to us because they don't have any leads. The kid's father is on his way up. Should be here any second."

"Okay, I'm in." She needed something and hoped that it was indeed juicy enough to keep her occupied.

Dani had gone through the past thirty-six hours partially anesthetized. She was familiar with the feeling—or lack thereof. She had experienced it plenty, years ago, but then it had come in cycles, followed closely by rage. This time, Dani wasn't sure if the anger would come. What did she have to be mad at? She already knew she had the capacity to be a horrible person. Becca hadn't told her anything new.

Her daily life was all part of a routine, so she went through the motions. The situation would have been much simpler if she'd been able to block everyone out, but she'd just started walking, and reverting back to crawling would only hamper her further. As a result, she added a smile and common courtesy to everyone she encountered, whether they returned the gesture or not. It wasn't much, but at least she was trying.

Home was a different story altogether. Unable to turn her mind off, she barely slept but spent hours trying to sift through the past ten years of her life, doing her best to catalogue her mistakes and failures and compare them to the victories to see which ones carried the most weight. In some cases, she found herself lacking. So tonight, instead of tossing, turning, and thinking, she had plans to work a double and do something positive with her time.

However, it was just past eight. Her focus should have been on her patients, charting, research, and various other activities, but the only information her brain could retain were thoughts of Becca, which vacillated between rewind and a slow playback of the night before last. Recalling the look on Becca's face and the conviction behind her words sent a stabbing pang right to the pit of her stomach. So maybe this time her cycle was going to be a combination of numbness and pain.

Becca wanted her. She wanted them. She wanted a relationship. This news didn't surprise Dani even though it should have, which led her to believe that somewhere deep down, she'd known. When it came down to it, Dani had no idea if she was capable of giving Becca what she needed. How would she find balance when that was something she never really had? There would always be a patient, an emergency, and the need to dedicate herself to whatever hospital she worked for. Rick understood all that, and Becca had initially tried. Obviously, Becca felt she'd changed enough to try again. Dani wasn't sure that was true.

As for the other things Becca had said, Dani closed her eyes and stopped pretending that she was working at all. She pushed her iPad away. The other things. There were many sides to a story, and theirs was no exception. The screaming matches, the hurt feelings, and near the end, there were times Dani hadn't even wanted to go home. Yes, she had participated, and at the time, Dani had been convinced that Becca was asking for the impossible: time she couldn't give and promises she couldn't keep.

Becca should have been prepared. They'd talked many, many times about the ways medical school, residency, and so on could be consuming, but the more Becca had demanded, the more Dani felt pushed beyond her limits. The anger had come then and hung around. This was Dani's perception of the entire awful mess, and no matter how many ways she looked at it, she came right back to where she started.

Dani stared at her cell phone. It lay face down on the table. She itched with the need to reach out for it. Becca had kept her word. She texted, but their texts seemed to be nothing more than obligatory. *How are you? How was your day?* No trips down memory lane to make her laugh. No charm or swagger. It was as if someone had hit a reset button so that she could get another look, another chance. Dani had to stop and find another way. The road she had taken so far had gotten her nowhere.

Compared to her, Becca had experienced something else completely. If Becca could have walked in her shoes, and vice versa, maybe things wouldn't have gotten so bad. Dani laughed out loud because that had been an issue then, and it was still an issue now. Her unwillingness to see things from Becca's point of view meant she *hadn't* been listening. Dani covered her face with her hands. Nothing that had been said was news to her. It was a lot to choke down through her own off-colored filter, but through Becca's?

Dani ripped her hands away from her face and leaned back in her chair. She shook her head as if the sense she needed would break free. It didn't. It didn't matter who was right, wrong, or even worse. Dani was in her last year of residency, but after that was three more years of fellowship training. Her life would be just as chaotic probably even more so that first year, with long hours and increased demands on her time. They would indeed end up exactly where they'd been before. Dani was so mentally tired, and therapy was a couple of days away. Not that there was some magic answer, because there wasn't.

She didn't know how to fix any of it, and she didn't know if she had the energy to keep trying. However, the thought of Becca being even farther out of reach gave her pause. Dani cared, of course she did, but she needed to sort her feelings out. She needed to breathe. She needed some resolution. She needed…so many things.

Her cell phone beeped. Dani picked it up quickly only to see a text from Rick.

Worked late but I'm gettin ready 2 leave. U home or at hospital?

She typed out her reply. *Working a double. In peds resident lounge.*

K. Stay put be up in a min

Dani was surprised he was going home instead of to Sandra's. Maybe she was working the graveyard shift. Everyone around her was going on with their lives. She wanted to know how to do that too. A few minutes later, the door swished open, and Dani glanced up.

Rick smiled. "Hey, stranger."

She smiled back. It was hard and maybe selfish not to. He looked so happy. "Hey, yourself. Sandra working late?"

He nodded. "Yeah, I still coulda crashed at her place, but I figured…" Rick shrugged. "Not that you're some kind of afterthought or anythin'."

"It's okay. I get it." Dani waved his words away.

"Well, since you're workin', I guess I'm on my own anyway. Why aren't you in one of the study rooms? More privacy."

"I'm usually good at tuning everyone out. Nobody bothers me anyway unless they need something."

"Huh, okay. I guess I could go see what Becca's up to."

Dani swallowed. "I guess you can." She did her best to keep her tone neutral.

Rick pulled out a chair and sat down. "So, Thanksgivin'."

"What about it?"

He stared at her and shook his head. "It's next week."

"No, it's not." It was a little disarming that time had passed so quickly.

"Fourth Thursday in November. That's when it always happens, but I'm way ahead of you. Ordered a fried turkey from Popeye's last month. Sandra is doin' a thing with her family earlier that day. She's still comin' over, and since you and Becca are tryin' to be whatever it is you're tryin' to be, she'd be comin' too. Maybe there won't be so many leftovers with four of us."

The thought of Becca sitting beside her at a family gathering both warmed her and sent her into a panic. "Uh, I'm working."

"So? I am too." Rick studied her. His eyes narrowed. "Never stopped us before." He continued to look at her. "Is it Sandra that's got you all hesitant? I thought you guys—"

"No, we're fine. Probably never going to be best friends."

Rick groaned. "It's Becca, isn't it? I thought you guys were at least bein' civil to—"

"We're just in a weird place right now," Dani interrupted.

"Well, yeah, but still it's Thanksgivin'. We're all the family she's got, no matter what's goin' on.".

When he put it like that… "Okay, I guess it's fried turkey for four."

Rebecca turned from her back to her side in an effort to get comfortable. Peyton blinked slowly at her. "What? Am I botherin' you?"

Peyton didn't answer. Rebecca rolled her eyes, and she wished that was followed by them closing so she could get some sleep. No such luck. Maybe if she actually turned off the bedroom light? Regardless, her head was heavy with thoughts and feelings all centered on Dani.

Work hadn't even offered her a break. The case with Alvin was over before it had started. What was up with people making false reports? And how had no one caught on to that? No one needed attention that badly, and what was with the way that father had kept trying to hug her? All the crying that guy had done could have won him an Oscar. He'd been snotty and pale already, so that probably helped. The penalty for lying about a crime should be much harsher than it actually was. Stupid bastard.

She flipped over to the other side. Her cell phone was right in her line of sight. Rebecca wanted so badly to call Dani just to hear her voice, but she was sure that right now that would wreck her. It was hard enough as it was checking herself when she sent a text, keeping them as straightforward as possible. Hell, even that hurt, but overall everything stung a bit.

Dani was going through a lot. Rebecca wanted to be there for her, to further show her who she was now, but could she pay the price? Sitting around waiting wasn't her thing. This was her life too, and it made Rebecca more than a little queasy that this aspect, at least, was out of her control. There was nothing else for her to do.

Her phone beeped. Rebecca snatched it off the nightstand and read the text.

Ur comin' ovr for Thanksgiving. It was from Rick.

It couldn't be time for that yet. She looked at the date. She had been better lately about being more aware of things.

What does Dani say? Rebecca texted back.

I'm sayin ur comin' ovr.

Well, that didn't sound good.

Idk.

I'm not tryin to hurt nebody but it's ur first real holiday home. Should b with some1 who cares. U and Dani hav survived each othr this long.

It felt like somebody was stabbing at her chest with a butter knife and they had broken skin. Rebecca sucked in a shaky breath.

I still don't kno. Let me think bout it.

I kno. If u can't come 2 us I guess u should go 2 Mark's.

K.

She could at least give him that. Even though Mark hadn't asked, it was a possibility.

Nite.

Rebecca peered down at her phone but didn't respond. She put it back on the nightstand face side up and reached for the lamp. Her cell beeped again. Rebecca glanced at it. That dull pain went up to a definite throb.

How was your day? Dani texted.

The words taunted her, but Rebecca was pretty sure she wasn't meant to take them that way. The question was as generic and harmless as their other texts, but the kicker was that Rebecca had always been the one to send them or at least start the conversation.

Hope flared in her stomach, balancing out everything else. Dani might have been unsure about them, but she'd just made one thing clear: she wanted at least one aspect of them to continue.

CHAPTER 25

DR. LUFT GLANCED AT DANI AND tried to smile. She didn't really succeed. "Maybe today will be the day." Dani patted her on the shoulder as they made their way to Jacob's room.

"We'll see."

She continued to look at her. "Thanks, by the way, for letting me do this with you. It's very nice of you and greatly appreciated. I feel a little more confident about things, but…" Dr. Luft shook her head. "I don't know. I just thought I'd be better at the whole interaction thing by now. What do you think?"

"About?"

"How I'm doing?"

Dani let out a hesitant chuckle. "I'm not sure I'm the best person to ask."

"Why not? You've always been brutally honest before."

"Yes, well, I'm trying to not be so brutal these days."

They stopped outside Jacob's door.

"That doesn't make me hopeful," she whispered.

"Luft, it's your career. Please don't base it on something I do or don't say."

"Who, then?" Her eyes were all shiny and pleading.

"Yourself."

She sucked in a deep breath and nodded. "I'm taking point?" Her voice went up on the end.

"Are you asking me or telling me?"

"Telling you?"

"Luft." Dani sighed.

"Okay, okay, telling you."

"That's better, but remember who you're dealing with—a concerned parent. You're not there to dictate."

She nodded again. "Got it."

Jacob's door was partially open. Dani pushed it further. Sheri looked up as they entered, and Jacob did his best to sit up and smile. "Doc D."

"Good morning."

"How you doing today, J?" Dr. Luft asked.

Jacob looked the other doctor's way. "Better than yesterday, I think."

Dr. Luft grinned. "Good, but you know the drill. We have to check you out anyway."

"I know. It's all good."

Quietly, Sheri stood and adjusted the pillows behind her son's back. She smiled as she helped him to get more comfortable.

Dani checked his vitals, his latest labs, and everything else in between while Sheri watched over them silently. Meeting her gaze a few times, Dani got what she expected—an unreadable mask—but the coldness toward her seemed to be lacking.

"Mrs. Cook, when we're done here, I'd like to give you latest breakdown on Jacob's condition," Dr. Luft informed her.

Sheri nodded once and turned her gaze toward her son.

"Ma, it's okay—they're gonna take that thing out and take good care of me."

The relief that washed over Dani was powerful enough to almost knock her over. She looked from mother to son and back again. Sheri's eyes were no longer unreadable. They were full of fear and resignation.

"He's right," Dani said. "We will."

Sheri's lips trembled. "Okay."

Dr. Luft clapped her hands. Dani turned to her and glared. She smiled sheepishly. "That's good news. Mrs. Cook, do you have any questions?"

She shook her head. "Not right now. No."

"What about you, J?" Dr. Luft asked.

"I'm gonna wake up and be fixed?" Jacob sounded so excited.

"You are, and with a little more chemo, you'll be good to go and just be a kid again," Dr. Luft said.

Sheri stared at Dr. Luft. Her mouth opened, but she didn't say anything.

"Okay, we'll get out of the way. Get some rest, Jacob. We'll see you this afternoon."

Jacob beamed. "Okay, Doc D."

Dani threw one last glance Sheri's way, but she was focused completely on her son—as it should be. They left the room.

"Wooo, that wasn't so bad." Luft clapped her hands again. "Things are a lot easier when parents use some common sense."

Staring at her, Dani was at a loss of words for all of three seconds. "Let me give you some honesty."

Her eyes widened.

"Being judgmental toward others who are scared and sometimes hopeless can seep through when talking to them." It was hard to keep the anger out of her voice, but she did because she wanted her to really listen. "Check your personal opinions about people at the door. I think it will give you a chance at being a better doctor."

Dr. Luft looked down at her feet then back up again. "You know, right now I can really understand why a lot of the residents don't like you."

Shocked by her words, Dani reexamined what she'd said and how she said it. She wasn't scathing or condescending. She'd asked for her opinion and after her statement, Dr. Luft's difficulties made sense. "No, you're not going to put this back on me. You're responsible for your own behavior. Think about what you just said."

Luft's face reddened. "I... Okay. Yeah, maybe that was a little inappropriate." She looked everywhere except at Dani. "Sorry, I'd better go."

"Good idea. We'll see where your head is in the morning."

She nodded and walked away.

Dani watched her go.

Her pocket vibrated. Automatically, she reached for her phone. It was a notification, reminding her of her therapy appointment in fifteen minutes. Knowing that paved the way for a whole different type of relief to settle onto her shoulders. Hopefully, in time, Peppermint Patti could help her see the light at the end of the tunnel Dani was in.

Rebecca opened her eyes, and the contents of the toilet was the last thing she wanted to see. Using her elbows, she pushed herself up and away from the commode. There was no way she could throw up anymore. Nothing was left. The room swirled, and her stomach heaved. Rebecca groaned as she leaned over the toilet yet again.

"Shit, shit, shit." Rebecca's voice was husky and squeaky. Slowly, she reached up and flushed. Rebecca wiped at her forehead. Her hand came away wet even though she had the chills. Moving more cautiously, she sat on her ass and scooted backward against the wall.

When she'd gotten up this morning, feeling achy, nauseous, shaky, and like her head was three times its size, Rebecca convinced herself that a Coke would settled her stomach. She'd been so fucking wrong. At least it had helped her scratchy throat for a hot minute. She leaned her head back and closed her eyes. When she opened them again, Peyton was in the doorway. She meowed loudly.

"I know…I know you're hungry." Rebecca swallowed. The thought of any type of food item almost made her puke again. "But it's gonna be a while."

Peyton meowed again and trotted inside. She rubbed her face against Rebecca's bare feet and then climbed into her lap, purring like a fine-tuned engine. Rebecca glanced down at her. "Am I dyin'? That's why you're bein' so nice to me?"

The cat blinked, and Rebecca blinked back. She sat there for several more minutes and then decided to try getting up again. She pushed Peyton out of the way and took some deep breaths, before using the wall to help herself stand. The bathroom tilted and went gray for a few seconds before coming back into focus.

"Whoa." Since the wall had gotten her this far, Rebecca made sure she had some kind of contact with it as she finally left the bathroom and hauled her ass down the hall toward the kitchen, where her phone and Peyton's breakfast was waiting. She got to her cell first and dialed Mark's number.

"What's up? Guess what I found at the gas station just now?"

Rebecca tried to clear her throat, but it still felt like something was in there.

"A Coke with your name on it. I bought it just so I could see you roll your eyes while you sucked it down," Mark continued as if she'd told him to. "Hello?"

"Mark?" Her voice was the same.

"Why does it sound like you've smoked a whole pack of cigarettes?"

"Sick."

"Oh, damn. You're not coming in, are you?"

"No."

"God, you sound like death. I'm gonna come check on you."

Rebecca gazed down at the floor. It looked really good right about now. "No, jus—" She licked her lips. "I'll be fine."

"Uh-huh, I'm sure. I'm not coming for *you*. It's for my own peace of mind. Now, I could either call you every hour or so to make sure you're still living or I can come see for myself." He paused. "I'm still gonna call, just to let you know, but just not as often."

She didn't have the energy. "Yeah, whatever." Rebecca hung up the phone and realized she'd have to get to the front door at least to unlock it. She groaned. The wall was fast becoming her best friend.

When the doorbell rang later, Rebecca said, "Come in," as loud as she could. She leaned heavily on the back of the couch, using it as a guide to get her to the front of it. Mark let himself in. Apparently, he'd heard her. Rebecca swayed when she got to the couch arm, but suddenly Mark was there.

"Careful." He put an arm around her waist. "Go slow." Mark helped her sit down and took the seat beside her.

She eased back against the cushion. "Probably contagious."

"I hardly ever get sick, so it's fine."

Neither did she.

"Jesus, Becca, I know you had a little headache last night, and it turned into this?" He stared at her and shook his head. "You look like the walking dead. You looked in the mirror, right?"

Rebecca tried to nod, but she was sure her head was going to fall off.

"Okay, I'm gonna get you to bed and throw some things together that'll help you get through the day. You have soup?"

She made a face and smacked her lips.

"Oh, it's like that. Broth, Gatorade, and water for you, then."

Rebecca made another face. "Don't have Gatorade."

"I'll go to the store once I get you situated."

"Feed Peyton," she added.

"I will."

"Hey."

Rebecca jolted awake to see Mark leaning over her. "Yeah?."

"Okay. Got lozenges for the throat. Advil for the fever. Crackers for the nausea, and plenty of liquids. Forget the broth. It's nasty anyway." He pointed to her nightstand and then at the trash can sitting beside it. She looked toward it blearily. "In case you get sick. Now, I need the code to your phone."

"134900." She didn't hesitate.

"I'm gonna text Benz and then Rick in case I end up working late."

"Don't text...Dani."

He looked up at her. "I wasn't going to, but are you sure?"

Rebecca sucked in a breath as tears stung her eyes. She was being a bit overdramatic, but she was too exhausted to wrangle her emotions for the moment. Hell, maybe this whole situation was what had made her sick. "Yeah, I'm sure."

"Okay, then." He held up her phone. "Let me finish this and then we'll get you some meds. You have two days to get over this. I don't care which house you go to for Thanksgiving, but you're not sitting alone at home with that creepy cat. You hear me?"

She nodded once and almost teared up again. God, Rebecca hated being sick.

The second time Dani stepped into Jacob's room, she wasn't shocked to see him sleeping. Sheri wasn't there, but she could hear running water coming from the bathroom. A few seconds later, the bathroom door opened. Dani looked up to see Sheri wiping her eyes with tissue. They were red rimmed like she'd been crying.

"I can come back later," Dani said softly.

Sheri shook her head and sniffed. She met Dani's gaze, and suddenly Sheri's tears were falling in earnest. They both glanced at the bed. Jacob hadn't batted an eye. Dani touched Sheri's shoulder. "Come with me. I'll make sure someone checks in on him."

Nodding, Sheri followed her.

Dani stopped at the nurses station to do what she'd promised. Then she ushered Sheri into the nearest empty room. Dani grabbed a box of Kleenex and gave it to Sheri, then encouraged her to sit.

"It must be strange seeing me like this." Sheri looked at her.

"Your son is sick. There's nothing strange about being emotional."

Sheri laughed, but her expression was sad and somehow angry. "You don't understand. This is my fault."

"What do you mean?"

"Jacob being sick."

"I've seen many parents blame themselves, but you can't control genetics. You had nothing to do with his tumor."

Sheri shook her head. "It didn't have to be this bad."

"His prognosis is very good, Sheri."

"But he has to have surgery." Her tears started again. "That's what the doctor said about his father too. His prognosis was good." Sheri covered her mouth with her hand as she continued to cry. She pulled her hand away. "It's my fault. The tumor could have been found earlier."

Dani kneeled in front of her and waited. Sheri seemed to have a lot more to say.

"After his father died, I worked. I put everything into that job. It was the only thing that kept me busy and kept my mind right. Jacob came to me. His stomach was always hurting. He wasn't eating much, and he slept all the time. I thought he was just still upset about his father and trying to get attention. One morning he woke up, and he was so swollen I knew something was really wrong. All that time, I should have been focusing on him. Oh, God…" Sheri leaned forward and pressed her face into her hands.

It took a moment for Dani to digest everything she'd heard, and when she finished, Dani was slightly nauseated out of sheer empathy. She moved toward Sheri and pulled her hands away from her face. "You have an amazing child who is going to grow up healthy and strong. I can't imagine the fear you're feeling, but you are doing the right thing. Every precaution will be taken."

Sheri met Dani's gaze. "I wanna believe you."

"Please try. It's okay to be scared, but you have to believe too."

Sheri nodded, and then the most remarkable thing happened—she hugged Dani. Swallowing down the tears clogging the back of her throat, Dani hugged her back. "It'll be okay." She said the words with conviction, but inside, Dani was shaken.

While Sheri's experience wasn't exactly like her own, there were some parallels. Out of her own fear, she was pretty much planning to put her life on hold until after fellowship training. Becca wasn't going to wait for her. No sane person would. Dani had always wanted to be a doctor as far back as she could remember, but looking at who she had become, all she'd done, and what she'd lost, Dani wondered if it was worth all the sacrifice.

Sheri squeezed her tight, and part of Dani screamed yes, based on this outcome and many like it. The other part whispered emphatically that cutting herself off from the rest of the world had never done her any favors in any of her private relationships. No. It was time for her own life to be just as important too, and Becca factored into that life somehow. Dani was certain. "It'll be okay," she repeated.

Rebecca whimpered and tried to reach around and swat away whoever's hand was on her shoulder, shaking her awake. They never stopped, so she obviously hadn't succeeded. Slowly, she rolled over on her back, moving her head separately. Any sudden movements and it was going to fall the hell off. The Advil she'd taken when Mark was here had helped earlier, but now it felt like she hadn't taken anything at all.

In an effort to open her eyes, Rebecca blinked. The light, wherever it was coming from, was blinding and sent a bolt of pain right through her eye sockets. So, she kept them closed and ended up drifting again.

"Becca, c'mon, try to sit up and open. You need more fluids and somethin' for your fever. I'm gonna give you Tamiflu too."

She waved Rick away. Maybe if she slept a little longer, she'd have the energy to do all that. Rebecca had to practically crawl to the bathroom earlier, which used up every bit of her reserves.

"I forgot how shitty a patient you are. I guess I'm gonna have to treat you like a rag doll."

Rebecca moaned as he slid his hands under her armpits. At least he was gentle. He shifted her this way and that. He pressed something against her lips. She opened slightly, then drank deeply from the bottle put there a few seconds later.

Rebecca blinked again and opened her eyes just a little to see Rick hovering over her with a mask covering his nose and mouth. "Dyin'?" she croaked.

"Don't be so dramatic. You're young and strong, but you more than likely have the flu. I don't know where you got it from. I love you and everythin', but you're not givin' it to me."

Her mind was sluggish, but she remembered the man with the fake kid and fake story. He'd obviously looked like death for a reason. Sleep pulled at her again. Rick talked to her, but his voice was muffled like it was far away. Her bedroom door closed, but the sound mingled with the others.

She heard another voice, a familiar female one. Rebecca tried to listen but gave up a few seconds later. Maybe her fever was worse than Rick thought, because she could have sworn she heard Dani.

CHAPTER 26

A COUGHING JAG PULLED REBECCA out of sleep. It felt like someone had her lungs in a vice grip. Unable to breathe properly, she did her best to sit up so that she could suck in some air. A hand touched her back, rubbing in large, soothing circles. Rebecca leaned into it. Even with her clogged nose, she caught a whiff of Midnight Pomegranate body spray, Dani's favorite, which had to be all in her head.

"Mucinex will help that cough and make it more productive."

Rebecca's eyes snapped open, and she scrambled away even though her achy body yelled in protest. She grabbed her head and moaned. Trying to relieve the pain, she squinted. No matter how she looked at it, Dani still sat on her bed. "Wh…what?"

"What am I doing here?"

Still holding her head up, Rebecca nodded slightly.

"You have the flu, and until you get past the initial stages where you feel like utter crap, it's best that someone check on you."

"Why?" Rebecca croaked.

With a gloved hand, Dani pushed her back against the bed. "You don't take care of yourself when you're sick, and because I wanted to."

All kinds of warmth shot through Rebecca. Made her think her fever was back. She stared at Dani as she eased back against the mattress. Her hair was loose and wavy around her shoulders, and her glasses looked askew. Her eyes were clear, soft, concerned, and focused only on her. Rebecca's fever had to be back. "Dyin'."

Dani smiled. "No, you're not."

"I am. Don't lie."

This time, Dani laughed. "I've seen worse cases in the ER. You're gonna be okay. I promise."

Rebecca noticed the face mask dangling around Dani's neck. She pointed at it. "Put it on."

Dani did. "I had the flu shot this year, and I started taking Tamiflu. Better?"

"Yea—" Rebecca broke into another coughing fit. When it was over, she looked around her bedroom. She had no idea what time it was, only that it was dark and one of her lamps was on. "Rick?"

"He switched shifts. He's working overnight so he can come stay with you during the day."

She felt strangely guilty and taken care of at the same time.

"I'll run to the store and get something more appropriate to treat your symptoms."

"Mucinex?" Rebecca repeated.

Dani nodded and stood. "And a couple of other things."

She tried really hard to keep her eyes open because she had a question to ask. "Aren't you mad at me?"

She was met with silence as Dani looked down at her.

Maybe she could have asked that a different way or something else entirely, but she didn't have the mental energy to use a filter.

"No, I'm more mad at myself." Dani paused. "Get some rest. We'll talk when you're feeling better."

Rebecca didn't know what that first part meant, but even as she drifted, she knew she had to find out.

Dani was awakened by the weight on her chest and loud purring. She blinked her eyes open. Peyton looked down at her and licked her paws. Dani froze and stared at the cat. She wasn't at all sure about her. "Nice kitty. I know I'm in your room, but you've got to learn to share." Dani had seen the cat tree by the window, but there was also an empty, ready-made bed.

Peyton stopped grooming herself and looked at Dani unblinkingly.

She tensed, ready to bolt from the bed at first sight of an extended claw or a hiss.

Peyton inched forward and purred louder than before, which made Dani relax slightly.

"Oh God." She sucked in a breath as Peyton pressed her nose against Dani's chin. Then, the sandpaper-like consistency of her tongue licking her face eased all of Dani's fears. Going on instinct, she reached up and petted the cat, who burrowed into her neck. Dani smiled. "You know I'm taking care of your mama. Don't you?"

Sitting up, Dani brought the cat with her, still curled around her neck. "You seemed creepy at first, but you haven't given me any trouble at all, even though you've seen me at my worst." She glanced at her phone. It was a little after six. "Good alarm clock too." Dani slowly stood. Peyton detached herself and jumped to the floor. She looked up at Dani and meowed loudly.

"I'm up. Thanks."

Peyton turned away and sashayed toward the door. She turned and meowed again. Suspicious, Dani glanced at her. "Did you do all that because it's time to eat?"

The cat swished her tail and meowed again before walking out in the hallway.

"Or...?" Panic seized Dani. Maybe the cat had woken her up because something was wrong with Becca. Moving quickly, Dani made her way down the hallway until she got to Becca's room. The door was open just like she'd left it. She peered at Becca's sleeping form, watching her chest rise and fall with only a modicum of difficulty. Becca's face looked dry, which meant her fever hadn't returned. Dani's shoulders sagged in relief. It was possible for the flu to have complications, but Becca was strong and otherwise healthy.

Unable to tear her eyes away, Dani leaned against the door and just watched. When she'd been in med school, Dani used to get up at the crack of dawn and do the exact same thing. Doing so gave her a measure of peace before the storm, so to speak. Right now, the sight settled her just the same. That feeling paved the way for something powerful to wash over her; in that moment, Dani knew she was doing the right thing, the only thing. She swallowed. That didn't mean she wasn't still scared. Becca deserved time and attention, and if they were going to give this relationship another try, Dani had to find a way to make things better and keep her own sanity while doing it.

They had a lot to talk about.

Peyton brushed against Dani's ankles and meowed once more. "Shhh." She glared at the cat. "You really did do all that for food, huh?" Peyton blinked slowly up at her, then she set off further down the hall. Halfway, she turned to Dani to see if she was following.

Dani rolled her eyes, "I'm coming." She paused. "After I shower and get dressed." She turned and pulled her T-shirt over her head.

Rick yawned as he opened the refrigerator. He took out a carton of orange juice and drank directly from it.

"She won't like that."

He wiped his mouth. "You gonna tell her?"

"I might."

Rick looked her up and down before smirking. "Uh-huh. Why are you here, again?"'

Dani leaned against the counter and looked up at him. "Cleveland. Remember?" For some reason, she laughed. It sounded shaky and nervous, which she was.

"Huh." He crossed his arms over his chest and stared at her curiously. "Yeah, Cleveland. It sure as hell wasn't easy, but somethin' big is happenin' isn't it?"

"Yes, I think so." Dani sucked in a breath. "It started a while back, but I think you being Cleveland was a good idea."

"It helped me a lot. Got me Northwestern and Sandra, but now I'm gonna need you to spill. For right now, just call me Hollywood. I'm up for anything.'"

"You sure?"

Rick nodded.

"Okay, but I'm not really sure how we got to this point. I was so angry with her, which somehow led to wanting her. Now, I can't seem to stay away. The last part happened more organically, I guess. We hit a lot of snags, but I hope we can get through them."

"Well, damn." He wrapped an arm around Dani and pulled her close. "Damn." Rick sucked in a deep breath and let it out slowly. "You sure about this?"

This was her life, and it was time for her to live all aspects of it. She'd had enough regret. "Yes, I am, and I want to be present this time. Do my part to make it work."

Rick smiled outright. "Then 'Ruswells' is official again."

Dani groaned. "No, please don't go there."

"Sorry. Have to."

The doorbell rang.

Dani pulled away from Rick. "I hope that doesn't wake her."

"Well, go answer it so whoever it is won't do it again."

She was already halfway across the kitchen. A minute later, she stared at the balding white man outside Becca's door. It had to be Mark. He was just as Becca had described him. Dani let him in.

"Happy Thanksgiving." He smiled as he stepped in the house. "My wife sent me to the store. Rick told me yesterday she was gonna be fine, but I decided to take a detour anyway."

Dani smiled back. "You must be Mark?"

"Yep, we met before, but I don't think you were paying much attention to me. Dani, am I right?"

Heat rushed Dani's face. Yes, she remembered almost everything about that night, but he was just a passing thought. She nodded and reached out a hand. "Nice to meet you, and happy Thanksgiving."

"Likewise. So, does our girl still think she's dying?"

Dani laughed and enjoyed the warmth that shot through her. Our girl. Becca had been talking to him. "As of last night, yes."

"It's a shame. Her first Thanksgiving back, and she's spending it in bed." He looked at her, and Dani suddenly felt like she was under a microscope. "But it's a good thing she's around the people she wants to be with."

Becca had been talking to him a lot.

Mark's gaze shifted to somewhere behind her. "Rick?"

"All day." Rick walked up beside Dani. He shook Mark's hand with gusto.

"Well, it's good to put some faces to the names. She talks about you two non-stop." Mark cut his eyes to Dani. "Especially you."

Rick snorted. "I'm hurt."

Dani elbowed him. He didn't even flinch.

"When she's feeling better, we should all get together. Get to know each other a little bit. I'll even invite the other guys. You might wanna pull your hair out five minutes later, but still."

Rick shrugged. "I'm good. Let's do it."

Dani looked up at him. "We should probably ask Becca about it first."

"She'll be…"

"She'll be…"

Rick and Mark said simultaneously.

A smile pulled at Dani's lips. "Fine with it?" she finished for them.

Mark and Rick glanced at each other and laughed.

Dani shook her head. "I'm going to go check on Becca again and then get to work. Mark, you should think about getting an antiviral so you won't get sick."

Not waiting for them to respond, Dani left the living room. She stood in Becca's doorway in almost the exact same place. Becca had turned over and was now facing the opposite wall. Disappointment grabbed hold of her.

Becca groaned and slowly switched to lying on her back. She coughed a couple times as she opened her eyes. When Becca finally met her gaze, Dani's heart clenched before nearly jumping out of her chest. Becca looked awful. Her eyes were puffy, and she wiped slobber from her mouth. Her hair stood up at weird angles. She should have wrapped Becca's hair in a scarf to preserve her hairstyle, but by the time Dani had gotten there, it was too late. Regardless, Dani was completely unaffected by it all—as was her heart. It continued to beat double time.

"Hey," Becca rasped. "I'm still alive."

"Good morning." Dani smiled and stepped deeper into the room.

Becca held up a hand and coughed. "You don't have on a mask or anythin'. Don't want you to get the kids sick."

Dani stopped. She was right. She shouldn't take chances even while on the Tamiflu. Becca would be contagious for a few more days. "Sorry, I wasn't thinking."

"Mmm." Becca stared at her. Her expression was pained but gentle. "Still wanna be here?"

"I do." Dani nodded.

"Why?" Becca asked softly.

"You asked me that already."

Becca lapsed into a coughing fit, and seconds later, Rick walked in with his mask and gloves in tow. "I'm here. I got her."

Dani really wanted to stay. She glanced at Becca, then at Rick.

"You're gonna be late."

Right now, Dani didn't care.

Rick sighed loudly and pushed her gently toward the hallway. "You can make googly eyes at her later. Hopefully, by the time you get here, she'll even look a little better."

Dani glared.

Rick smiled with his eyes.

"Fine. Tell her I'll call and check on her later."

"She heard you," Becca called out throatily, then immediately started coughing again.

"I'm gonna put Vicks VapoRub on the bottom of her feet. Clear all this right up." Rick crossed his arms over his chest.

"Oh my God, what is wrong with you?" Dani asked.

"Kiddin', unless you don't get outta here."

Dani backed away. "Okay, bye." When she turned, Dani ran right into Mark. "Oh, sorry."

"It's okay. I just wanted to poke my head in."

"Not without gloves and a mask. You walked right past them on the kitchen counter."

"Okay, I can do that." Mark followed her back to the kitchen. "She's gonna be fine, right?" he asked again.

Dani smiled. He really cared about her. "Yes, she is."

Rebecca woke up slowly and tried her best to take a deep breath, but she wasn't quite able. "Shit."

"Your breathing isn't as bad as it could be. Trust me." Dani's voice was slightly muffled through her mask, but she was still understandable.

"I can't tell."

Dani held up a finger as she finished writing in the notebook in her lap. "My stethoscope tells me so."

Rebecca didn't really feel any better, but with Rick's help earlier, she felt cleaner. She turned toward Dani, who was sitting in a folding chair on the other side of the bedroom. Rebecca was pretty sure Dani didn't have to camp out in her room, but nonetheless, she was glad she was. She had a ton of questions, but it seemed every time Rebecca tried to ask, they were interrupted or Dani stopped the conversation altogether. Dani being here meant something. It meant a lot, but she wanted to hear her say it. She wanted to hear that Dani understood. Maybe Rebecca needed to do this a different way.

Dani closed her notebook.

"You workin' on patient stuff?"

"No." Dani looked away. "I was making a list." She recapped her pen. "It's important, so I wanted to do it the old-fashioned way."

"I really regret not puttin' a TV in here, especially since I'm stuck for a while." Rebecca tried to stave off a coughing fit, but she didn't succeed. It only lasted for a few seconds. She sucked in a breath. "Readin' your grocery list would be interestin'."

Dani's face flushed. "That's not what it is."

"Don't care what it is."

"Becca…"

"Please?" God, she sounded pitiful. She hated being sick.

Dani met her gaze. Her eyes were wide and panicked. Her face was redder than it had been a second ago.

"If it's that personal, then—" Rebecca suddenly felt like an ass.

"It is, but I was trying to wait until you felt better before talking to you about it."

"I wanna talk now."

Dani opened her notebook. She glanced at Rebecca and released a shaky breath before looking down. "Call her everyday no matter how busy I get." Dani cleared her throat. "Call her and let her know I'm going to be late as soon as I find out. Switch with someone once a month so I'll have at least thirty-six hours or more to spend with her all at once. Take her to Samuel L. Jackson's movies as soon as they open. Meet her friends because they're family…" Dani read on.

Rebecca couldn't breathe, and it had nothing to do with her being sick. For a minute, she didn't think any of this was real, which made it all the more powerful. To know that Dani was trying and making plans were actions that spoke a hell of lot louder than any words, but Rebecca was greedy. She wanted it all.

"That's all I have so far."

Their eyes met, and even with Dani's stupid mask on, Rebecca was mesmerized by what she saw. Sadness, happiness, and fear. Rebecca opened her mouth to speak, but thought better of it. She needed to wait and let Dani have her say. Tiredness tugged at her, but she beat it back. Her energy level was a little better tonight, but not by much.

"You were right. I knew I hurt you. I didn't know how much until you left, and I wasn't ready to face it. I don't want to do that to you again. I don't want you to do it to me. If we try this..." Dani sucked in a breath. "Whatever this... Whatever we turn into, I want to be present for it. I need to be. It can't be like it was before."

Rebecca nodded.

"You deserve better. We deserve better."

She nodded some more and started to cough. Seconds later, Dani was on the bed rubbing her back. When it was over, Rebecca turned to look at her.

Dani's chest heaved, and her eyes were shiny. "I'm scared and nervous, but this is bigger than all that." She waved a gloved hand between them. "Can you please say something now?"

Rebecca said the first thing to come to mind. "I really wish I could kiss you right now."

Dani made a sound. It was somewhere between a sob and a laugh. She moved closer, wrapping her arms around Rebecca from behind.

Some missing piece slid home for Rebecca and locked itself in place. She caressed Dani's forearms. Feeling goosebumps rise made her smile. Not wanting to but knowing she had to, Rebecca untangled herself. "Contagious," she whispered. "But I won't be in four days."

"Four more days." Dani's eyes burned her.

"Then I can touch you the way I want." The air around them flared to life with all kinds of heat. Smothering the energy between them was no longer an option. It was time to let it rage.

Dani swallowed. It was loud. "Yes."

Yes. That word was Rebecca's favorite. Right behind the phrase, "I want to be present."

CHAPTER 27

As she walked away from the nurses station, Dani's pocket vibrated. She fished out her phone to see Becca's name flashing back at her. Despite a pang of concern, she smiled as she answered, "What are you doing up? It's almost three a.m."

"Couldn't sleep." Becca shifted around in bed, rustling the covers. "You got a minute?"

Dani made her way down the hall toward the on-call rooms. "I can give you more than that."

"I know you're busy."

"I am, but it's you. And even though it's been a week since you got sick, you're not at a hundred percent yet." It was amazing how those words just fell from Dani's lips.

"I'm fine. The Delsym works wonders for my cough. I got a lot done today, and I'm definitely going to work on Monday."

"I guess how you do at Mark's this afternoon will help you see if that's possible."

"Mmm, maybe. You comin' over after work?"

"I was planning on going home to get a few hours' sleep."

"You can sleep here." Becca's tone was suggestive but light.

Dani tried to push away a flash of doubt to make room for the shiver Becca's words caused. Maybe all of this was just for sex. She closed her eyes, knowing that didn't make sense, but something still lingered inside her. "This is too easy. Us, I mean. That doesn't scare you?"

"Things don't have to be hard. You know that, right? I take it as a good sign. Means we're not forcin' the issue. It's natural... We're natural."

Becca sounded so sure. She wanted, needed, to believe her. "I know, and I hear you."

"You don't sound irritated to hear from me."

"Wait. What?" Dani wanted to understand where Becca was coming from with that statement.

"I mean when we were together before. Sometimes when I called, you sounded aggravated."

"I did?"

"Yeah, but I could tell you were happy to hear from me today. You were smilin'."

Dani smiled once more. "Maybe."

"There it is again. So, what does Peppermint Patti think about us?" Becca asked.

"I won't see her until next week. She's on vacation."

"You made some pretty big choices."

"I did, and despite me being a little wishy washy they felt...feel right." Dani had to slam that point home. "I'm about to make another one right now."

"What's that?"

"I'll come over after work."

"Well, good. You have three bedrooms to choose from."

"Including yours, huh?" Dani asked playfully.

"Oh yeah." Becca cleared her throat. "Trust me, I'm not tryin' to charm you into it, but maybe touchin' you, bein' inside you, will get rid of those doubts and convince that part of you that we really do feel right."

Dani bit her bottom lip. "Is that right?"

"Yeah, maybe that's why you wouldn't let me touch you before."

She let the words seep into her. "You could be right." Dani looked down at her lap. "I'm sorr—"

"I know you are, but I think about it all the time. The way you just... mmm. I couldn't have said no even if I wanted to. Sex between us has always been good, but that was next level."

Dani's stomach clenched as heat invaded her. She licked suddenly dry lips. "Yes."

Becca exhaled noisily. "Yes, what?"

"Becca." Dani's nipples hardened to tingling points.

"You gonna answer me?" Becca's tone was soft, deep, and raspy.

The door to the on-call room burst open. Two people laughed as they almost fell inside.

"Excuse me?" Dani said loudly, as though it wasn't her fault that she hadn't locked the door.

"Oh God, sorry!" They backed away quickly.

Becca chuckled. "Whatever room you decide to pick, I'll see you in a few hours."

"You'll probably be sleeping." Saying those words didn't squash Dani's level of excitement.

"You know where the spare key is. Wake me up. "

The warm touch fluttering underneath her T-shirt and over her stomach jolted Dani awake. "Wha…?"

"Told you to wake me," Becca whispered directly into Dani's ear, which resulted in a hard shiver.

Becca's hand skimmed the edges of Dani's pajama pants before shifting upward again between her breasts. Dani whimpered. "You needed your rest for Mark's party."

"Maybe. Is that why you didn't come to my room?" Becca covered a breast, kneading it firmly before pulling at Dani's nipple.

Dani hissed and arched into the touch. "Becca."

She bit into Dani's shoulder, causing a massive chain reaction of sensations that settled firmly between Dani's legs.

Becca tugged at her T-shirt, inching it upward. Dani wrestled to be free of it. When Becca pressed against her, Dani moaned hoarsely and then froze at the feel of Becca naked against her.

"We can stop." Becca's breathing was ragged, but she kissed Dani's ear gently. Then she slowly removed her hand.

Dani grabbed her arm. "I want this." She did, but Dani had no idea if her mind was going to rebel on her when her body was at its most pliant.

"I'll try to go slow, but Dani, I don't know if…" Becca pulled her arm away and grasped Dani by the hips, thrusting against her from behind. Becca whimpered, and the sound, along with her movements, cut through Dani, leaving her fiercely aroused.

She reached back, grabbing Becca's ass and encouraging the urgent movement. Her breathing stuttered as Becca increased the force of her thrusts.

Becca pulled at the waist of her pajama bottoms. "Can I take them off?"

For some reason, Becca asking permission was the sexiest thing she'd ever heard. "Yes."

Leisurely, Becca pulled the pants down her hips. Dani wiggled in an effort to move them lower. Becca's breath washed over her face, and she turned toward it. She reached back, tangling a hand in Becca's hair, and pulled her forward.

Their lips met, and everything else was forgotten. Becca's kiss was desperate, thirsty, and utterly messy. Becca moaned into her mouth when their tongues touched. Her hand slid between Dani's thighs, cupping her, and Dani's sense of urgency careened upward. She pushed at her remaining clothing and kicked them away from her legs.

Feeling Becca completely naked against her made Dani cry out. She ripped her mouth away and tried to breathe. Becca's hands squeezed teasingly, and in one smooth motion, she was back at Dani's breast, tugging and pulling on her nipple.

"Becca! Fuck!" She slammed her eyes closed and tried her best to hold on as jagged light flashed behind her eyelids.

So much for slow, but Dani was more than okay with it.

"Hands and knees." Becca whispered the words in Dani's ear.

Her world tilted, and she nearly fell off it. Dani needed to see her and look her in the eyes. She turned over on her back. When their gazes met, Dani knew for a fact that Becca had been right. Her doubts were invalid.

Becca looked at her as if her world had shifted too. Her eyes were dark and so full of awe. Her face was flushed. Her mouth swollen and wet.

Dani reached up, trailing her fingertips down Becca's cheek. Becca closed her eyes, following the touch, and when she opened them, Dani had already reared up, pulling her into a kiss that made everything right side up again.

Minutes later, Becca ended the kiss and pressed her forehead into Dani's. Then she scooted back, giving Dani room to move. Finally, Dani did as she was told. She trembled on the inside, but it traveled outward quickly. Becca obviously had plans, and she was sure it involved leaving her a quivering mess.

Dani turned her head to the side and wrapped her arms around a pillow. The rest of her body was held up by her knees. She spread them as wide as she could. For a second, there was nothing, no touch and hardly any sound over her own ragged breathing. Had she dreamt it all? It wouldn't be the first time. Maybe Becca had gotten into her head somehow and saw what she wanted, needed.

Becca's hands slid over the curve of her ass.

Dani gasped.

Her hands moved downward, parting Dani's cheeks and pulling her open. Her thumbs brushed against Dani's swollen labia. Her body bucked, and something inside her snapped. She reached between her own legs, rubbing her clit furiously.

"Please! Becc—"

Before she could finish, Becca moaned as her fingers sank into Dani.

Dani screamed. One, two, three deep, twisting thrusts, and her body was ripping itself apart. Becca's arm wrapped around her torso, bringing them together from behind. Dani's hips undulated wildly as orgasm rolled through her. "Don't stop. Oh, God!"

Becca listened.

Rebecca could still taste herself on Dani's tongue. She sucked on it, and Dani's hips twitched. Rebecca walked her hands down Dani's back and grasped her hips, urging Dani into a soft grind. Gasping, Dani whispered, "I can't."

She squeezed Dani's ass and thrusted harder.

"Jesus!" Dani's gasp became a moan.

"I did again. So can you, and I'm the one recoverin'."

"I know," Dani whined. "But I just need to sleep for a little while. Maybe we'll have time before Mark's. What time is it?"

Rebecca reached toward the nightstand for the phone she'd brought with her. "Ugh, we have to leave in about two hours."

Dani whimpered and pushed playfully at Rebecca's shoulder.

She chuckled. "That leaves you with an hour and half. We can be fashionably late."

Dani gave her a bleary eyed stare. "You're going to let me sleep?"

Rebecca brushed sweat soaked strands of dark hair off Dani's forehead. "Promise."

Dani gave a goofy smile. "When we get back, we can go for round fifty-seven." She flopped over to the empty side of the bed.

Pushing up on her elbow, Rebecca looked down at Dani and snorted. Dani's eyes were already closing. She studied her, comparing the way this Dani looked spent to the one she'd known years ago. There was no competition. In their core, the women were the same, but the layers were different.

Rebecca let go of the past. With all she had in her life now, it was as easy as breathing. She took a deep breath and promptly started to cough.

Dani's eyes popped open.

Rebecca laughed.

Dani groaned and turned away from her, but she didn't resist when Rebecca pulled her into her arms.

Seeing Rick drive up just as they were getting out of her car, Rebecca waved as he and Sandra closed their car doors and turned toward them. She stopped waving. "What the hell?"

Dani bent over laughing. Rebecca continued to stare at Rick as he walked closer. His eyes were bright with amusement. Sandra reached out a hand introducing herself. "I'm Sandra, by the way. Don't ask me anything about what he's doing because I don't know." She nodded in Dani's direction as Rebecca shook Sandra's hand.

"I'm Rebecca. Nice to finally meet you." She glanced at Sandra, but her gaze gravitated back to Rick. "Why do you have that stupid mask on?"

Rick shrugged. "I didn't think you'd recognize me otherwise."

Dani laughed even harder.

"Why do you have to be so extra?" Rebecca glared, but she was finding it hard to keep a straight face, especially with Dani cackling away in her ear.

Rick took off his face mask. His smile was huge. "I like to keep things interestin'."

Sandra sighed and rolled her eyes. Regardless of her slight coldness toward Dani, Rebecca liked her already.

"Well, you're gonna fit right in with these guys," Rebecca said.

"Sooo, you're sayin' I should keep the mask?"

Rebecca snatched it out of Rick's hand. Dani snorted. Rick stared at them, especially at their linked hands. He smirked. "Don't y'all look fresh like daisies. Hope y'all didn't scare poor Peyton too much."

She pressed her lips together, but her smile broke through. "Shut up. We're late." Rebecca glanced at Dani. She couldn't help herself. The happiness in her eyes overtook the exhaustion she could see there as well. Apparently, the feeling was as contagious as her flu had been. It seeped through her cell by cell.

Without warning, Dani leaned forward and kissed her.

"Awww, God, I'm glad to see that, but I'm tellin' you, we need to contact Shonda. We could make her a rich woman."

Rebecca walked toward Mark's porch. "She's already rich," she called over her shoulder.

"Richer. You know what I meant."

She didn't respond, choosing to ring the doorbell instead. A few seconds later, it opened and Emmet enveloped Rebecca in a hug, along with the smell of Axe body spray. She stood stiffly at first but then raised her arm, hugging him back. Just as quickly as the embrace started, it ended. Emmet moved away. "Hey! It's been weird without you. Feeling better?"

Rebecca cleared her throat. "Hey, Emmet. Yeah, I am."

His smile was big, goofy and one hundred percent genuine. "Oh, sorry, I wasn't trying to be rude. I'm Emmet. Nice to meet you."

Dani stepped closer to Rebecca again and accepted his handshake. "You too. I'm Dani."

Rebecca wrapped her arm around Dani's waist. "You gonna let us in?"

Emmet's eyes widened. "You're gay?" He smiled again.

Her mouth twitched. "Bisexual." Rebecca aimed her thumb over her shoulder. "That asshole back there is Rick, and the woman is his lovely girlfriend Sandra."

Emmet waved and moved aside, letting everybody in.

The smells of home hit her square in the face—cooking food, air freshener, and cleaning products. Rebecca headed straight for the kitchen, pulling Dani along with her. Feeling Dani's eyes on her, she met her gaze. "What?" she asked softly.

"You look happy."

"I am." Rebecca grinned.

Rick sighed loudly and moved around them, bringing Sandra with him. He smiled as he looked over his shoulder. "I'm starvin'. My stomach is practically yellin' at me."

"Ignore him and his hypoglycemia," Dani muttered.

"I already am," Rebecca said.

As they got closer to the kitchen, Alvin made his way out. "Wells, you don't seem like the type of woman to be late to her own party." His eyes twinkled. "Good to see you, though."

"Alvin," Rebecca grumbled. "Leavin' already?"

He chuckled. "Don't sound so broken up."

Rebecca grinned. "Can't help it."

"Uh-huh, well, it's my weekend, but did you know there's a woman draped all over you? Never felt any lesbian vibes comin' from you. Damn, I'm sorry I'm gonna miss the show." Alvin paused. "Who is this, by the way?"

He just had to be an ass. Rebecca opened her mouth.

"*This* would be Dr. Russell," Dani said, beating her to the punch. "But you can call me Dani."

"Oh, feisty. That figures. Good to meet you." Alvin smiled. " I already met your Rick. Interesting crowd."

"I agree totally."

"Okay, maybe we'll be able to dance around each other some other time." Surprisingly, he stepped closer, pulling Rebecca into an awkward hug. "Gotta go."

She patted him on the back. He pulled away seconds later and left.

Rebecca blinked.

"That was nice. I think," Dani said.

"Yeah, maybe." Rebecca smiled. She was sure he'd left her guessing on purpose.

An unfamiliar laugh pulled Rebecca back toward the kitchen. When they walked in, Lieutenant Benz was the last person she expected to see. Wasn't it weird for authority figures to mingle with the peons? Apparently,

Benz hadn't gotten the memo. She clinked her glass with Mark's and laughed again at something he said.

"Who's that?" Dani asked.

"My Lieutenant."

"Oh, you have an Olivia Benson."

"I guess I probably do," Rebecca agreed.

Mark looked up. He smiled and waved them over.

Lieutenant Benz downed the rest of her drink. "So, Wells, here we are. Everyone is buzzing about you. Turns out you're a talker when you need to be." She raised her empty glass toward Rebecca. "Perfect fit." Benz turned her gaze toward Dani. "Now don't be rude. Introduce your guest."

Rebecca scraped her fork across her plate. She'd eaten way too much and would probably regret it later. She looked around. Rick laughed at something Emmet said. Mark smiled down at his daughter, and Sheila eyed them both affectionately before turning back to her conversation with the Lieutenant. While Dani and Sandra had been talking earlier, they weren't now. Sandra drained her wine glass and reached for the bottle.

Dani slumped against Rebecca, who put her arm over Dani's shoulders and pulled her closer.

"You still with me?" Rebecca asked.

"Mmm, trying."

Rebecca kissed her on the side of the head. "We'll go back to my place soon. Round fifty-seven, remember?"

Dani smiled sleepily. "I remember."

Looking up, Rebecca caught Rick watching them. He smiled. Rebecca smiled back and took in everything and everyone around her once more. She had something old and something new, but it was all precious.

She was where she needed to be—home, starting again.

As Morning Report ended, Dani slipped out quietly. She could usually be patient, but not today. She pulled the door open to the stairwell and took the stairs down, two at a time. Dani should have been meeting with her team to start morning rounds, but this was more important. She could have waited and delivered the news with Dr. Meda and the rest of the team in tow, but Dani didn't want to. She had a vested interest in Jacob and Sheri. When she was just a flight of stairs away from the pediatric oncology wing, Dani started to smile and found that she couldn't stop.

With her iPad tucked into her side, she practically ran past the nurses station toward Jacob's room. Dani didn't bother to knock before swooping in. She stopped abruptly at the sight before her.

How could he be sleeping at a time like this?

Sheri pressed her finger to her lips but tilted her head slightly as she studied Dani. Then her eyes widened. Dani held up her iPad, pointed to it, and then waved her toward the hallway. With a smile still firmly planted on her face, Dani gave Jacob one last glance before stepping out. She could have woken him, but as a kid, he deserved the huge amount of attention he was about to get from his entire treatment team. After all that Jacob had been through, he needed the party. This moment was for his mother.

After pushing the door almost closed, Sheri stepped out into the hallway. She pressed a hand to her chest and stared at Dani. Her eyes remained wide, and her lips trembled. Sheri's gaze was so full of trust and hope that her eyes started to spill over. She wiped her tears away and smiled, transforming from a concerned mother to an ecstatic one. "It's good news."

Dani nodded and chuckled. "Yes—am I that obvious?"

"Well, I've never seen you smile like that."

"I could say the same," Dani responded. "Your face is going to hurt by the time I'm done. There was no lymph node involvement, and the histology of the tumor was favorable. We're sticking with the plan for a round of post-operative chemo, but other than that, he's a very lucky and incredible boy."

Sheri blinked rapidly. "What...what did you just say to me?"

Since it would probably be unprofessional to whoop like she was at a basketball game, Dani grinned and took a step closer to Sheri. She reached out and touched her arm. "He's going to be fi—"

"Shut up." Sheri closed the distance between them, engulfing Dani in a hug. She squeezed tight and whispered, "Just...thank you."

Dani sucked in a surprised breath and returned the hug with fervor. It would have been easy and expected to tell her "you're welcome," but the situation with this family went deeper than that. Dani thought of Becca, Rick, and who she, herself, had become.

Somehow, Sheri and Jacob had helped her break down the hard parts and realize that it was okay to be human, to feel just like everybody else. "Thank *you*."

EPILOGUE

"SANDRA'S RUNNIN' LATE," RICK ANNOUNCED. "She'll get here soon as she can. We might as well get started. What's our movie choices?"

"*Imitation of Life* or *The Hitman's Bodyguard*." Rebecca reached for her Coke.

"Wait. *Imitation of Life*? The first or second version?" Dani asked.

Rebecca turned toward Dani. It was really hard not to glare, so she didn't fight it.

Dani laughed as she stuck her hand in the huge bowl of popcorn on the coffee table. "So, the second version, then."

"I guess you know me after all." Rebecca grinned.

"I try." Dani's gaze smoldered. "Really hard sometimes."

"Ugh, will you two stop. I know what y'all are talkin' about. I'm a doctor, so I'm not stupid." Rick dug into the popcorn. "*The Hitman's Bodyguard,* that's with Samuel L. Jackson, right?"

"Yeah. Dani took me to see it when it was in theatres, but still."

"Well, you did that shit on purpose." He leaned away and stared at Rebecca.

"What are you talkin' about?"

"Who the hell wants to watch *Imitation of Life* and end up bawlin' like a baby and depressed at the end?" Rick asked.

"It has a good overall message," Rebecca shot back, but it was difficult to keep a straight face. "Plus it's my house and my TV, so I get some say in the choices."

"Whatever! I'm here visitin', so that should count for somethin'."

It did. Rebecca was happy as hell to see him, but when it came to movies....

Rick pointed his finger in Rebecca's face. "Besides, we've supported your Samuel L. Jackson obsession and even added to it, so don't even go there." He narrowed his eyes but grinned as well.

Dani brushed her lips against Rebecca's cheek and slid her arm into the crook of hers. "Just give it up."

"I'm puttin' our votes in for *The Hitman's Bodyguard*." Rick crossed his arms over his chest. "So you win."

"I knew I would." Rebecca bumped his shoulder.

"Well, you got the woman. All kinds of winnin' right there." Rick's voice was soft, and his expression even more so.

Rebecca turned toward Dani. "Yeah, I did." She leaned in for a kiss.

Rick stood and put in the Blu-ray.

Rebecca snagged some popcorn for herself. The bowl was already half gone. The good-natured bickering between them made Rebecca smile, but the bond between them was something she'd never take for granted again.

He sat back down and started looking around the living room. "Where's that crazy-ass cat of yours? Hidin' in a dark corner?"

"What? Don't talk about Peyton like that. She can be a real sweetie," Dani chimed in.

As if she'd heard her name, a series of meows started and got closer and louder with each one. Peyton sprinted into the living room and jumped onto Rebecca's lap. She meowed again and began purring like a freight train. Peyton rubbed herself against Rebecca and then jumped into Dani's lap to do the same.

"See? I told you." Dani stroked the cat's head.

A few seconds later, Peyton ended up in Rick's lap.

"Dani's right. She's mellowed out a little," Rebecca added.

"Maybe." Rick looked down at her. He raised his hand, and before he could even touch Peyton, she hissed at him. "Goddammit!" Rick pushed her off and pressed himself against the arm of the couch.

Rebecca laughed.

"Don't women go crazy for this Ryan Reynolds guy?" Rick asked about halfway through the movie.

"I feel the same way about Samuel L. Jackson," Rebecca said.

"I don't think you feel *exactly* the same." Rick leaned back and glanced at her.

"Eh, you're right. Probably not."

Rick shook his head slowly.

"Anybody want more popcorn?" Dani asked.

"Yeah, we should pop a couple more bags. I'll come help and get more drinks too." Rebecca jumped in before anyone could answer.

Dani grabbed the bowl, stood, and headed for the kitchen. Rebecca was right behind her.

"Hurry up!" Rick called out.

Taking a moment to have Dani closer without interruption, she wrapped her arms around her from behind as they entered the kitchen. "You stayin' tonight?"

After setting the bowl on the counter, Dani turned in her arms. "I was thinking more of staying the weekend. I have to work, but still."

"I think I can live with that."

"I thought you could. If Rick is busy while I'm working, you can always go over to Mark's."

Rebecca paused but continued to hold Dani's gaze. "I might, but I'll be fine here on my own too, if that's how it ends up."

"It's ending up a lot like that lately."

That's when it hit her, and Rebecca's insides melted. "You're tryin' to look out for me."

"My fellowship just started, so I'm going to be stretched thin. I don't want—"

Instead of letting Dani finish, Rebecca pulled her into a kiss. One that was deep enough and hot enough to leave her flustered. Their foreheads touched.

Dani's eyes were still closed, and she seemed to be trying to catch her breath. Rebecca's own breathing was ragged, but she found the words she needed to say. "We talked about this."

"I know." Dani opened her eyes. "I just...worry."

"It doesn't feel like it did before, does it?"

Dani shook her head.

"Because it's not. We're not."

"I understand that, but it's best that I check in with you. Not take anything for granted."

"Patti encourage that?"

Dani sighed. "No, she said to be careful not to become hypervigilant."

"Mmm."

"Aaand, I'm already there." Dani looked heavenward.

Rebecca smiled. "I wouldn't say that."

"What would you say, then?"

"That I can tell you're where you wanna be." Rebecca leaned forward close enough for their lips to almost touch.

Dani nodded and slid her arms back around Rebecca's neck. "Yes."

Rebecca brushed Dani's mouth with her own, teasing it open in hopes that by speaking to her this way, each word would be absorbed and etched in finality. "I can tell I'm important...we're important."

"Yes." Dani's expression was open, vulnerable, and her voice dripped with emotion. She looked at Rebecca like she wanted to crawl inside her.

"I can tell that you love me."

Dani whimpered and exhaled shakily over her lips. "God, yes."

Rebecca wasn't naïve enough to think they'd made all their mistakes the first time around, but any new ones they stumbled on were going to be handled by different people. Their foundation was strong. There was concrete beneath Rebecca's feet, not shifting sand. Rebecca kissed her with that confidence and conviction.

One of Dani's hands fisted in Rebecca's hair as she gave back everything she got and plenty of her own.

"I don't smell pop... Jesus Christ, move! I'll do it." Rick sounded amused. He pushed them out of the way and opened the cabinet, hunting for the popcorn.

Dani grinned as they continued to kiss.

"When y'all are done, think you can manage to bring out the drinks? Or do I need to do that too?" Rick smirked.

Rebecca pulled back and glanced at Dani. "We done here? We understand each other?"

"We're done." Dani didn't hesitate.

Smiling, Rebecca met Rick's gaze. "Yeah, we're good."

ABOUT KD WILLIAMSON

KD is a Southerner and a former nomad, taking up residence in the Midwest, east coast, and New Orleans over the years. She is also a Hurricane Katrina survivor. Displaced to the mountains of North Carolina, she found her way back to New Orleans, where she lives with her partner of ten years and the strangest dogs and cats in existence.

KD enjoys all things geek, from video games to super heroes. She is a veteran in the mental health field, working with children and their families for more than ten years. She found that she had a talent for writing as a teenager, and through fits and starts, fostered it over the years.

OTHER BOOKS FROM YLVA PUBLISHING

www.ylva-publishing.com

BLURRED LINES
(Cops and Docs – Book 1)
KD Williamson

ISBN: 978-3-95533-493-2
Length: 283 pages (92,000 words)

Wounded in a police shootout, Detective Kelli McCabe spends weeks in the hospital recovering. Her only entertainment is verbal sparring matches with Dr. Nora Whitmore, the talented and reclusive surgeon. Two very different women living in two different worlds. When the lines between them begin to blur, will they run from the possibilities or embrace the changes they bring to each other's lives?

IN A HEARTBEAT
(The L.A. Metro Series – Book 3)
RJ Nolan

ISBN: 978-3-95533-159-7
Length: 370 pages (97,000 pages)

Officer Sam McKenna has no trouble facing down criminals but breaks out in a sweat at the mere mention of commitment. Trauma surgeon Riley Connolly tries to measure up to her family's expectations and hides her sexuality from them. A life-and-death situation at the hospital binds them together. But can there be any future for a commitment-phobic cop and a closeted, workaholic doctor?

CODE OF CONDUCT
Cheyenne Blue

ISBN: 978-3-96324-030-0
Length: 264 pages (91,000 words)

Top ten tennis player Viva Jones had the world at her feet. Then a lineswoman's bad call knocked her out of the US Open, and injury crushed her career. While battling to return to the game, a chance meeting with the same sexy lineswoman forces Viva to rethink the past...and the present. There's just one problem: players and officials can't date.

A lesbian romance about breaking all the rules.

IN FASHION
Jody Klaire

ISBN: 978-3-96324-090-4
Length: 220 pages (68,000 words)

Celebrity Darcy knows all about perfection. She's famous for stripping bare and restyling women on her UK TV show, Style Surgeon. Fans hang off her #EmbraceDesigner tweets and there's no challenge she can't meet. That is, until security guard Kate struts into her changing room. Suddenly Darcy's the one who feels exposed.

A lesbian romance about facing and embracing your own unique design.

Credits
Edited by Lee Winter and Amanda Jean
Cover Design and Print Layout by Streetlight Graphics

Printed in Great Britain
by Amazon